M000206668

THE LAST ROMAN

BOOK ONE: EXILE

B.K. GREENWOOD

COPYRIGHT

BAT CITY PRESS

Cover Design by **Dusan Arsenic**

Edited by **Dan Szczesny, Gareth Clegg**

This book would not be possible without the incredible support and encouragement from my wife, Sonya, and children, Chris and McKenna.

And a special thanks to those that helped me cross the finish line with this completed novel; Joe, Keri, and Jessica. Also, a heartfelt thank you to all the beta readers throughout the years. Your inputs and constructive feedback have been essential to my journey.

DEDICATED TO:

My grandfather, Roy "Bud" Hutchins.
You taught me to never stop learning
and always to reach for the stars.

CONTENTS

PROLOGUE

For if the trumpet give an uncertain sound,
who shall prepare himself to the battle?
—I CORINTHIANS 14:8

THUMP. THUMP.

Each strike of the mallet further aggravated the hangover that had plagued Marcus all morning. Worse than the sound of the mallet were the cries of anguish, but he knew from experience that those cries would become whimpers. The sooner that happened, the better, Marcus thought. Honestly, the sooner he finished this assignment and left this godforsaken city, the better.

By his count, this was the ninth crucifixion Marcus had administered since arriving in Jerusalem. He was a combat veteran and had witnessed firsthand the unadulterated violence of war. But he had never understood the brutality of the crucifixion. To kill a man in battle was one thing but nailing him to a cross was cruel by any measure. Several days of suffocating punishment before dying of exposure might be appropriate for those guilty of the most heinous of crimes. But, when applied to thieves and would-be kings, the practice seemed gratuitous—even for Romans. Marcus pushed the thought

1

from his mind and watched as they lifted the prisoner and attached the crossbeam to the post.

Thump. Thump.

Marcus winced, closing his eyes and rubbing his temples. When the soldier finished hammering, he opened them and looked up at the figure nailed to the cross. He was naked, except for a cloth wrapped around his legs and waist. His head, ordained with a crown of thorns, slumped forward, blood dripping from his hair and down his shoulders and chest. The prisoner lifted his head and looked at Marcus. He would never forget those eyes. Where was the pain or hatred? Why were they perfect displays of compassion and pity? Those eyes burned directly into Marcus's soul.

FALL 37 A.D.
GAUL

Eyes fluttering open, Marcus stared at the canvas ceiling. He closed them again, but all he could see was the image of the Galilean. After a few minutes, Marcus decided his restless night of sleep was over. It had been four years, yet he was still having the dreams. He wondered if they would ever stop. He sat up and stretched his arms, his aching joints reminding him it was time to give up this army life. The blanket fell away as his feet swung to the dirt floor.

Marcus stood and groped for his nearby tunic, dressing in the darkness. He was tall for a Roman, with broad shoulders and a narrow waist, both of which he inherited from his father. From his mother, he had received his aquiline nose, a set of piercing, dark-brown eyes, and a sturdy, sharp jawline. From the pair, he had gained his fanatical sense of determination. Perhaps that was why he still campaigned. He sat on the cot to put on his sandals, then stood and stepped into the next room.

2

A candle was burning next to a platter of fruits, cheese, and dried meats on a small wooden table.

"Good morning, sir."

Marcus had not seen Nicodemus sitting on a stool in the darkened corner of the room. The older man stood as Marcus moved to the table.

"Good morning," Marcus replied.

"Did you sleep well?"

"Not really." He pulled out the chair and sat down. "But that's not unusual."

"You didn't eat at all last night—" Nicodemus pushed the platter toward Marcus. "You'll need your strength. It sounds like there will be a fight today."

"Most likely." Marcus picked a dried date from the platter and popped it into his mouth.

"We're not waiting for Caligula?" Nicodemus poured Marcus a cup of spiced wine.

"No. Quintus thinks this is our best chance to 'fix' the barbarian problem." He took a long swig from the cup. "I'm not sure he shares my sense of caution when dealing with the emperor. But then again, it's been several years since Quintus was in Rome."

"Ignoring the emperor..." Nicodemus frowned. "That hasn't worked out so well for others."

"No, it hasn't." Marcus grabbed a piece of cheese and changed the subject. "I need to write a letter."

"Of course." Nicodemus moved to a nearby trunk and pulled out parchment, reed, and vial. He placed them next to Marcus. "Let me know if you need anything else, sir."

Nodding, Marcus unrolled a piece of parchment and, pulling the cork from the vial, dipped the reed into the ink. He paused, his mind drifting for a while. After a few moments, he wrote.

To my wife and love Natalia,

I hope you are in good health! And things are well for the children. Has Cato returned from the academy? Be sure he stays on top of his studies while away from school. And Julia? Tell her I still have the drawing she made for me and carry it at all times.

I'm so happy you joined me here in Gaul. I know it was an arduous journey for you and the children but having you here will negate this land's dreariness.

We have been chasing this raiding party for a month now. Our scouts say they have stopped running, and hopefully, this will mark the end of the campaign. If so, I will meet you in Lutetia, two weeks from now. Do not worry; Quintus is an excellent general, and the men are well-trained and ready for a fight.

My love, I miss the comfort of your company and the tenderness of your touch. The longer we are apart, the more I realize how much I need you by my side. Though the words I am now writing will be cold by the time they reach you, please remember that they once burned with the passion of my heart.

I have thought long and hard about my station in the army. Although I wish to serve my empire, each assignment I accept carries me farther from you. With this in mind, I have decided that this will be my last appointment. My father has confirmed that he can find me a position in the Senate. Once secured, I shall never again leave your side, for the thought of a life without you is unbearable and represents a future that I have no desire to face.

All my love,
Marcus

Marcus set down the reed and took another sip from his cup as he waited for the ink to dry. He looked to the tent's entrance and the faint sunlight seeping in from beyond. He rolled up the parchment, tied it with a rawhide strip, then took the candle and poured hot liquid wax onto the knot.

"Nicodemus?"

The servant reentered the room as Marcus stood up from the table.

"Sir?"

"Make sure this letter goes out this morning."

"Of course, sir."

Marcus lifted his cup, and before taking a swig, looked down into its dark contents. His mind drifted back to his dream and the prisoner with the crown of thorns.

"Is there something...wrong, sir?"

Marcus looked up. "No. My wife and children are in Lutetia."

"That's outstanding, sir. I'm sure you're excited to see them."

"Yes, I am." Marcus set down his cup and looked back at Nicodemus. "Do you believe in the gods?"

"No, I'm Jewish. I believe in the one true God."

"One god?" Marcus grinned. "He must be busy."

"I believe he manages." Nicodemus smiled, but it faded. "Why do you ask?"

"I sometimes wonder what they have in store for me." He shrugged. "My family has never been so close when I've gone into battle. I guess it puts things into perspective."

"Hmmm." Nicodemus looked down at the table.

"What?" Marcus studied the older man. "We've been together long enough. You can speak your mind with me."

"Sir, it's a natural feeling. We all struggle with our mortality and what might happen when we die." His expression hardened. "But you need to forget about all of that. Those thoughts are dangerous. That's how men lose battles, and that's how men die. You need to be the soldier that has stayed alive all these years."

"You're right." Marcus met his gaze. "I think it's time for my armor."

The trumpet blast shattered the peaceful dawn and had the men scrambling from their tents. Marcus stood at his tent's opening and watched as the centurions assembled the men. Satisfied, he turned to a nearby horse, which anxiously sniffed at the gentle breeze. The mount's ears twitched, a natural reaction to the tension that had settled upon the army like the heavy morning fog.

Marcus ran one hand down the horse's chin, then took the reins from a grubby-faced stable boy. He swung into the saddle and glanced down at the child, who smiled back at him with a toothy grin. The youngster was the product of the legion's brothel, a permanent reminder of a fleeting relationship. None of the legionaries could claim him as their own, yet they would collectively see to his upbringing. Someday he would gain his citizenship by serving in this very legion, but for now, he performed whatever tasks were required.

Another short blast from the trumpet sent the boy scurrying away. Silence settled upon the men—then a familiar voice echoed across the camp.

"Legionaries, are you ready for war?"

A loud cheer erupted from the ranks as the soldiers thrust their swords high into the air. Marcus scanned the crowd, finding the man responsible for this question. It was General Quintus Ligarius Melus, mounted on a giant white stallion.

Twice more, Quintus bellowed, "Legionaries, are you ready for war?"

The cheer grew louder each time the men responded.

Quintus nudged his horse through the frenzied troops, stopping next to Marcus.

The general was a close friend of Marcus's father, despite their differences in temperament. Quintus had lived in the shadow of the Imperial banner, meeting his enemies with the blunt force of a Roman legion. Marcus's father roamed the equally dangerous Senate floor and met his enemies with cunning and intuition. Marcus detested the latter's politics, so here he was in the middle of Gaul.

"Impressive speech," Marcus said.

"I thought so." Quintus crossed his hands over the horse's neck.

"Up all night writing it?"

Quintus chuckled.

"How are you feeling?" Marcus asked.

"I've been better." A troubled expression gripped the general's rugged features. "I just spoke with our scouts; this is not the raiding party we've been chasing. It's now an army."

Marcus nodded. It looked like these barbarians *wanted* to be chased. "How many?"

"Good question." Quintus turned his head toward the forest beyond the camp walls. "Forty, maybe fifty thousand."

Marcus frowned and did a quick calculation; they were outnumbered three to one.

"That's a lot of fucking barbarians."

"Yeah, it is." Quintus shrugged. "But what else can we do? The nearest legion is ten days march."

"Desperate soldiers are dangerous soldiers."

"Yes, they are." Quintus agreed. "I'm glad they stopped running. I'm sick of these fucking woods. Too many trees."

"And I miss the sun." Marcus looked up at the dull gray sky. "Even when it shines, it's still cold."

"Then let's get it over with. Marcus, keep in close contact with the Fifteenth. The boys will be eager—too eager. Discipline is the only advantage we have."

"I know."

"I'm sure you do. But it may not matter; these barbarians may kill us all." Quintus smiled and guided his mount away, calling back over his shoulder. "Then again, who wants to live forever?"

Marcus nodded to his lead centurion, Gaius, who motioned to the other centurions. The order swept down the line, and the column lumbered forward, the squeak of leather and the clang of iron filling the morning air. Marcus spurred his horse forward and overtook the soldier that bore the legion's eagle, then galloped past their sister legion, which had assembled on the far side of the palisade opening. Quintus watched the procession from a slight rise, surrounded by his advisors. Marcus passed through the wooden gate and onto the open field beyond. Turning to his left, he galloped along the freshly cut logs that served as their hasty battlements. Catapults loomed above the barricade, poised to wreak havoc on the enemy.

Marcus halted his horse about a hundred yards short of a narrow stream, twisting back to watch the progress of his legion. The men were quiet as they plodded along the broken field. Many of them would not see nightfall; still, they marched on. Marcus had a deep respect for the common legionary. They would spend twenty-five years of their life fighting, bleeding, and dying for the empire. They built roads, walls, and bridges, endured extreme weather, long marches, and isolated assignments. The discipline was harsh but fair. If they survived their enlistment, they would receive a small parcel of land or its equivalent in gold. That reward would prove elusive for many of these men. As he watched the familiar faces pass by, he felt more than a little guilty with his decision to leave the army.

He pushed the feeling aside and directed his horse to a nearby cluster of officers. One man, Lucius Sentius Tantalus, the eldest son of a powerful senator, stepped forward as Marcus dismounted. Appointed by the emperor, the *tribunus laticlavius* was technically the senior tribune. A new arrival to the legion, he was wise enough to yield to the veteran officers. Based on his plump, childish face, Marcus judged him to be in his early twenties. The other officers, *tribunus angusticlavius*, were veterans, having risen through the ranks over several years.

"Good morning, gentlemen. Sleep well?"

"Sir, how could we?" Lucius pointed toward the barbarian camp. "Those bastards were up all-night yelling and screaming. When do they sleep?"

"They don't," Faustus, the older tribune, replied. "They're like wolves, always on the hunt...craving human flesh."

The color drained from Lucius' face as the others nodded in agreement.

"Well," Marcus interjected, knowing the veterans would have the young man pissing in his sandals. "There'll be no human flesh consumed today."

If they were disappointed that Marcus had interrupted their fun, they hid it well.

"Have you walked the field?" Marcus looked around the circle.

They all nodded in unison.

"Questions?"

"No sir," Faustus spoke for them all.

"Good. Lucius, you'll be part of the reserves. Take your cohort to the staging area near the general."

"Yes, sir." He started to walk away but stopped. "I've heard there are a hundred thousand barbarians—"

9

"Probably, but don't worry...they rarely cook the officers," Marcus said.

"You're right," Septimus agreed. "They eat them raw!"

The officers chuckled. The mouth of the young tribune moved, but no words came.

"Get going." Marcus patted him on the shoulder. "Find Titus —he'll issue the orders."

The young man turned away but stopped to execute a hasty salute. Nodding in return, Marcus looked back to the others and shook his head.

"Let's pray to the gods that we don't need our reserves."

The men grinned, but the smiles faded as they looked at one another. It was clear they faced a much larger force.

"You've done this a hundred times. Keep the formations tight. I want crisp execution. And most of all, discipline. Understood?"

They nodded in unison.

"Good." He looked around the small group. "I do not know why the emperor wants this godforsaken land, but we're going to get it for him."

They all snickered, but the rumble of distant war drums recalled their somber mood.

Tullus echoed the sentiment of the others. "Don't worry, Marcus, we'll teach these fucking bastards a lesson in warfare."

"I'm sure you will. May the Gods be with us."

The yellow orb that promised to be the morning sun slowly devoured the heavy fog, and it revealed the faint outlines of the surrounding forest. To the left lay a stream, its sparkling current hidden beneath a mass of reeds that clung to the steep embankment. It emerged from the trees near a boulder in a far corner of the field, meandering toward their camp before cutting back and disappearing into the dense foliage.

The ground was clear for the thirty yards that led up to the fortifications behind them. In front, the wildflowers and golden grass swayed in the morning breeze, a peaceful setting that was a stark contrast to the impending slaughter. A dark forest loomed in the distance, concealing the enemy who was sure to be watching them as well. Fields like this were uncommon in Gaul, and it surprised Marcus the barbarians had agreed to meet them on such favorable ground.

From his jittery steed, Marcus watched the centurions organize the cohorts. They adjusted the spacing between the rows and columns, ensuring each man was three feet from his companion in all directions. This spacing allowed each man ample room to maneuver while still providing support to his neighbor. He swiveled in his saddle to check the status of their auxiliaries.

The cavalry troop was stationed near the end of the formation. The troopers, like their commander Octavius, waited for the battle to begin. Archers, deployed behind the legion, performed last-minute checks on their equipment. Each bowman had stuck an allotment of arrows into the soft ground before him, allowing for easy access once the battle had begun. Beyond the archers and within the palisade walls, Marcus could see the various crews working to prepare the war machines.

A murmur from the nearby troops interrupted his inspection. Marcus sat up in his saddle and peered toward the distant tree line, where a group of shadowy figures had emerged from the woods.

The Suebi were huge; even the average barbarian towered above most Romans. Their extraordinary stature was matched only by their tenacity in battle. And they did not take well to subjugation.

A smile crept across his lips; if Marcus was fighting for *his* freedom, he wouldn't give up either.

The mob of warriors moved from the safety of the woods and began their trek across the open field, pale sunlight glittering off their shields and weapons. One command from the centurions prompted the men to ready their javelin. From behind, Marcus heard the archer's commander order his men to nock their missiles. He dismounted and handed the reins to the young boy that had followed from the camp. Marcus drew his sword as he stepped toward the line, but Gaius grabbed his wrist and frowned.

"I don't think you'll be needing that." He spat on the ground. "And if you do, then we're fucked."

Without waiting for a reply, the centurion moved off to reposition a young soldier who had strayed out of line. Marcus grinned, slid his sword back into its sheath, and watched the enemy advance. The barbarians were scattered across the field, but not as many as he had expected. A nagging feeling crept over him, but it vanished with the sudden appearance of enemy cavalry. Marcus turned in time to see the Roman cavalry commander, Octavius, waving his sword above his head and leading his troops forward. The two groups met forty yards from the line, crashing together in a tangle of man and horse. A Roman cavalryman slew their leader, and soon, the Suebi warriors were galloping for the safety of the distant woods. Caught up in the heat of battle, the victorious horsemen followed hot on their heels. The legionaries thrust their swords into the air as they cheered the victors.

"Not too far, Octavius."

The whisper escaped his lips as Marcus watched their cavalry disappear into the trees. He shook his head and shifted his attention back to the field where the enemy infantry had advanced to within a hundred paces of their line. They were now close enough to distinguish the fearsome war paint that covered their upper bodies.

A series of muffled thumps signaled the catapults had joined the day. Goat-sized boulders sailed through the air, smashing into their loose formations. Groups of men disappeared as the stones tumbled across the meadow, leaving clouds of bloody mist in their wake. The ballistae were next to join the fight. These machines launched giant darts that sliced through flesh and bone, often pinning their unfortunate victims to the ground. One such missile skewered two men, who struggled to free themselves from the thick wooden shaft.

The Suebi pressed on, knowing the barrage would ease if they could get close enough to the Roman line. But the carnage had just begun. Marcus heard the order, followed by the twang, as hundreds of archers released their bows in unison. The arrows streaked overhead, raining down among the advancing men as they hunkered beneath round wooden shields. Shrieks of dying men punctuated the air as the lethal missiles repeatedly found their targets.

Still, they advanced. The hair on the back of Marcus's neck stood up as the barbarians let out a blood-curdling scream and closed the distance between the lines. On the centurion's command, the front ranks of soldiers launched their pilums toward the advancing enemy. Hurled with deadly accuracy, the six-foot javelins pierced through shield, flesh, and bone. Finally, the Romans unsheathed their swords and met the exhausted attackers. Marcus realized the initial attack would fail and looked across the bloody field to the woods beyond.

Where was the second wave? He peered toward the distant woods to see if Octavius had returned, but saw no sign of the cavalrymen. Marcus ran toward Gaius, who was urging the men forward.

"Gaius, order a halt!"

"Sir? We've broken the bastards!"

13

"Did we? You think that was the main attack?"

"You're right." He shook his head. "I'll try to hold 'em back, but it won't be easy."

Just as he finished speaking, the attackers spun around and ran—many of the Romans in steady pursuit.

"Order the stand down!" Gaius called to the drummer as he rushed toward the nearest soldiers. "Get in line!"

"We're not peasants—we're legionaries!" Another centurion grabbed a nearby trooper and thrust him back toward the formation. "You'll get back in line, or I'll cane each one of your lousy hides!"

Confident that the veterans would halt the advance, Marcus scanned the dense forest across the field. Turning to the left, he looked beyond the stream, focusing on the pasture. The grass moved in a circular motion, not back and forth as one would expect from the slight breeze. Then it dawned on Marcus what was happening.

"Gaius!" Marcus peered into the mass of soldiers. "Gaius!"

Marcus spun around and frantically motioned for his horse just as the centurion appeared by his side.

"The boys are reforming," Gaius panted.

"Good." Marcus pointed to the formation. "Find as many centurions as you can—quickly!"

Years of taking orders had set the habit, and Gaius sprinted away as Marcus turned toward the boy who held his horse.

"Can you ride?"

"Yes, sir! Very well."

"Good." He lifted him into the saddle. "Do something for me; it's very important."

"Will I be a legionary?"

"What?" Marcus grinned, despite the dire circumstances. "Of course! But you must find the general. He'll be surrounded by a lot of men on horses. I need you to say these exact words:

'Marcus says the left flank is under attack.' Do you understand?"

The boy nodded.

"Repeat it to me."

"Marcus says the left flank is under attack." He trembled with excitement or fear, probably both. "You can trust me."

"I don't have any other choice." Marcus slapped the rump of the horse, and it bolted toward the center of the line.

When he turned back, he saw several centurions sprinting toward him. They gathered around as Marcus fell to one knee.

"Listen to me...do not question or hesitate." Marcus drew a line in the soil with a twig. "Here's our line. I want the second row of cohorts to execute an about-face. They will swing out, pivoting on the third, which will anchor on the First. That new line will advance until it is perpendicular to the rest of the formation, almost like two walls coming together. This will leave the ninth positioned—" He stood and pointed to a mound of rocks. "There. Do you understand?"

They all nodded in unison.

"Go!"

They left, bellowing orders as they reached their men. Thanks to years of drilling, the men executed the order with Roman precision—and not a moment too soon. As Marcus reached the newly formed line, the grass stopped moving. There was a moment of surreal silence before the meadow disappeared, replaced by a thousand men covered in long stalks of grass. They glared at the Romans and let out the same spine-chilling scream that had ushered the previous charge. His men could barely unleash their pilums before the two sides collided in a tangled mass. The struggle grew desperate as wave after wave of warriors emerged from the woods beyond the stream. They now faced the bulk of the barbarian army, and Marcus watched in horror as his weakened line buckled under the weight of the onslaught. Knowing that it may crumble at any moment, Marcus ordered the archers into the melee. Despite their lack of armor, the brave souls threw down their bows and joined the fray.

Marcus moved along the faltering line and soon encountered the largest man he had ever seen, hacking his way through the thinning ranks. A legionary tried to bar his path, but the ogre swung his massive blade, catching the soldier just below his jaw. A crimson arc of blood sprayed from the fatal wound, much of it splattering across Marcus' face and chest. Behind the giant, more barbarians advanced to exploit the breach.

Marcus grabbed the shield of a fallen soldier and rushed the behemoth, who welcomed the attack with a vicious blow. The force drove Marcus to one knee and nearly knocked him unconscious. Marcus raised the shield to protect his head and shoulders and thrust his sword upward. The point struck metal, so he shoved it harder until he felt the blade dig into the soft underside of a trunk-like arm. Marcus could hear the giant's howl above the din of the battle and knew that retribution was near. Another thunderous blast crashed into the shield, the metal and banded leather splintering from the attack. The next blow would rip Marcus asunder.

Desperate, Marcus hastily covered his head with the remains of his ruined shield. He mustered all his strength and drove forward into the beast. The shield thudded against his waist, eliciting an angry grunt. Marcus reached around the barbarian's leg with the blade of his sword, finding the naked thigh. Though never meant as a weapon for slashing, the edge of his sword was still razor-sharp. He drew it across the giant's hamstring, cutting through flesh and sinew as Marcus pushed forward. The Suebi screamed in agony as the two men crumpled to the ground. The barbarian smashed the hilt of his sword into Marcus's head, knocking off his helmet. The world spun as Marcus stood and staggered away. Blood flowed down his face, blurring his vision. His opponent, writhing in pain, screamed at him.

Marcus heard several men shout, "The giant is down!"

A loud cheer erupted from the Romans, but that only encouraged the other barbarians. Marcus raised his sword in time to block another attack, but the force knocked him to the ground. The barbarian raised his sword to strike a death blow when Gaius appeared out of nowhere and ran him through. With great effort, Marcus regained his footing, lumbering forward to rejoin the melee. He lost his balance again and had to lean on his sword to keep from falling. As he stood watching the raging battle, a sharp pain shot through his side.

He looked down and saw the blade of the stricken giant sliding beneath his armor. The barbarian was sitting on his haunches, trying to stab him again. Marcus summoned his remaining strength and, swinging for the neck, felt the cold steel bite into flesh, then bone. A low gurgle escaped the laceration as the colossal body slumped forward, and the barbarian's head fell to the ground.

Marcus dropped the sword, trying in vain to reach his wound and stem the flow of blood. His breath grew labored, and he coughed, a coppery trace spilling into his mouth. He slumped to his knees as scores of legionaries rushed past. Marcus watched the reinforcements plug holes in the line and stem the barbarian attack. More cohorts arrived, and the battle devolved into a desperate struggle. Even with both legions engaged, the outcome was uncertain.

Marcus watched as the ranks dwindled, the men stubbornly giving way to the onslaught. It looked like they may break at any moment when a commotion drew his attention to the right side of the battle. A cheer rose from the legionaries as the forgotten Roman cavalry rejoined the fight and rolled up the exposed barbarian flank. Within minutes, the Suebi army was in full flight, and the mounted troopers were cutting down the stragglers. As the centurions rushed to put the men back in formation, Marcus slipped to the ground, his gaze fixed on the gray, sunless sky.

Moments later, Gaius knelt beside him. He tried to undo the bloody clasp of his armor, but Marcus pushed his hand away. Their eyes met.

"The men did good," Marcus said.

"Yes, they did."

Marcus continued, but it was inaudible.

Gaius leaned over, and Marcus whispered, "Tell my wife—" He coughed up specks of blood onto Gaius's soiled cheek. "I'm so sorry..." Marcus swallowed back the warm fluid rising in his throat, "sorry I left her."

"I will," he promised. "I will tell her myself."

Marcus nodded as a white horse arrived, the rider dismounting. Somewhere in the distance, he could hear the general's voice.

"Gaius?"

The old centurion did not reply, but the answer was written on his troubled face. Quintus knelt to the ground.

"Marcus, your actions have saved the day. I plan on submitting your name to the Senate..."

Quintus paused when their eyes met, then shifted to the pool of blood gathering around them. As the general spoke of honor rolls and victory marches, Marcus looked beyond him to the sky above. There was a shimmer in the cloud that resembled a bird. He tried to focus on the form as it grew closer, but he could not keep his eyes open. As he slipped into the darkness, he thought of his wife and the fact that he would never see her again.

CHAPTER ONE

*It is easier to find men who will volunteer to die,
than to find those who are willing to endure pain with patience.*
—JULIUS CAESAR

THE ROMAN OFFICER SQUINTED *at the setting sun, then looked over at
a cluster of priests. The tallest glared at him down a long, crooked
nose. The officer shook his head and turned to the centurion standing
next to him, a grizzled veteran who spat on the ground and shrugged.
Frustrated, the officer glanced back at the prisoners hanging on the
crosses; the two thieves were awake but silent. A third—the so-called
prophet—appeared to be unconscious.*

*"Shit," Marcus said beneath his breath as he walked to the edge of
the rocky knoll. The centurion followed close behind, his shadow
stretching down the barren hillside.*

"Marcus, only you could fuck up a crucifixion."

*"Shut up, Gaius." Marcus glanced back at the priests, then to the
centurion. "What do you think?"*

*"Me? I think we should kill them all, even the priests. But that's
probably why I'm not an officer."*

"Yeah, probably." Marcus nodded.

19

"Here's how I see it: if you ignore their request—and if they had an agreement with Pilate—you know how that will go down. And if they are lying? We can handle that later, our way."

"You're right, but I still don't like it."

"What's there to like?" The centurion's scarred face softened. "Once we like this part of the job, well...let's just say things couldn't get much worse."

"I get it." Marcus cast his gaze toward the prisoners, where it lingered for a moment before he said, "Alright, let's get on with it."

Marcus crossed the knoll, stopping before the high priest. "I will honor your request, but a Roman soldier will carry it out."

The priest raised his chin. "That is acceptable."

Marcus glared at him. This priest didn't act like a conquered man, which was the real problem with these Jews. They didn't know when they were beaten.

Turning to the centurion, Marcus motioned to a nearby plank. "That should do."

Gaius pointed to a soldier who picked up the piece of wood and started toward the closest thief. The prisoner glanced from the soldier to the board, unsure of his intentions, which soon became apparent as the legionary planted both feet and swung the board forward, shattering the prisoner's legs with a single blow. The man slumped forward, the weight of his body crushing his lungs and squeezing the life from his limp form.

Without hesitation, the soldier moved on to the other thief who begged to be spared. The pleas intensified to screams as the soldier struck his blow. This time, the force was enough to break the board as well. As the prisoner slowly suffocated, the soldier looked down at the splintered plank, then at Marcus. The latter glanced around the hillock, but there were no other boards.

His eyes fell upon a nearby soldier and the weapon he held. "Longinus, your spear."

The young man handed him the lance. Marcus balanced the hefty weapon and decided that it would suffice. The priest rushed forward, his entourage scrambling to keep pace. Two soldiers stepped in front of him, their spears crossed to block his advance.

"You must break his legs!" demanded the priest.

Marcus spun around, scowling. "What did you say?"

The priest licked his lips and pressed his point. "I said you must break his legs. That was the agreement with Pilate."

"Are you giving me an order?" Marcus glared at the priest.

"Well, no—I mean, yes..."

Marcus closed the gap between them, the spear clenched in his fist. The two soldiers stepped aside as the priest tried to stand his ground. He was no match for the angry Roman, and he shuffled back a few steps, bumping into his companions.

"Look around, you stinking bastard," Marcus spat. "I'm an officer in the Roman army, and I'd burn this fucking city to the ground before I took a single order from a scraggly little shit like you."

The priest met his gaze but could not hold it. He started licking his lips again, then turned toward one of his companions. He leaned over, whispering something into his ear, and smirked in satisfaction as the young man scurried off.

Marcus watched as the man disappeared into the crowd and thought; well, I'm certainly not going to break his legs now.

His eyes dropped to the spear. The shaft was nicked in a dozen places; the wood had long ago lost its grainy hue. Near the blade, the surface was stained a dark brown from blood, mud, or both. The blade was six inches long, its dull gray surface pitted and worn. But the meticulously honed edge gleamed in the fading light. Marcus grasped the thick shaft near the middle, balancing it as he stepped toward the last prisoner.

Marcus stopped at the foot of the cross, his attention drawn to a dozen mourners huddled just beyond the guards. Most of the group were weeping, unable to look at the man hanging on the cross. But one glared back at him, her piercing green eyes filled with hatred.

He returned to the task at hand and studied the bloody torso, choosing not to look up at the prisoner's face. Marcus leaned forward, *plunging the spear between two ribs. The blade disappeared into the flesh, sliding toward his unseen heart. As Marcus pulled the weapon free, a mixture of blood and fluid flowed down the shaft and onto his hand. Gasping, Marcus dropped the spear and buckled to the ground.*

The sky darkened as if the hand of one of the gods had reached down and blotted out the sun. The desert flowers sagged and exhaled, and a soft breeze whispered across the rocky mount. As the ground shook, a deep, narrow fissure split the barren earth and crept toward the distant city walls.

The stunned crowd peered at the fading sky, then down at the jagged crevice. Most fled toward the city, while others fell to their knees, tearing at their clothes as they wailed. A few stared at the slumped body of Jesus and wept.

The centurion knelt beside Marcus and looked up at the Galilean.

"Maybe he was the son of their god."

Marcus was awake, but he could not move. His eyes fixed on the angry sky and a cluster of shimmering raindrops. The raindrops grew more prominent as they descended, only to assume the shape of two winged figures. They hovered just above the cross and looked down on the fallen Roman. They seemed surprised when he met their gaze, and they stared back at him for what seemed an eternity before turning their attention to the dead Galilean. The two reached down and lifted what looked like a spirit from the sagging body. As they disappeared into the approaching night, the storm unleashed its fury.

MODERN DAY
BOSTON

Marcus bolted upright, the bedsheet sticking to his sweat-covered chest. He drew a deep breath and looked down at his hands, half expecting them to be covered in blood. He looked over at a pill bottle sitting on the nearby nightstand. Marcus debated whether to reach for it when his cell phone buzzed. He glanced at the clock and picked up the phone but didn't recognize the foreign number.

He accepted the call. "Yeah?"

"Marcus?"

"Yes...who's this?"

"Julien Courbet, Interpol. We chatted a few months ago."

"I don't remember."

"You worked with my boss, Naomi."

"Naomi? Oh, yeah, I remember her."

"Well, we have an update for you."

It piqued his interest. "Really? I wasn't expecting any help from Interpol."

"Naomi appreciated your support with the ambassador's daughter and wanted to return the favor."

"What do you have?"

"We found a body, a young woman, here in Paris. Several elements of the crime matched the case files you sent. Based on the security tape, we think it's the man you're looking for. I sent a file to your email."

"Thanks, I'll check it out."

"Just to be clear, this conversation never happened."

The agent hung up without waiting for a response.

Marcus yawned and rubbed his hand through his disheveled hair, then grabbed a pack of cigarettes from the nightstand. Lighting one up, he took a long pull and moved to a dresser near the window, stopping to pour himself a glass of scotch. He sat at the nearby desk, took a sip of his drink, and picked up his iPad to check his email. He found one from an unknown Gmail account, opened the attachment, and scanned through crime scene photos until he reached a surveillance photo.

Levi was staring right into the camera.

Marcus took a deep breath, swallowed the rest of his scotch, and looked back at the half-empty bottle. He decided to shower instead. Entering the bathroom, he undressed and relieved himself, a cigarette dangling from his lip. The heavy odor of stale scotch drifted up from the bowl. He took one last puff, dropped the cigarette and flushed. As he waited for the water to warm up, he again ran his finger over the scar on his ribcage and shook his head. Although he had been cut a thousand times, this was the only wound that would not fade. He should have died on that miserable field, but he had not. And two-thousand years later, he still did not know why.

He stepped into the shower and prepared himself to face another day.

After showering, Marcus grabbed some coffee from the kitchen and headed to the garage. A black SUV was parked in the closest space, and next to it was a dark gray BMW. Marcus made his way to a door at the back of the garage. Inside was a well-stocked workshop with a variety of metal and woodworking tools. He continued through another door into a small armory. Here, a dark-suited man stood at a table, loading supplies into a duffle bag. Various pieces of tactical equipment and automatic weapons covered the walls of the room. Several spaces were empty, accounting for the contents of the bag.

"How much ammo did you pack?" Marcus looked at the bulging bag.

"For you? Never enough."

Marcus could not help but smile whenever Cormac said the word *never*, *car* or *fork*. He could drag Cormac round the world, but he would never drag the Boston accent from the older man. Nor would he want to.

Cormac was about 5'7", but you could tell by the way his

24

shoulders slumped he used to be taller. He had a wiry frame, and his head was bald and shiny. In thirty years, Marcus had never seen the man with hair, but Cormac's face was nearly wrinkle-free, a surprise given his age. His nose was flat, with a single bump in the middle, a memento from his years in the boxing ring. His eyes were foam green and seemed to hint they were once much brighter. He lifted a magazine and inspected it before slipping it into the bag. Marcus could see his bright white knuckles, a visual reminder of the painful arthritis that was now ravaging his weathered body.

Marcus leaned forward, placing both hands on the stainless-steel table. "Are you sure she's ready?"

"What? Sam?" Cormac shoved two iPhone boxes into the bag. "We've talked about this. She's been out a dozen times, and she saved your ass in London—lord knows you were useless."

"Both my legs were broken."

"Yeah, like I said, fuckin' useless."

"How did you become a priest? You swear like a sailor."

"Hey!" Cormac pointed a crooked finger at Marcus. "I don't swear during mass or around kids or widows."

Marcus shook his head and crossed his arms.

"Look," Cormac shoved another couple of magazines into the bag, "she's my niece, and I wouldn't let her go if she weren't ready. She's tough as nails and smarter than the both of us put together. Plus, she can do all that tech stuff you refuse to learn."

"You're right, but she hasn't been there when..." His voice trailed off.

"What? When you get stinking drunk? Your metabolism is so crazy, it never lasts."

"No." Marcus glared at him. "You know that's not what I'm talking about."

"Ah, the dying thing. No, she hasn't." He zipped up the bag and looked Marcus in the eyes. "I went over everything. She knows what to do if you come back, you know, all fucked up."

"Are you sure? It can be pretty ugly."

"I'm sure." He pushed the bag toward Marcus. "I don't carry this shit anymore."

Marcus picked it up and slung it over his shoulder.

"You want me to call Father Pierre in Paris?"

"Nah," Marcus shook his head. "Let's do this one off the books."

"Something bothering you?"

"Just a feeling. I don't trust the new Cardinal."

"You and me both. That guy is wicked fuckin' corrupt."

"And a dick."

"Yeah, that too." Cormac met him near the end of the table, "So, what's the plan?"

"Go to Paris, stake out the club. Levi is a creature of habit. He'll strike again."

"And then what? You gonna kill that bastard?"

"I need him to find Thomas."

"You shoulda killed that bastard years ago."

"I know, I know." Marcus shook his head as he moved toward the door. "You get some breakfast. We'll keep you posted."

"Will do."

Marcus sat staring out the window of the chartered jet, holding his second glass of scotch. The dull gray clouds below were growing brighter by the minute. As he took another sip, Sam came out of the cockpit and stopped in the galley to grab a bottle of water.

"We should be in Paris by early evening." She sat across from him, twisting the top off and taking a drink. "Hopefully, make it to the club by midnight."

Marcus nodded and took another swig. Samantha, or Sam,

was the same height as her uncle now that he had shrunk in stature. But she got her looks from her mother, who was French. Short, jet-black hair, piercing brown eyes, and sharp, clean features that would not be described as beautiful, but most men would find her attractive. She was smart, like her mother, but her stubbornness came from her father's family.

Sam's mother and father were killed in a car accident when she was eight years old. She had no other family, so she came to live with her uncle, Cormac. Which meant she also lived with Marcus. Cormac had done his best to raise her, but he was not always up to the task. Luckily, they had found a wonderful nanny to help. Somehow, they got Sam through her teens and graduated from high school. There may have been a boyfriend or two who received unexpected visits from Cormac or Marcus, and on one occasion both, but it all worked out. She went to Carnegie Mellon and studied pre-med, then switched to cybersecurity, with a minor in poetry, which Marcus never understood. Cormac said it helped her write code. Marcus was skeptical.

Marcus had never planned for her to take over for Cormac, but the longer he lived, the more he realized that life never goes as planned. They had always tried to shield her from their line of work, but she was as bright as she was nosy. By the time Sam was 14, there were few secrets. It was amazing that she finished high school or college, as she was constantly butting into their clandestine activities. Sam was managing missions remotely by 17. By 21, she was going along.

"So..." Sam settled into her seat and took a sip from her bottle. She looked up. "I asked my uncle, but he said I needed to talk to you. That it should come from you."

"And what is that?"

"Everything." She took a deep breath. "Now that I'm fully on board, I think I need to know everything."

He grimaced, then took another swig. "Okay, fair. Fire away."

"The immortality thing. If you get killed, you come back three days later."

"Yes."

"But others don't? Like this guy we are chasing, Levi. If you kill him, he stays dead? Why?"

"I'm not sure why, but there's a difference." He set down his glass. "Anyone who Christ healed was transformed. Lepers, the blind, the dead. They stopped aging, they don't get sick, and they heal almost immediately. They're also stronger and faster than normal people."

"But they can be killed?"

"Yes, but it's pretty tough to do. It's got to be traumatic. Decapitation, falling from a tall building, an explosion. If they survive, even for a moment, their body will begin to heal."

"How many are there?"

"I don't know. I wasn't with him those three years. I would guess dozens, maybe more."

"And how many are left?"

"Four, that I know of. Not including Thomas or myself."

"Because you guys are different?"

"Yes, we weren't healed. I'm the one that put the spear into Christ's side."

"And that transformed you?" She frowned.

"Yes, but I didn't know. Several years later, I was killed in Gaul. I resurrected after three days, and I haven't aged since. I've died more times than I care to count, but I always come back."

"So, you're like a super immortal."

"I guess if you want to put it that way."

"Well, that makes it sound cooler." She shifted in her chair. "Why do you think you come back?"

"I don't know. Perhaps it's my punishment for taking part in the crucifixion?" He shrugged. "Or maybe they haven't decided where I'm supposed to go."

28

"You're exiled."

Marcus paused, a curious look on his face. He bit his lip, then said, "You're right. I never thought of it that way."

"And Thomas?"

There was a long pause, and it was as if Marcus did not hear the question. Then he nodded. "He's in the same situation. He was one of the twelve disciples, but his faith wavered."

"Doubting Thomas."

"That's him. And he's stuck here, just like me."

"So, what is he up to?"

"I don't know. But Levi will tell us what he knows before I kill him."

There was little traffic as they drove through the bright heart of Paris. Marcus said nothing as they crossed the Seine and pulled into a parking spot across from Notre Dame Cathedral. It was drizzling as Marcus shifted the car into park.

"Are you meeting someone?" Sam asked.

"No, not really."

"Not really? What does that mean?"

"It means I don't want to talk about it," Marcus said as he opened the door but paused, his eyes focused on the wet pavement. The rain dripped into the car. "I'm sorry...I didn't sleep on the flight. I'm just tired. I'll be back in a few minutes, and we can go to the club."

Before Sam could reply, Marcus closed the door and disappeared into the darkness.

He pulled his trench coat tight and moved into the shadows. High above, spotlights bathed the damaged cathedral in a steady, rapturous glow. The contrast made the darkness seem even darker. He slipped through the trees, following the path to a walkway overlooking the Seine. As he approached a

29

short wall, Marcus could hear, and then see, one of the restaurant boats gliding up the river. A dozen photograph flashes erupted along its length as it passed the cathedral. Marcus turned his back to the boat and continued down the trail, over the Archbishop's Bridge and under several streetlights that tried and failed to hold back the deepening night.

By the time Marcus reached the tip of the island, the drizzle had increased to a steady downpour. He sought and found a boulder near the water's edge. Marcus ignored the chilling rain, sat down, and let his gaze settle on the far bank as he drifted into the past. The city lights faded into the darkness.

CHAPTER TWO

Without a family, man, alone in the world,
trembles with the cold.
—ANDRE MAUROIS

FALL 37 A.D.
GAUL

MARCUS WAS ALIVE.

He wondered why, but he had more important issues. Something heavy pressed down on his entire body. He tried to take in a breath, but his mouth and nose filled up with dirt. As he choked and coughed, his anxiety intensified. His entire body squirmed, his hands clawing at the loose soil. He seemed to make some progress, but the exertion only made the lack of air more pronounced. He tried not to take another breath, but he was light-headed and seconds from passing out. As his body weakened, he felt his hand punch through the soil and into the open air beyond. But it was too late.

Or was it? Someone grabbed his hand and pulled him from the earth. His head broke the surface and he emptied his

31

bursting lungs, dirt flying from his mouth and nose. Marcus wiped his face, squinting against the sunlight as he looked around for the hand that helped him.

Nicodemus was kneeling beside him, a smile on his weathered face.

"Welcome back."

Marcus tried to reply, but his throat was too dry. Nodding, he looked down and realized his lower body was still buried in the dark, soggy earth. He wiggled his legs back and forth, and with help, squirmed free.

His servant handed him a cloth to wipe his face, and then a water skin. Marcus took a short pull, swishing the water around in his mouth to clear the dirt. He spat it out, and then took a long drink, the cool water burning like fire as it flowed down his parched throat.

"Can you stand?" Nicodemus asked.

"I think so." Marcus stood on wobbly legs, his eyes shifting to the surrounding field. That's when it hit him.

The stench of death. A stench that lingered for days after a battle. A stench that drew dozens of crows and vultures to pick at the bloated corpses. There were hundreds, if not thousands, of bodies scattered across the field. All of them were barbarians, as the Romans had already gathered their dead.

"What happened?" Marcus pulled his gaze from the field.

"Not here. The barbarians could come back. We need to leave." Nicodemus's tone had changed. He no longer talked like a servant.

He handed Marcus a tunic and sandals.

"Where's my legion?" Marcus slipped the tunic over his head.

"Gone." Nicodemus picked up a small bag and walked away. "Left yesterday."

Marcus stumbled after him, the two walking around the abandoned Roman camp and into the forest beyond.

Nicodemus led them to a pair of horses tied to a tree. He secured the bag to one, then moved to help Marcus up into the saddle of the other.

Within minutes, they were making their way back along the road they had traveled a week earlier when chasing the war party. As they rode side by side, Marcus looked over at his companion.

"What happened?"

"How much do you remember?" Nicodemus glanced over at him.

"The barbarian stabbed me. I killed him. Then it gets fuzzy."

"Sending the young boy to the general was genius. The reserves arrived just as the line was going to break. They redeployed the second legion, and it was touch and go. Then our cavalry reappeared and outflanked the barbarians. They were pinned between the legions and the streams." He looked down, shaking his head. "It was a slaughter."

Marcus nodded, the stench of the field still clinging to his nostrils.

"So, who buried me?"

"They didn't bury you, Marcus. They cremated you."

"That's impossible."

"I watched them light the pyre. The night of the battle, as both legions watched. You were a celebrated hero."

"Then how did I end up in the ground? Is this the afterlife?"

"No, no. That would mean I'm dead too." He grinned. "And I'm very much alive. I can't explain how. But perhaps I can explain why." He guided the horse around a slight bend in the road. "Back in Judea, you were the commander at a crucifixion."

"I commanded many. More than I can count."

"This one had a Galilean. One that you stabbed with a spear."

Marcus pulled on the reins of his horse, and Nicodemus followed suit.

"Yes." Marcus studied the older man.

"Something happened to you that day."

"I fainted."

"Did you?" He shrugged. "Perhaps. But something changed. That Galilean was the Son of God."

"That's what they said."

"No, he is real. I'm living proof."

"How is that?"

"I was born blind, and that Galilean healed me when I was fifty years old."

"You will forgive me if I'm skeptical of that."

"Of course you would be." Nicodemus pulled a small dagger from his belt. "I abhor blood, but you need to be convinced."

Before Marcus could reply, Nicodemus ran the blade across his palm.

"What are you doing?"

"Watch!" Nicodemus grimaced and held out his hand to Marcus.

It was just deep enough to draw a steady flow of blood that dripped off the side of his palm. But within a minute, the bleeding had slowed. After another few breathless minutes, it had stopped.

Marcus looked up at Nicodemus. "I don't understand."

"We should keep moving." He urged his horse forward, Marcus beside him. "None of us understand. We've just come to accept it. And you must as well."

"I wasn't healed."

"No. You are different. But there is one other like you."

"Who?"

"A man named Thomas. He was at the crucifixion, and soon after, had a similar encounter to yours. He realized you were transformed as well. That is why he asked me to go with you... to be there when you came back."

They passed through the shadows of a giant oak, Marcus doing his best to process his alternative world. They had just picked their way across a narrow stream when he broke the silence.

"So, what now?"

"We have to get you out of the empire."

"What? My family?"

"Them too."

"Why?"

"Caligula arrived the day after the battle. He was livid that the general did not wait for him. The emperor had him executed on the spot."

"Quintus is dead?"

"And all the tribunes," Nicodemus said. "Caligula ordered the battle wiped from history. That is why I said you *were* a hero."

Marcus pulled up his steed again and turned to Nicodemus. "I wrote my wife about the battle."

The blood drained from Nicodemus's face. "Where is she?"

"She was coming to Lutetia."

Nicodemus looked down the path and back at Marcus. Without a word, they both urged their horses forward, picking up the pace until they were galloping down the trail.

They reached the outskirts of Lutetia a few hours after sundown. They slowed as they exited the forest, the path cutting across a small field. A long, wooden bridge spanned the dark river that separated them from the small town. As they approached the bridge, Nicodemus reined in his horse.

"Stop!" he called to Marcus.

"Why?" Marcus spun his horse around to face Nicodemus.

"You can't go in there. You're dead."

Marcus started to reply but then closed his mouth.

"Someone will recognize you. I'll go." He handed Marcus his bag. "There is some food in here. Wait for me over there." He pointed to the tip of the island where a small grove of trees crept up to the river's edge.

Nodding, Marcus watched him go, the soft pounding of horse hooves on the wooden planks echoing through the night. When Nicodemus had faded from sight, Marcus guided his horse to the trees. Once there, he tied his mount and took the bag to a large boulder overlooking the river. He sat on the rock and chewed on a dried piece of meat.

An hour later, Marcus heard the familiar sound of hooves on planks. Unsure if it was Nicodemus, he walked back to the trees and looked out across the field. His hand fell to his side, only to realize he had no weapon.

But no weapon would be needed. A rider and horse took shape in the darkness, and though there was no moonlight, Marcus could tell it was Nicodemus. He stepped from the trees, grabbing the reins of his horse.

"So?"

Marcus's heart sank when he saw the older man's expression. His response only confirmed what Marcus feared.

"Gone. Two days ago."

"Where?" Marcus's jaw clenched.

"Massilia, they're to be sold to a slaver."

Marcus fought the rage building inside him. He took a shallow breath and looked back toward Lutetia.

"I'll go after them. I might get lucky and catch them before they reach the coast." He looked back up at Nicodemus. "But I need a sword. And gold."

Nicodemus dismounted and untied a blanket from behind the saddle. He unfolded it, exposing a sword and scabbard within.

"I hoped you wouldn't need this." He handed the sword to Marcus, along with a small pouch of coins. "And this is all I have."

"Thank you." Marcus took the sword and wrapped the belt

around his waist. He opened the pouch and poured a few coins out, which he handed back to Nicodemus. He then closed up the bag and tied it to his belt.

"Go back to town. In my house will be my family papers. Bring them to Massilia. If needed, we can use them to secure more gold."

Marcus disappeared into the trees, emerging soon after with a horse in tow. He vaulted onto his steed, and using both heels, urged the beast into a gallop.

As he thundered past, Nicodemus whispered. "Godspeed."

Marcus stood on the dock, fists clenched, and watched the galley fade into the sunset. He had missed them by an hour, maybe less.

Looking around, he clutched the arm of a nearby dock worker. "Where is that ship going?"

"Fuck you!"

Marcus grabbed him by the throat, stifling his cry. He clawed at the Roman's grip but could not break it. The worker nodded frantically, willing to give up the destination. Marcus let him go, and he fell to his knees, rubbing his throat.

"Sardinia," he gulped.

"Where can I hire a boat?"

The man pointed to a nearby building. Turning, Marcus watched several sailors enter a door beneath a small sign.

"You can have that." Marcus nodded toward the winded horse and tossed the worker a gold coin. "I won't be needing it."

As he made his way across the quay, he squinted to make out the faded letters on the sign.

Hades Den. Appropriate.

CHAPTER THREE

Whoever fights monsters should see to it that in the process he does not become a monster. And if you gaze long enough into an abyss, the abyss will gaze back into you.
—FRIEDRICH NIETZSCHE

MODERN DAY
PARIS

MARCUS WATCHED SAM from the top level of the club, ignoring the strobe lights and thumping techno music. She stood near the bar, a drink in hand for show.

Scanning the crowd, Marcus spotted Levi as he pulled two young women across the dance floor. He was in his late-thirties, with greasy black hair and cinnamon-colored skin. A hawk nose dominated his shallow face, set below a pair of menacing eyes. His six-foot frame was lean and sharp.

Levi arrived at the bar and motioned for his tab. Sam set down her drink and turned toward the exit, bumping into Levi as she passed. He looked up as Sam placed her hand on his shoulder and leaned forward to say something into his ear. Levi looked her up and down, then reached for her, but she was already walking away.

Confident she had placed the bug, Marcus slipped through the crowd and down the narrow steps. He stepped into the crisp Paris night and took a deep breath to clear his smoke-filled lungs. Sam waited for him near the end of the line of people waiting to get in.

"You got it?"

Marcus frowned at the screen. "I think so."

"Let me see." She took the phone from him. "You really need to get better at these things."

"I know."

"It's good, see?" She showed him the dot on the screen. "He'll be out soon."

They started down the sidewalk, and when traffic allowed, crossed the street.

"You see he had two girls?" Sam said.

"Yeah, it's normal for him to escalate."

"Should we just grab him now?"

"We talked about this, Sam." Marcus stopped in front of a black sedan, leaning his arms on the roof as he looked over at her. "We need to know where he's staying."

"Yeah, but I'm sure we could find that out..." Her voice trailed off when she realized Marcus was scowling at her.

"We stick to the plan." He opened the door and slipped into the driver's seat.

Sam shook her head, opened the passenger's side and got inside.

She grabbed the iPad from the dash and opened up the tracking app. "Here he comes."

Levi emerged with the girls in tow. He handed a slip to a valet, and soon, his red BMW pulled up to the curb. A few minutes later, they were speeding down the street.

Marcus switched on the headlights and pulled onto the

rain-soaked street. They drove along the empty boulevards, following the signal on the map. Now and then, they could see the taillights of the BMW as it moved through the darkness. They were entering a seedy part of Paris, full of abandoned warehouses and run-down tenements. Sam could see dark figures huddled in the shadows, the orange glow of a cigarette piercing the night.

As the signal came to a stop, Marcus flicked off his lights and pulled the car to the curb. The BMW, brake lights reflecting off the shallow puddles, had stopped in front of a warehouse as it waited for the garage door to open. A few seconds later, the lights disappeared, and the car slipped inside. Sam handed Marcus a pair of infrared binoculars, and he scanned the four-story building. He located several warm signatures around the perimeter and a couple more behind the various windows.

"Who owns this place?" Marcus scanned the surrounding buildings.

"Hold on...I don't have the best signal. Why don't we have 5G?"

"I don't even know what that is."

"Never mind." She clicked through a series of documents. "It belongs to Lumex, Inc., kinda—it went into foreclosure six years ago. Gideon Bank holds the lien—but," she scanned the transaction history, "they never listed it for sale."

"I'm sure Thomas owns both companies." Marcus set down the binoculars. "Time to go."

"Yeah, we don't have all night."

"What, you got a hot date?"

"Tinder—"

"Jesus!" Marcus grimaced at her, then inserted a miniature receiver into his ear and adjusted the microphone strapped around his neck. "Testing, testing—"

"Got it." Sam had slipped on a pair of earbuds and was

punching up more data on the iPad. "City records show this place has four levels. The bottom floor is shipping, docks, and ramps. The second and third floors are cold storage. The top is an office. A stairwell and freight elevator go up to all levels. There might be a stairwell to the roof. Should have fire escapes on all the floors."

"Negative—" Marcus inspected the building again, this time using the night vision setting on the binoculars. "They're gone."

"Well, that's not very safe..."

"Call in the fire marshal; maybe we can ticket them into giving us what we want." Marcus leveled his glasses on the top floor windows. "Alright, looks like he's settling in. Are we ready to go?"

"Yep, I downloaded the blueprints." Sam handed him an iPhone with a cable. "If you find his computer, connect this to the USB port. You know...the oblong connector?"

"I know what a USB port is..."

"Well, I can never tell..."

"Sam."

"That will get me remote access to his hard drive. The script will run after you plug it in. I'm sure it's encrypted, so a password would be helpful."

"Got it."

"Good...break a leg."

"Not funny."

"I know, last time was two legs," Sam said. "One is better."

Marcus muttered something indiscernible beneath his breath as he stuck the phone into his jacket. Marcus switched off the dome light, popped the trunk, and exited the car. He lifted the lid and dropped a few items into his pockets before slipping into the shadow of the nearest building. Marcus could see his breath billowing out before him as his eyes adjusted to the night. He clung to the darkness and made his way down the empty street. At this hour, he was counting on the guards being less attentive.

"Sam?"

"Yeah?"

"Watch the guards; I need to know if I'm spotted."

"I think you'll know when they shoot at you."

"Just watch."

Marcus reached an alley where he stopped and studied the building next to the warehouse, across from him. Both buildings were the same height. He shoved his hands into his pockets, walked across the street and up a set of stone steps, kneeling in the doorway. The door was chained shut, but he could push it open just enough to squeeze inside.

The windows were covered with plywood, but some moonlight slipped through. It was just enough to allow Marcus to move around without stumbling into the scattered debris. He reached the far wall and spotted a recess that looked like a stairwell. He started up the staircase, careful to avoid the gaping holes in the steps. The wood was spongy, but it held, and after three rickety flights, he reached the roof.

A strong breeze met him as he emerged from the doorway and walked up to a low brick wall on the edge of the roof. He studied the opposite building and, satisfied it was deserted, opened his coat and produced a narrow metal cylinder connected to a bundle of cable. When engaged, four sharp spikes extended from the casing to form a grappling hook. He gathered the thin line into his left hand and swung the hook in a tight circle, launching it towards a short ventilation pipe just beyond the distant roofline. The fixture landed about two feet beyond the target, so Marcus moved to his left and pulled the cable until the hook wedged onto the pipe. He took up the slack, walked to a nearby fire escape ladder, and wrapped the wire around the metal frame, securing it in place. He lowered himself onto the wire and shimmied across the opening, pulling himself onto the roof.

"I'm on top of the building, about to move in." Marcus knelt to catch his breath.

"Gotcha, everything's quiet." After a brief pause, Sam said, "It's probably a trap."

Marcus ignored her, moved to the square hut that held the staircase door, and tested the knob. It was locked. He knelt and took out his penlight, placing it in his mouth so he could inspect the knob. He used several tools from a small pouch, began working on the lock, and within a minute, he was putting the tools away and pulling a silenced pistol from his coat. He opened the door, stepped inside, and waited for his eyes to adjust before proceeding down the steps. When he reached the bottom of the staircase, he could hear voices in the room ahead. He pulled out his phone and flicked through a building floor plan, stopping at the top floor. The door was in the room's corner, next to a door leading to the interior staircase.

He reached down and twisted the handle, relieved to find it unlocked. He pulled the door open and slipped into the shadows of the corner.

"More than you expected, huh, bitch?" He could hear the question, but the response was more of a moan. "I'm just disappointed your friend is no longer with us."

Wow, that was fast. Marcus drove the thought from his mind and moved into the light, pausing for a moment to ensure the deadbolt on the main door was locked. After taking a couple of steps, he could see the entire room. The voices came from behind a row of fabric panels that segregated one part of the floor into what he assumed was a bedroom. A kitchen stood on his right, built along the outside wall. The middle of the room had a couple of sofas and a huge TV, its volume muted.

A girl's body was sprawled across one sofa, strips of blood-

43

splattered clothing clinging to her lifeless body. Marcus moved around the couch, keeping a wary eye on the bedroom opening. She was young, nineteen or twenty, with pale skin and long blonde hair. Her throat was sliced open from ear to ear, a look of terror frozen on her pretty face. Marcus reached down to close her eyelids and then walked over to the bedroom.

It took up the entire end of the floor, with massive windows that dominated the wall. Underneath the windows lay a sprawling bed, at the foot of which stood Levi holding a long, curved knife. He was staring down at a girl, her wrists and ankles tied to the bedposts. She was covered in blood, but it did not look like she was bleeding.

"Hello, Levi."

"I said no—" Turning, the color drained from his face. Levi looked down at the naked girl and then dropped his weapon.

"Now why did you do that?" Marcus circled him.

"I don't know."

"You never were that smart."

Eyes squinting, Levi scanned the room, pausing on a pistol sitting on the nightstand.

"You won't make it."

Levi was fast, but Marcus was faster. The first slug tore into Levi's shoulder, knocking him away from the nightstand and onto the floor. He rolled to a stop, blood gushing from the wound. Undeterred, he sprang up and ran toward the weapon.

The second slug shattered his kneecap. Levi crumpled to the floor, clutching his bleeding leg. Marcus walked over to him, gun leveled.

"I told you."

"Fuck off!"

Marcus waved the weapon toward the door. "Let's go."

Levi glared up at him.

"Suit yourself."

Marcus caught his chin with the point of his boot,

sending blood and teeth flying across the room as Levi collapsed into a heap. Marcus leaned over and grabbed the collar of his shirt, dragging him across the wooden floor. He pulled him into the living room, stopping in front of a wooden chair. Marcus set his weapon down on a nearby table and lifted the limp body into the seat. He reached into his coat, producing a roll of duct tape, and taped Levi's arms and legs to the chair.

Marcus tossed the tape onto the couch and scanned the rest of the room for Levi's computer. He saw it on a desk near the window. Marcus moved over to the laptop, tapped on the keyboard, and watched the screen flicker to life. He knelt beside the desk, pulled out the phone, and plugged it into the USB port. The tiny screen sprung to life as the script ran.

Marcus was about to get up when he noticed a small leather case sitting on the desk. He opened it and found four sealed vials of blood. He pulled one out and read the small label. It had a date and time, but nothing else. He frowned and put the vial back, slipping the case into his jacket pocket.

"Sam, you should have remote access."

"Yep. I need the password."

"You already told me that."

"I know, but my uncle said you forget the important things."

Marcus shook his head and glanced back at Levi, who was still sitting unconscious in the chair. He moved back toward the bedroom and peeked back into the opening. The girl glared at him. Marcus moved into the room, picked up a blanket from the floor, and used it to cover her naked body.

"It's going to be alright," he said in French. "I'm going to cut you free, but I need you to be very quiet. Understand?"

She trembled. Fear and distrust filled her glistening eyes as Marcus produced a small knife from his pocket. He held up one hand to calm her and cut the bonds that held her feet, allowing her to curl her legs up into her chest. Marcus then moved forward and cut the ropes that held her wrists. She clung to the thin blanket and recoiled into the fetal position.

"I know this is hard, but I need to ask you some questions." Marcus sat on the bed.

She stared back at him.

"What's your name?"

"Camille."

"All right, Camille. My name is Marcus." He took a moment to look around the room. "If I find your clothes, do you think you can walk?"

She nodded.

"Good. I'm leaving so you can get dressed. Please come out when you're finished. And I need you to do this quickly, understand?"

She nodded again. Marcus stood up, gathered her scattered clothes, and placed them next to her. He found her high heels under the corner of the bed, and scanning the room, found what he was looking for near the far wall. He moved to a tall dresser and rifled through the drawers until he found a couple of pairs of socks. Camille sat up when he returned to the bed.

"Your shoes are useless. Put these on."

Marcus dropped the socks on the bed and started back to the living room. He stopped when he felt a tug on his coat. He looked down to find her tear-stained face staring up at him.

"Thank you."

"You're welcome. Please hurry." He turned away before she could respond. Levi was awake when he stepped into the living room.

"Are you keeping my *guessst* company?" He had a lisp from the missing teeth.

Marcus pulled up another chair and sat down and glared at Levi.

"What?" Levi pressed.

Marcus replied with silence.

"Is *thisss* the part where you *ssscare* me? Intimidate me?"

"Where is Thomas?"

"Who?"

"And I'm also gonna need the password," he waved his gun toward the desk, "to your laptop."

"I forgot it."

"Easy or painful."

"Fuck off."

"You need to get more original with your insults. Painful it is."

Marcus set his gun down on the table and reached into his jacket, pulling out a small black case. He opened the case, picked out one of several needles and a small glass bottle. Levi watched as Marcus stuck the needle through the lid of the bottle and filled the syringe.

"This is sulfuric acid, mixed with saline. It would turn a normal person's nervous system to ash." Marcus glanced at the man's shoulder wound, which had already stopped bleeding. "But you're not normal, are you?"

Levi watched the needle from the corner of his eye.

"Once this starts moving through your bloodstream, your entire body will be on fire." Marcus set down the needle and picked up the roll of duct tape from the coffee table, ripping off a six-inch strip. "Last chance."

"I got *nottthhing.*"

"Brave, but stupid." Marcus put the tape over his mouth and tapped his forehead. "To be honest, I was hoping you'd chose painful."

He knelt beside Levi and emptied the contents of the syringe into his jugular. Levi strained against the tape, his body stiffening. Marcus tossed the needle onto the couch and glanced back at Levi.

"Give me the password, and I'll make it quick."

He was waiting for some sort of response from Levi when

Camille walked into the room. A question formed on her lips, but Marcus cut her off.

"Camille, I need you to go to those stairs." Marcus pointed to the door that led to the ceiling. "Go up to the roof and wait for me. I'll be there in a minute."

She stood still, watching Levi convulse.

"Camille!"

She snapped back to life and nodded as she headed for the door. Marcus turned his attention back to Levi, whose skin was dark purple in a dozen places.

"You ready?"

Levi's head bobbed up and down, so Marcus ripped the tape from his mouth.

"Fuuuuck off!" he groaned and passed out.

That was the problem with immortals, Marcus thought. *They get used to pain.* He picked up his gun and walked over to the computer to check on the download's progress.

"Sam, I think it's finished. But I couldn't get the password."

"That's not the only problem you have. Three cars just pulled up to the building."

"For fuck's sake," he said.

Marcus unplugged the iPhone and dropped it into his pocket. There was also a cellphone on the table which he took as well. It came to life when he picked it up, and he realized he would need another password. Or...

He looked toward Levi, who had rocked himself back and forth enough to push the chair over backward. As he fell to the floor, the chair broke into several pieces. Levi scrambled to his feet and then toward the door, the pieces of wood still taped to his arms and legs. Marcus followed him up the steps and reached Levi just as he pushed a black intercom button. A red light blinked as Levi spun back toward Marcus, a smile on his bloody face.

His victory was short-lived. Marcus smirked and fired a

48

round into his forehead. As Levi's body fell to the ground, Marcus turned toward the exit. Camille was standing next to the door. He was going to say something when she bent over and vomited.

"Fuck me." Marcus looked down and put five more rounds into Levi's head.

"I heard that," Sam said. "What happened?"

"Nothing."

He knelt, pulled out his knife, and laid Levi's hand flat on the floor, severing his thumb with the sharp blade. He wrapped the thumb in a piece of Levi's shirt and stuffed it into his pocket, along with the knife. He sprinted toward Camille, pulling out his pistol on the way. As he neared the exit, he could hear shouts coming from the stairwell beyond, followed by a pounding on the metal door. He looked over at Camille, who wiped her mouth with the back of her hand.

"Get up the stairs."

Her eyes shifted from him to Levi.

"Now!"

As she started up the stairs to the roof, Marcus fired several rounds through the main door. The titanium-tipped bullets ripped through the metal panel, and the shouts beyond fell silent. The spent casings were still skittering across the floor as Marcus disappeared up the stairwell.

Camille was just ahead of him, slowly climbing the steps.

"Faster!"

Below, he could hear muffled gunfire, followed by heavy thuds, as the guards battered against the door.

"Sam, I need a way out."

"Jesus Christ, there must be two-dozen men running around out here." She paused for a moment. "Can you get out the way you came in? I can get to the far side of that building with the car."

"I can try...nice plan."

"Hey, it's not my fault you didn't have an exit strategy, again."

Marcus fired several more shots down the stairwell, just as the first guard stepped through the opening. The rounds hammered him back against the wall. Marcus tossed the empty weapon down the steps, pulled out his other pistol, and followed the girl out the door. He turned and looked back down the stairs as two men rounded the corner with their guns raised. Marcus fired down at them and pulled a grenade from the webbing under his coat. He flicked the pin with his thumb and dropped it down the stairwell. He slammed the door shut and pulled Camille to the side as the blast shook the building.

Marcus looked at the girl. She was in shock, and the frosty night air was not helping. He took her hand, leading her to the cable connecting the two buildings. Marcus glanced back toward the doorway, knowing the guards would spill out at any moment. He pulled his knife out and severed the cable with the serrated edge of the blade, then dropped the knife and moved back to the edge of the roof with the line in one hand. He gauged the distance, wrapped a length of the wire around his arm and brought the rest back up to grip in his hand. With his left hand, he motioned for the girl to join him.

As she inched toward him, Marcus wrapped one arm around her. "Hold on to me."

"What!" She tried to step away. "Are you crazy?"

"Yes, but you have to trust me, or you're going to die on this roof."

Pausing, she glanced back at the menacing doorway behind them and nodded as she draped her arms around him.

Marcus wrapped his coat around her body and clenched the cable with his other hand. Together, they stepped onto the short wall and shimmied to the right, lining themselves up with a window on the opposite side.

"God, I hope this works—" he said.

"What works?" Sam said in his earpiece.

"You don't want to know."

He looked up at the star-filled sky, took a deep breath and stepped off the ledge. The girl screamed as they plummeted through the darkness. They were still picking up speed when they crashed through the plywood and glass covering the window. Marcus grunted as the shards of wood and glass dug into his hands and face.

They landed with a thud, debris settling all around them. As Marcus uncoiled the wire from his arm, a sharp pain shot through his lower back. In the pale moonlight, he could see a piece of wood protruding from his side, just above his waistline. Groaning, he sat up and slid his hand along his back. The other end of the shard was sticking out an inch or so from his skin. Marcus rolled to his knees and used the windowsill to pull himself up. He looked back at the roof and could see several men raising their weapons to fire toward the window.

Camille stood a couple of feet from the opening, waiting for Marcus. He ignored the sharp pain exploding from his side and sprang toward the girl, bullets tearing up the surrounding floor. As they tumbled to the ground, Marcus felt a round slam into his shoulder. The Spectra fabric of his jacket absorbed most of the force, but the bullet penetrated the material and lodged in his muscle. Marcus grimaced as he rolled to his side, then to his knees, one hand covering the wound in his side. He took several shallow breaths before reaching for Camille.

She did not respond.

In the faint moonlight, he could see that she was staring at the ceiling. He scanned her body and found a single entry wound near her heart and noticed a large pool of blood gathering around her body. Marcus shook his head, then closed her eyes and studied her peaceful expression for a moment before he heard a distant voice calling his name. He looked down and realized his earpiece had fallen out and was dangling by his chest. He used two bloody fingers to slip the piece back into his ear.

"Marcus? Are you there?" Sam was getting frantic. "Marcus!"

"I'm here—" He peered around the darkened room. "I'm on the third floor, getting ready to head down. I expect a lot of trouble, so I'm going to exit on the second floor."

"Okay. Some windows have fire escapes."

"Some?" He moved away from the body and deeper into the building. "If I can't find one, I'll jump."

"Isn't that how you broke your legs last time?"

"Shut up."

After a few minutes, he found the stairwell. He could see flashlights from guards making their way up. As he reached the first landing, his foot plunged through the rotted wood. He pulled it out and thought about turning back, but decided against it. As he took another step, the weakened floor disintegrated around him. He lunged for the railing, but it was out of reach.

"Oh shit."

He pulled in his arms, letting his body fall through the rotting wood. A few seconds later, he landed among a group of men making their way up the staircase. There was a moment of total silence as they stood in the darkness, then the creaking and groaning staircase collapsed. The others scrambled to escape the crumbling structure, but Marcus grabbed one of them, shoving him to the floor. He was perched on top of the man when the framework gave way and they all plunged into the abyss. As they hit the ground, the guard's body cushioned most of the impact, allowing Marcus to roll off him and come to a kneeling position among the ruins.

There were a dozen groaning bodies lying around him. Marcus stood, hoping to reach the window before more guards showed up. But he was not so lucky. Within seconds, several flashlights were scanning the room, and one fell upon him.

Marcus pulled out his pistol and fired at the light. He realized the muzzle blasts had given away his position, so he dropped the weapon and sprinted toward the moonlight seeping through a nearby window.

Splinters peppered him as the bullets chewed up the floor and ceiling. One round sliced through his calf. Another grazed his wrist. He covered his head with his hands and dove through the window. For a moment, he enjoyed the cool night breeze, knowing the cold, hard street was soon to follow. He lowered his good shoulder and grunted as his body crashed into the cobblestone, tumbling into a grove of trash cans.

Marcus came to a stop against a brick wall, surrounded by decaying rubbish. He heard the angry screech of tires and looked up to see a pair of glowing red lights bearing down upon him. The shouts from inside the building grew louder as the car stopped and the passenger door swung open. He crawled forward and pulled himself up into the seat. As they catapulted back down the alley, the door slammed shut, and bullets clunked into the heavy chassis.

Marcus shifted in his seat, stifling a groan.

Sam spun the car onto the street, then glanced over at Marcus. "The girls?"

"Dead." Marcus grimaced. "Tell me you got the files."

"Yeah, I got them, but they're encrypted." She paused. "What happened?"

Sam looked over at her partner. Marcus was staring through the passenger window, a blank look on his bloody face. Turning back to the road, she drove them to their flat.

CHAPTER FOUR

Heaven is high, Earth Wide.
Bitter between them flies my sorrow.
—Li Po

Summer 38 A.D.
Carthage, Ifrīqiyyah

Marcus leaned back in his chair, nursed his cup of wine and studied the man seated in the far corner. Shadows from the nearby fireplace danced across the man's sweaty, pockmarked face. He was engaged in a lively discussion with several others that grew louder with each pitcher of wine.

Outside, the sultry summer night pressed on, but it made no difference to Marcus. He had no place to be and an eternity to get there. He took another swig, set his cup down and waited. Two pitchers later, the room was almost empty, and the fire was a pile of fading embers. The owner wasn't adding more wood. Even bartenders have to sleep.

Marcus, realizing the end was near, stood and drained his cup. He dropped several coins on the bar on his way to the door

54

and headed out into the night. A breeze, dry and lonely, swept across the dark street. Marcus looked up to the cloudless sky; it would be months before it rained again. By then, he would be in another dark corner of the empire. He looked around the alley and found a dark niche in a nearby building, which he occupied.

Marcus settled into the silence, a place he always dreaded. The last thing he wanted to do was be alone with his thoughts. He tried to clear his mind and focus on the tavern. The promise of the pain he was going to inflict brought him a measure of solace.

The tavern door swung outwards, and three men staggered from the entrance. The trio gathered for one last salutation, then parted ways. Two of the men walked past Marcus and disappeared. The third swayed for a moment, somehow staying upright, then stumbled away. Marcus moved forward, slipping from shadow to shadow as he stalked his prey. He was just about to make his move when the man lurched into an opening between two slumping buildings.

Marcus thought he might have been noticed, but then realized the man was vomiting. Marcus approached the gap and saw his target bent over with his hands on his knees. The sickening odor of stale wine drifted from the alley as the man emptied his stomach again. Marcus retreated from the opening and waited.

The retching stopped, and the man stepped back into the street. Marcus grabbed him by his tunic and spun him through the air, slamming him into the wall.

"What the hell!" the man cried.

"Shut up!" Marcus shoved one hand over his mouth.

The man squirmed, his bloodshot eyes straining. The more he fought, the harder Marcus pushed his head into the wall. As they struggled in silence, the moon crept over the nearest rooftop and chased away the shadows. The silver glow reflected off his sweaty forehead as the man finally gave up the fight.

Marcus placed his forearm across the man's throat and lowered his hand. "What's your name?"

"Huh?"

Marcus slapped him. "Your name!"

"Mi, Mi–"

"Well?"

"Miltiades!"

"Are you the captain of the Hesperides?"

"Yes!"

"Did you pick up a group of slaves in Massilia three months ago?"

"No–" Marcus pulled back his hand to strike again. "I mean yes—yes, I did."

Marcus snarled through clenched teeth, "Where did you take them?"

"Alexandria...always Alexandria. My brother runs a slave market there."

"A name!"

"What?"

Marcus pulled him from the wall and slammed his head into the stone. The heavy thud sounded like a melon cracking, which meant his skull was fractured. *I better hurry before he blacks out*, Marcus thought. He leaned forward. "What is his name!"

"Sappho...His name is Sappho." His voice slurred.

Marcus held up a gold coin. "For Charon."

Marcus pressed the coin into his mouth and clamped it shut. He held it closed with one hand and used his other to shove a dagger into the Greek's midsection. Eyes bulging, Miltiades tried to squirm away. Unrelenting, Marcus slid the blade to the side, watching as the life drained from his countenance. As Marcus stepped back, Miltiades buckled to the ground. His mouth fell open, the coin glinting in the moonlight.

Marcus looked at the knife, clutched in his blood-soaked hand. He dropped the knife, disappearing into the darkness. He would need to catch the tide if he wanted to sail tonight.

For more than a week, the galley skirted the dark African coast. Marcus paced the worn deck like a wounded animal, stopping now and then to look up at the billowing sail. Just after sundown on the eighth day, a string of fireflies appeared on the horizon. The captain was summoned, and after conferring with his first mate, they agreed it was Alexandria. Marcus was standing near the railing when the captain gave the order to lower the sail.

Marcus frowned at him. "Why are we reducing sail?"

"It's too dark. We shall slow our approach and enter the city at sunrise."

The sailors stopped to watch their exchange. He turned his gaze toward Alexandria, his hands on his hips, grinding his teeth. So close.

Marcus studied the captain. He was a short and stocky Sicilian with thick leather skin from years beneath the blistering sun. Beside him stood the first mate, a tall Phoenician with a mangled left ear and a lazy eye. The second man shifted closer to the captain, offering moral support.

Marcus glared at them. They were not the same men he had hired three months ago. After selling his family's assets in Massilia, Marcus had plenty of gold, and he used it. The captain and his crew, having been paid twice the going rate, were eager to please. But in the ensuing three months, they had sailed farther than most ships would in a year. And Marcus was an impatient client, often pushing the captain to ignore customary discretion in favor of expediency. They could tell another such request was forthcoming. The captain preempted the Roman.

"I cannot navigate the harbor at night...the entrance is too narrow." He looked up at the sliver of a moon. "With better light, I might try such a thing. But it's too dark for that tonight."

Marcus glowered at him, the lines of his face sharpening. Only the night stood between them as the boat rolled in the shallow swells. The creaking of the old ship and the occasional ripple of the sail magnified the silence.

Nodding, Marcus looked away. "Very well. I want to be moving into the harbor as the sun rises."

"Of course."

Marcus ignored him, just as he ignored the hatred in his heart. It would have to wait one more day.

Once they docked, it did not take Marcus long to find Sappho. There were hundreds of slave traders in Alexandria, but few were Greek, and only one was named Sappho. It turned out that he traded in all commodities, not just slaves. But Marcus didn't care; he was after one thing and one thing only. Sappho would provide that before he died.

Marcus waited in the shade of a fruit stand, chewing on a handful of dried dates as he studied a two-story building across the dusty plaza. It was one of a dozen similar buildings that served as slaver's row. Marcus had learned that the slaves were sold and traded twice a week in auctions held in the plaza he was now surveying.

Over the next few hours, he watched a dozen men enter and leave the building. The afternoon was giving way to the night when Marcus abandoned the stand, leaving a few coins with the vendor. It had been at least thirty minutes since the last customer had left the building, and Marcus was convinced the Greek would soon close shop for the day. Sappho was not aware that he would receive one more customer.

Marcus slipped through the thinning crowd and stopped before the building, checking both directions before pushing open the door.

The interior was dark and cool and would have felt refreshing in any other circumstance. As the door swung closed behind Marcus, he glanced around the shop. It was full of various trinkets, junk mostly, from all over the empire. An extended counter stood before the back wall, with a bead-covered arch leading to a backroom. Marcus reached back to the door and secured the latch. As he turned back into the shop, the beads split open to reveal a half-dressed man with an annoyed expression on his sweaty face.

"I'm closed. Come back tomorrow." He said in Egyptian. Sappho didn't bother entering the room until he noticed Marcus did not appear to be leaving. He tried again in broken Latin. "I'm closed. Come back tomorrow."

"I think I'll stay," Marcus replied in Greek.

Disgruntled, Sappho pushed his way through the beads as he tied the drawstring of his trousers. He was taller than his brother but had the same shiny, pockmarked complexion. They must have shared the disease as children. Marcus grinned as he thought about what else they would soon share.

"What are you smiling about?" Sappho stepped further into the room. "Get out of here!"

Marcus punched him in the chest. Grunting, the Greek spun around and stumbled into the counter. Sappho fought to catch his breath, clawing at the bar to keep from falling. Marcus stepped forward and kicked him between the shoulder blades, driving his chest into the edge of the countertop. Sappho would have screamed, but his lungs were empty. Gasping, he slid to the ground.

Marcus pulled him to his feet and dragged him through the beads. That's when he realized why Sappho was half-dressed.

A large bed, occupied by a young, frightened girl, was

pushed up against the far wall. She could not have been over twelve and was probably younger. She sat on the edge of the straw mattress and tried to reposition her dirty, ripped tunic to cover her thin body. Marcus pulled his eyes from the girl and settled them on the wheezing Greek.

Sappho, trying to recover, glanced at the girl, then at Marcus. His eyes bulged.

"Wait, I can ex–"

Marcus grabbed his jaw and mouth with one hand, cutting off his excuse. As Sappho struggled to free himself, Marcus turned toward the girl. "Go into the other room and wait for me."

She stared at him, a blank expression on her face. So Marcus repeated the instructions in Greek. She still didn't understand. Exasperated, Marcus glanced down at Sappho, who was close to passing out. Marcus dropped his body to the floor and looked at the girl. Again, he repeated the instructions, this time in stilted Egyptian. She seemed to understand, stood, and crossed the room. Her focus shifted back and forth between Sappho and Marcus.

When she disappeared through the beads, Marcus leaned over and pulled the Greek to his feet. He was still groggy when Marcus shoved him into a nearby chair. Sappho squinted and looked up at Marcus.

"Who are you?"

Marcus slapped him. "I ask the questions."

Sappho rubbed the side of his face and scowled at Marcus. "Do you know who I am?"

Marcus slapped him again, this time almost knocking Sappho from the chair. He climbed back into the seat, glaring at Marcus. His lips trembled as he swallowed another question.

Marcus picked up a nearby broom and snapped off the handle. "You will answer me immediately, or I'm going to break one of your bones. Understand?"

Sappho nodded.

"Your brother sold you a shipment of slaves he picked up in Massilia. Do you remember?"

"He brings me many slaves," Sappho said.

"These would have been Roman. A woman, with two..." His voice trembled. Marcus had to stop and swallow, before going on, "two children. A boy and a girl. Both young teenagers. Do you remember them?"

"Yes." Sappho stared at Marcus, his dark eyes probing. Marcus resented the intrusion and pulled back the handle. "Don't look at me!"

Sappho dropped his eyes to the floor.

"Where did they go?"

"I don't know."

Marcus smashed his right shin with the stick, shattering the tibia. Sappho bent over, howling in agony. Marcus grabbed his hair and yanked him back into the chair.

"Where did they go!"

"I don't remember!"

"Wrong answer."

Marcus shattered the kneecap on his other leg. Sappho threw back his head and squealed. Marcus clenched his jaw and watched him squirm.

"Where?"

"I...I..." Sappho looked up at Marcus. "A Syrian bought the children."

"Who?"

"Calimade...He's a merchant from Antioch."

Calimade. Always another name, Marcus thought.

"And the woman?"

Sappho took short, stunted breaths, sweat pouring down his face.

"You're going to kill me."

"Yes, but how much pain you suffer is up to you."

Sappho took a deep breath, sitting up in the chair. Exhaling, he nodded and looked up at Marcus. "She went to a local brothel owner. His name is Sayid."

The room spun. Light-headed, Marcus focused on standing upright. She was in the city! He took a sharp breath and studied the Greek. To Marcus, it sounded as if a stranger was asking the question.

"Where is this brothel?"

"It is near the docks. Ask any sailor; he will know." Knowing his fate gave him a little courage. "You should hurry. Women don't last very long in a place like that."

Marcus clenched his jaw and pulled a gold coin from his pocket. He looked down at the coin as he rubbed the smooth surface with his thumb. His eyes shifted to the sharp end of the broken stick, then to Sappho. The latter shook his head and sobbed, but Marcus ignored his pleas and spun the rod around, plunging it down through his collarbone and into his torso. Sappho screamed and tried to push Marcus away, but the Roman was too strong. He pushed the stick down until it punctured Sappho's heart. A few moments later, he stopped struggling and crumpled to the floor.

Marcus moved to the bed, using the blanket to wipe the blood from his hands. Tossing it aside, he grabbed a clay lantern from the table and shattered it on the floor near the bed. The fish oil inside splattered across the bedding, and soon the flames were climbing up the walls.

Smoke was pouring from the building by the time Marcus led the young girl across the plaza. He handed her a small bag of coins and motioned for her to leave. As the sun disappeared into the blood orange sky, flames poked from the doors and windows of the slave shop. Marcus watched the shopkeepers scurry like rats as the fire spread to the surrounding buildings.

Turning toward the docks, Marcus began the longest walk of his life.

Marcus had been sitting at the bar for an hour yet had not worked up the courage to speak.

He looked down into the wooden cup of cheap wine and raised it to his mouth. It took every ounce of energy to keep his hand from shaking. The bartender, a skinny Egyptian with only a couple of teeth, studied him from behind the bar. Marcus choked down the wine, wiping his mouth with the back of his hand. Marcus shifted his attention to the black opening in the far corner and clenched his teeth. He glanced up at the bartender.

"Girls?" Marcus mumbled.

The bartender took a step forward and squinted at Marcus. "What?"

Marcus cleared his throat. "Girls?"

He nodded and then tilted his head toward the opening. "In there."

Marcus pushed himself away from the counter and forced himself to walk toward the doorway. The narrow hallway beyond smelled like stale urine and sweat. Marcus fought the bile rising in his throat and continued into the small room beyond. There seemed to be several corridors, each leading down a hallway with more doors. Another skinny Egyptian sat on a stool in the shadow of a slow-burning torch.

He studied Marcus with dull, black eyes. "One girl or two?"

"Ah," Marcus stuttered.

"Just one?"

Marcus wiped his sweating forehead and blurted out, "I'm looking for a woman..."

"Yes, yes, of course." He stood.

Marcus put his shaking hand on the other man's chest. "A special woman."

The man looked down at his hand, then up at Marcus. The Roman was a good eight inches taller than him.

"What special woman?"

"A Roman."

His expression dropped, the blood draining from his face. "No woman like that here. No Romans, they're illegal."

Marcus could feel the Egyptian's heart pounding. He grabbed a fistful of tunic and growled, "Where is she?"

The man shrunk away, his eyes shifting toward the corridor. Marcus turned just as the bartender smashed a stool across his back. The chair shattered into a dozen pieces. Unfazed, Marcus flung the man he held at the bartender, knocking them both to the ground. The bartender tried to stand, but Marcus kicked him in the face. As he slumped to the ground, Marcus used both hands to grab the other man's tunic and lifted him off the ground as he repeated his earlier demand.

"Where is she!"

The man clawed at his iron grip, but Marcus just lifted him higher. As the man struggled, Marcus saw the bartender move, so he kicked him again, then again.

Moving toward the opening in the back of the room, Marcus dragged the Egyptian with him. There were no other doors in this narrow hallway, just a tall archway near the end. He advanced and emerged into some sort of lounge, filled with a dozen startled women. Heart skipping, Marcus scanned their faces. He saw a mixture of fear and curiosity, but nothing familiar. The Egyptian had stopped struggling, so Marcus dropped his limp body.

"Does anyone speak Latin?"

"I do." One woman raised her hand. She could have been twenty or forty; it was impossible to tell.

"I have gold, and I'll free all of you if you help me."

Standing, she studied him for a moment and took a few steps forward. "What do you want?"

"I'm here for a...friend."

"Natalia?"

The sound of her name knocked the wind out of him. Marcus bit his lip and nodded.

Without waiting for an answer, she said, "How much gold?"

"More than you need...and I can get you out of the city as well."

She looked around at the other girls as Marcus waited for her to answer.

"We will do it."

"Good. How many others?"

"Three. Two are with clients, and Natalia is upstairs...she is very sick."

Marcus swallowed hard. Nodding, he looked at the nearby staircase.

"Is there another exit?"

"Through there." She pointed to a dark opening in the corner.

"Very good, ah..." he looked at her.

"Sabrina."

"Sabrina...tie him up." Marcus nodded to the Egyptian. "I'll bring the other one."

"And then?"

"Then you get the other two girls away from their clients. Have them collect their things, only what they can carry. Do it all quietly."

She spoke to the others. Marcus recognized the Egyptian word for gold, and their response was immediate. The man was waking up when two of the ladies pounced on him. He screamed, but they shoved a cloth down into his mouth and, flipping him over, bound his hands and feet together.

Marcus moved back down the hallway and grabbed the bartender by his collar. He dragged him to the lounge and flung him next to the other man. The girls secured him as well.

"I have sent for the other girls," Sabrina said.

"Good." Marcus glanced at the staircase.

"I'll take you to her." Sabrina started for the stairs.

Marcus willed his legs to follow Sabrina as she climbed the steps. They moved down a long hallway with a half-dozen doors. Several of them were open, and Marcus could see women gathering their belongings. Sabrina led him to a closed door at the end of the hallway. She paused and turned back to him.

"As I mentioned, she is very sick. It happened almost as soon as she got here," she said.

Marcus only nodded. She looked away from his tear-filled eyes and opened the door, stepping aside so he could enter.

The room was dark and small, a single candle flickering near a tiny window. The faint scent of jasmine failed to hide the heavy mildew smell. In the corner, nestled into a pile of ragged cushions, lay a woman. Marcus licked his lips with a dry tongue and took several steps forward and fell to his knees. She was facing the wall, so Marcus reached forward and placed his hand on her shoulder. He could feel her fever through the thin fabric.

"Natalia?" His voice cracked.

She stirred but did not reply. Marcus pulled her toward him.

She mumbled something he could not understand, rolling over onto her other shoulder, thick black hair falling across her gaunt and sallow face.

Tears were rolling down his cheek. "Natalia?"

As her eyes fluttered open, he brushed the hair back from her face and lay down beside her. She somehow managed a weak smile. "Marcus."

He pulled her into his arms and sobbed. He rocked back and forth and ran a hand through her hair and whispered, "I'm here, baby...it's going to be alright."

66

Sabrina, watching the exchange from the door, turned and disappeared down the hallway.

Fifteen minutes later, Marcus emerged from the room, his eyes puffy and red, his jaw clenched. Sabrina was waiting for him in the hallway. He met her gaze but could not speak.

"They're all waiting in the kitchen, ready to go," she said.

Marcus nodded and disappeared back into the room.

Marcus led them through the shadows, pausing now and then to let a pack of drunken sailors stumble past. At the corner of a large warehouse, Marcus looked down and studied Natalia's face in the shallow light. He held her nestled against his chest, her shallow breath rising and falling in rhythm with his. She had not spoken since she first said his name. He shifted her frail body in his arms and led the others across the narrow street and onto the creaking wooden jetty.

Passing several ships, Marcus climbed up a narrow gangway. His stern expression silenced the sailor standing at the railing.

"Get the captain," Marcus snapped.

Nodding, the man glanced at the strange party and disappeared into the darkness. A few moments later, the disheveled and groggy captain appeared. His expression grew from surprise to concern as he studied the group of women huddled behind Marcus.

"What's going on?"

"We're leaving, now," Marcus said.

"We can't leave now! It's the middle of the damn night!"

"I don't care what time it is." Marcus paused, deciding that greed would trump fear. "If you get us to the open sea by dawn, I'll double your payment."

The Sicilian squinted in the darkness, the surrounding

sailors awaiting his reply. He looked down at the bundle Marcus carried, then at the girls standing behind him.

He nodded to the sailor next to him. "Awaken the crew; we sail now. And show these passengers to the cargo hold." He turned back toward Marcus. "That's all the space we have available."

"Not a problem."

"Where do we sail next?"

"Antioch."

"Very well."

"I'll be in my cabin. I don't want to be disturbed." Without waiting for a reply, Marcus disappeared toward the stairway and down into the hold.

They were slicing through open water by daybreak, the galley swaying as they plowed through the rolling breakers. Marcus sat on the edge of a narrow bunk and studied Natalia in the growing daylight. As he moved a thin strand of hair from her cheek, her eyes flickered. A smile crept onto her lips as she recognized him.

"Hi sweetie," he said.

"Hello." She looked around the small cabin. "Where are we?"

"Safe."

She nodded. "Are the children with your father?"

He forced a smile. "Yes, they are."

"Good," she whispered. "I'm so tired."

"You rest, sweetie." He leaned forward and kissed her forehead.

As the sun set, Marcus stood near the bow and watched seagulls swoop back and forth across the ship's path. He sensed Sabrina come up beside him, but he didn't turn to greet her.

"I'm sorry."

Marcus looked down at the railing, then squinted back at one of the plunging gulls. "At least she didn't die in that...in that place."

"Who was she to you?"

"My wife."

"Ah. You're Marcus. She talked about you all the time." Sabrina reached out and took his hand. "She never stopped loving you, and she knew that one day you'd be reunited."

Marcus pursed his lips and fought back the tears as he nodded.

She squeezed his hand and walked away.

He turned back to the choppy seas. Yesterday, rage consumed his every moment. That rage was gone, and it left behind an emptiness. He knew it would take forever to fill that emptiness.

He was right.

CHAPTER FIVE

All spirits are enslaved that serve things evil.
—Percy Bysshe Shelley, 1819

Thomas picked at the table and then took a drink from his small wooden cup. The wine was stale and bitter. Just like us, he thought as he glanced at the others sitting around the room.

It was amazing how things could change so quickly. Less than two weeks ago, they had enjoyed a groundswell of support and were about to make a triumphant entrance into Jerusalem. Now they were cowering from both Roman and Jewish authorities, unsure of how to proceed. And his companions were buckling under the stress. They believed Jesus was resurrected, and that he had appeared to them. Thomas shook his head and took another swig, this one long enough to drain his cup.

He reached forward and grabbed the nearby pitcher, but it was empty. Thomas looked beyond the table to the locked door, wondering if it was safe to go down to the tavern and get more wine. He had yet to decide when a familiar voice broke the silence.

"Peace be with you!"

The men stumbled to their feet. There, in their midst, stood the

70

Master. His gentle eyes drifted between them, smiling at each one of his disciples. It settled on Thomas, and Jesus motioned for him to stand. Thomas pushed his chair back and stood, head lowered. The others crowded around as Jesus pulled his tunic aside, revealing an angry, open wound.

"See my wounds. I want you to touch them," Jesus instructed. "Stop doubting and believe."

Tears filled Thomas's eyes, but he could not reply.

"You must do so."

Thomas nodded and extended his right hand forward, fingers slipping into the wound. He stiffened, eyes looking up at his Savior as he slumped to the ground. "My Lord and my God!"

"Because you have seen me, you have believed; blessed are those who have not seen and yet believed," Jesus said.

Thomas slipped from consciousness; he would never see the Master again.

MODERN DAY
MONACO

A crash of thunder snapped Thomas awake. It was followed by the steady patter of falling rain that filled the darkened chamber, rising each time the wind drove the downpour against the heavy glass. He sat beneath a massive window, facing the abyss. A bolt of lightning crackled through the night, lighting up his stoic features. The storm was now moving away, having released its heavy burden upon the city.

Another flash lit up the darkness, followed by a rumble that almost masked the soft buzzer.

He spun his chair toward a black marble desk and pushed a button. "Yes?"

"Lazarus is here," a voice said.

"Send him in."

As the door swung forward, light from the anteroom spilled into the chamber. Lazarus crossed the room, his footsteps echoing before him. He was of medium height with short black hair and a more prominent nose than his face required. He carried himself with a confidence that did not always stand the test.

"What happened?" Thomas reached forward and poured himself a drink.

"Levi was an imbecile," Lazarus stated. "I told you his extracurricular activities were going to get him killed."

"Yes, it was bound to happen." Thomas took a sip. "What did Marcus get?"

"Pretty much everything. Files, samples, and Levi's phone."

"Any idea where he is?"

"Not yet. I have a team working on it."

"We need to take care of this, once and for all."

"I've tried a half-dozen times," Lazarus said. "He's one elusive motherfucker."

"Well, it's time we up the ante."

"What do you want to do?"

"We've talked about it for a while." Thomas nodded. "Burn it down."

"Everything?"

"Yep. Take it all away."

"Will do." Lazarus started to walk away, then stopped. "Are you sure?"

There was a long pause as Thomas looked up. "Absolutely."

PARIS

Muted rays from the morning sun leaked past the heavy curtain and crept into Marcus' muddled dreams. As he shifted beneath the covers, the dull ache in his shoulder took him back to the night before. It was not a pleasant journey. He pushed the covers aside, reached back, and felt the edges of a bandage. He looked down and saw another just below his ribcage. Marcus sat up, peeled off the latter and inspected the wound. It was neatly stitched, the flesh puckered and light pink. It would be fully healed by lunchtime and nothing but a faint scar by evening. Lord knows he had plenty of them.

He lifted the blankets and swung his feet to the cold wooden floor. He reached for a nearby pack of cigarettes, lit one up, and after several puffs, stood and walked to the bathroom. Turning on the light, he started the shower. Cigarette dangling from his lips, he peeled off the other bandages and threw them into the trash can.

He tossed the butt into the toilet, stepped out of his sweats and into the shower. He placed both hands on the wall, lowering his head to soak his entire body. His mind drifted back to the girls. They were dead because he had let Levi take them home. There was a time when he might not have made that decision, but somewhere along the way, he had changed. Marcus closed his eyes and waited for their faces to fade. He gave up when the hot water ran out.

He dried off and wrapped a towel around his waist. After getting dressed, he exited the bedroom to find Sam pouring a cup of coffee in the kitchen.

"How are you feeling?" She held up the cup for him.

"Sore. And a headache."

"Well, this won't help." She handed him his phone. "You have a text from Ramirez? He wants to Facetime as soon as you are awake."

"Fuck me."

"Who is he?"

"The Cardinal Secretary of State."

"Wow, sounds important."

"It is. His office runs all the political and diplomatic functions for the Vatican."

"What does he want?"

"We *unofficially liaise* with his office."

"You work for him?"

"No." Marcus scowled. "He makes requests; we sometimes help. We try to stay aligned. It worked much smoother with his predecessors."

"So, you sometimes work for him."

Marcus glared at her and took a sip of coffee.

"You gonna call him?"

"Yeah, I'll be out in a minute."

"Okay."

Marcus moved back into the bedroom, pulled up the text, then began a Facetime call with Ramirez.

"Hello?" A young-looking priest answered the call.

"Yes. The Cardinal wanted me to call him. It's Marcus."

"Hold, please." The screen went black as he set it faced down. A few minutes later, the Cardinal glared into the camera, his chubby cheeks flushed.

"Marcus! Are you in Paris?"

"Maybe."

"Why? I don't remember discussing that. Or the trip to London last week, for that matter."

"I don't have to clear my travel plans with you," Marcus snapped back.

"We have an agreement. You are not to jeopardize the Church with your activities." The Cardinal leaned forward, his face filling the screen. "Your antics are drawing attention, and I can't risk exposing the Church to your...*indiscretions.* Go back to Boston until I decide what to do next."

"Let's be clear. I don't give a fuck what you think, and I don't take orders from you. I've bled a thousand times for the Church, and I'll be damned if I let you lecture me on what's best for it."

"You're dangerously close—"

"Close to what?"

"Go home, Marcus." The call ended.

Standing, he grabbed the phone and threw it against the brick wall. It shattered into a dozen pieces. Startled by the sound, Sam came storming into the room.

"Everything okay?"

"Yeah." Marcus rubbed his chin.

"I see that call went well." Her eyes fell to the broken pieces scattered across the wooden floor.

"It was great. And we need a new phone." He exhaled. "Tell me you had some luck with the files."

"Not without the password. It's beyond my skill set."

"Who's our Paris contact? Simon?"

"Dead."

Marcus frowned. "When?"

"Two months ago. Skiing accident."

"Antonin?"

"Prison," she countered.

"Okay, this isn't working. Who do you suggest?"

"Sebastien."

"He's in Paris? I thought he was in some castle in Transylvania."

"He's from Albania, not Romania," she corrected. "And he moved here about five months ago. Family issues."

"I don't know. He's pretty good, but there's something strange about him. Seems immature."

"He's better than you think. And he's not dead or in prison."

75

"Good point. Let's get a hold of him."

"Already did. We meet in an hour."

"Why didn't you say so?"

She just shrugged. "Want to get a crepe before we go?"

"Duh, of course."

"Here we are." She took the last bite of her crepe.

They had walked about twenty minutes from their apartment, stopping at a vendor along the way. Marcus wiped his mouth and hands with a napkin and dropped it into a nearby trash can. Looking back at the building, he noticed a gold placard.

"Is this the Albanian Embassy?"

"Yep." She motioned him toward the door.

"Are you serious?"

"Ah, yeah."

He rolled his eyes, stepped through the revolving door and entered a small lobby. To the right was a desk with a single guard, whose eyes narrowed as he watched them enter the room. Next to him was a metal detector; the rest of the area roped off except for an opening for people to exit. A couch and two chairs stood to the left, one of which was occupied by a teenage boy with his face buried in his phone.

"So, now what?"

Sam was already texting on her phone and looked up after finishing. "He should be here."

"Sam?"

Sam looked up to see the teenage boy standing next to her. He was about five-foot-tall, with short black hair and bright blue eyes. He had on a black Ramones t-shirt and a pair of ripped skinny jeans.

"Yes, can I help you?"

76

"Are you here to meet with Sebastien?" His English was perfect, with just a hint of an eastern European accent.

"Yes," Marcus said. "Do you know him?"

"I'm Sebastien."

Marcus looked over at Sam, who had a stunned look on her face.

Before they could respond, Sebastien nodded toward the desk. "Not here, follow me."

They stopped in front of the guard.

"You'll need to leave your weapons. You can pick them up later."

Marcus frowned and retrieved his pistol from his waistband, along with several extra magazines. He set them in a metal case the guard opened for them. Sebastien looked toward Sam.

"I don't need a gun. I've got him." She tilted her head toward Marcus.

The guard locked the box and put it under the desk. Then he stood and held out a plastic tub for their phones. They walked through the detector, retrieving their phones afterward. They followed Sebastien down a long hallway before stopping at an elevator near the end. Sebastian checked his phone several times as they waited for the door to open.

Once inside, Sebastien put his thumb over a pad as the door closed. The pad turned green, and the elevator descended for what seemed like three or four floors. Sebastien watched the puzzled expression on Marcus' face in the elevator's stainless-steel walls.

"We've only gone down two floors. It's a slow elevator because it's old. Like everything else in this stupid building."

"I didn't know there were basements that deep."

"They built this one on top of an old catacomb. It was easy to go deeper."

Marcus nodded but could not help himself. "I'm sorry. How long have you been doing this?"

The door opened, and Sebastien stepped out.

"What do you mean, *this*? Hacking? Since I was like eight years old."

"I mean doing jobs for other people." Marcus followed him out.

"I don't know. Four years? I went to this prep school for ex-pats. That's where I learned English and how to make money by stealing and breaking into shit online." He led them down a hallway and into an office/game room/bedroom. "Then my dad got a job in the government, and I met some different dudes. That's when my biz took off."

He motioned for them to sit down, then sat in a chair in front of an enormous desk. Multiple screens filled the wall above them. One was a split feed of all the security cameras in the building. Another was playing South Park, and a third was a YouTube channel of some first-person shooter game.

"How did you end up in Paris?" Sam, having wandered around the room, stopped and looked at some comics on a table.

"My dad became the ambassador. Totally sucks. The internet here is shit."

"I'm sorry to hear that." Marcus glanced over at Sam.

Sebastien stared at Marcus. "Is there a problem?"

Marcus' eyes shifted from Sam to Sebastien and then back. Sam shook her head.

"No problem," Marcus said.

"Good, because I don't meet in person, for this precise reason. Adults can be dicks."

"No, we're good." Sam tilted her head toward Marcus. "He's the only dick."

"Okay, cool. I already cracked the files you sent me. I'd be almost embarrassed to charge you for that." He turned toward the desk. "But it still looks like a bunch of useless shit to me."

"Can you get into his email?" Marcus leaned over his shoulder.

"Does he use email?"

"I doubt it," Sam cut in. "See if he had WhatsApp on his laptop."

"He does." Sebastien opened WhatsApp and logged in using the computer's autosave password data. "Ok, what are we looking for?"

"No dick pics," Sam warned.

"Got it."

Marcus looked over the teenager's shoulder, scanning the conversations.

"There—'T'."

T
What's your status?

I found him. I'll send the files.

T
Good. And the samples?

They're safe.

T
Take them to him in Rome.

Why does he need them?

T
Just do it.

79

"Good start. It looks like he used email. Can you find that?" Sam asked.

"Yeah, give me a few minutes. You guys want something to eat or drink? There's a refrigerator over there." He casually pointed to the other side of the room. "If you could grab me a Yoo-hoo, that would be great."

Sam stood up, looking at Marcus. "Do you want anything?"

"No, thanks."

"OK, I think I'm in his email." Sebastien opened an email with some attachments. "We have multiple files. Anything look tasty?"

He sat back and looked at Marcus, who scanned the contents and pointed out one from the list.

"Open that one, *DNA Stabilizer.*"

"K."

A 3D rendition of a chemical formula popped up on the screen. Sam returned and handed Sebastien his drink.

"What is that?" Marcus asked.

"No clue, man," Sebastian said.

"It's a formula for a drug." Sam took a sip from a water bottle she had opened.

"How do you know?" Marcus was surprised.

"I was pre-med, remember?"

"No."

"Well, you paid for it." Sam pointed to the following file. "What about that, *Growth accelerator?*"

Again, another formula.

They found several more in the same folder.

"Anything else to look for?" Sebastien glanced from Marcus to Sam.

Marcus remembered something. "What about his phone?"

"Oh, yeah." Sam dug into her backpack and pulled out the dead man's phone, handing it to Sebastien. "Can we unlock this?"

"Give him the, you know..." Marcus said.

She pulled a baggy from her backpack and held it up for Sebastien.

"Whoa, is that a thumb?" he asked.

"Yep." Marcus smiled.

"Gnarly!" Sebastien held up the iPhone. "Well, this doesn't have a fingerprint sensor. It uses facial recognition. And even if it did, it requires an electrical circuit...a live hand."

Sam glared at Marcus.

"What can I say? I was in a hurry," Marcus grumbled.

"Anyway, I'll see if I can reset his phone from his email. Give me a few minutes."

Marcus and Sam moved a few feet away and conferred as Sebastien worked.

"Drugs?" Marcus frowned. "I don't get it. Was Schumacher stealing these formulas to sell?"

"Possibly, but it doesn't seem to fit his profile."

"And the blood?"

"Samples of the drugs or the effects of the drugs?" she said. "But why would Thomas have the formulas in the first place? To make money?"

"I don't think so...he's made plenty through the more traditional methods. But, he doesn't want to be rich, just to be rich. He wants to use that money to achieve his actual goals."

"And what are they?"

Marcus paused. "I don't know, but I know who will."

"Someone in Rome?"

"Yep. I have an idea."

Before she could reply, Sebastian called them over.

"Guys."

"Wow, that was quick." Sam walked back toward the desk.

"No, we got a problem." He pointed to a security camera. A group of four men was in the lobby. The outside camera showed two black Suburbans.

"How do you know they are looking for us?" Marcus said.

"Look," Sebastien pulled up another screen. It was the revolving door, except it was an x-ray screen. "I have a scanner in the door."

The video showed two of the men in the doorway as it revolved. The silhouette of handguns and submachine guns glowed bright white against the screen.

"How could they have found us?" Sam set down her water bottle.

Sebastien looked at the phone in his hand. "Did you take this from one of them?"

"Yes, but I turned it off," Marcus said.

"The battery is still attached. The phone will still be in standby mode. If they installed tracking software, they could activate it anytime."

"Well, why did they wait so long?" Sam asked.

"They could have been waiting to see where we went," Marcus said.

"Or, it took them time to gain access to the network. They would need to hack in or get a government order to get access." Sebastien handed Marcus back the phone. "Either way, you need to take that and get out of here."

"Of course." Marcus looked up at the camera and the desk within the screen. "My gun is there."

He looked back at Sebastien.

"Don't look at me; I'm just a teenager. I don't have any guns."

"Yeah..." Marcus looked around. "I don't suppose you have a secret exit?"

"Do I seem like someone who doesn't have a secret exit?" He scoffed. "Follow me."

Sebastien led them away from the elevator.

"Take the phone for a few blocks or a mile, then ditch it." Sebastien pushed open a door that led into the bathroom. A small panel on the wall opened to allow access to shut off the water pipe.

"I don't think we're going to fit in there," Sam said.

Sebastien faked a smile, then reached inside and pulled a lever. A portion of the tile wall swung back.

"This leads to the bathroom of the Starbucks down the street. When you reach the end wall, if the light is green, the bathroom is empty. You can pull the latch, and a door will open."

"Okay, thanks." Sam stepped inside.

"You gonna be alright?" Marcus paused.

"Yeah, they won't suspect a 14-year-old kid."

Nodding, Marcus ducked into the opening.

"Hey," Sebastien called after them. "Make sure you send my money!"

The bathroom was empty, so Sam crept out first. Marcus waited a minute before following. Several customers watched them slip past the counter and stop near the front door. Marcus peered outside the window, then at Sam.

"I'm going to take the phone downtown. You wait 10 or 15 minutes and head to the safe house. Don't go back to the apartment."

"Are you sure we should split up?"

"Yes, I have more options when I'm alone." He met her gaze. "If you don't hear from me within four hours, get out of Paris. You know what to do after that."

She swallowed and nodded. "Be careful."

"You too."

With that, he disappeared out the door.

CHAPTER SIX

Darkness cannot drive out darkness; only light can do that.
Hate cannot drive out hate; only love can do that.
—MARTIN LUTHER KING

64 A.D.
ROME, ITALY

"IN HERE."

Thomas turned his attention to the cell door. He waited for the voice to continue, but all he could hear was the growls of hungry lions. He stood and moved to the door, looking out through the rusty bars. It was not morning yet, but they must be coming for them early. Standing tall, he brushed the hay from his tunic and faced the door.

The flicker of torchlight filled the small opening as a key slipped into the lock. A few moments later, the hinges groaned in protest as the door swung open. By now, the others in the cell were beginning to stir, some moving to stand beside Thomas. A few moments later, a pair of men stepped through the door, the taller of the two holding a torch. A smile erupted from Thomas's face when he recognized one of them.

"Nico!" Thomas hugged his old friend.

"Thomas!" Nico returned his embrace, then pulled away, a look of relief on his face. "Thank God we aren't too late!"

"No, I think we go tomorrow."

"Rebecca? Isabella?"

"We are here." Isabella stepped forward, then turned and motioned back toward the corner of the room.

A woman sat on the floor, her back against the wall. Two small children lay in the straw, their heads resting on her lap. Nico closed the distance between them and knelt beside her. The flickering torchlight danced across her delicate features.

"How are you?" Nico asked.

"I'm fine," Rebecca replied and looked down at the pair of dirty faces. "We have to get them out of here."

"I know. We will." Nico stood and glanced around the room, trying to count the shadowy figures. His face twisted into a grimace as he turned toward his companion, a man with dark features and a darker scowl. The man shook his head.

Frowning, Nico asked Thomas, "How many?"

"Twenty adults and two children."

"Too many!" growled the stranger. "We'll never make it out."

Nico pulled the man aside, but Thomas could still hear the conversation.

"You know what they are doing to these people...we cannot leave them."

Thomas watched the man scan the group and decided it was time they met.

"You must be Marcus?" Thomas stepped forward, hand extended.

"Yes." Marcus returned his grip. "He didn't say there would be so many."

"There were nearly fifty yesterday." Thomas lowered his voice so the others could not hear. "Nero burned half of them alive. Like human torches. His punishment for setting Rome on fire."

Marcus's expression was cold, hard. "We'd never make it out."

"What if we go in small groups?" Nico asked.

Marcus looked back through the door, shaking his head. "There are soldiers everywhere. It's not worth the risk." He looked back at Thomas. "I can take one group, no more than five. You choose which."

Very calculating, Thomas thought, *typical Roman*.

"What if we create a diversion?" Isabella had been lingering just outside their group.

"Like what?" Nico stepped aside so she could join them.

"The lion cages are right across the hallway...what if we released them?" She looked from Nico to Marcus. "Wouldn't that keep the guards occupied?"

Thomas watched the Roman. Marcus had a strange expression on his face that might have been mistaken for a smile.

"Stay here." Marcus disappeared out the door, pulling it shut behind him.

"That's him?" Isabella asked. "He looks different...but the same."

"We've all changed," Nico replied. "I'll explain more later when everyone is safe."

Thomas and Nico were giving instructions to the group when the angry roar of a lion interrupted them. It was soon followed by several more hisses and sputters. The entire group held its breath, staring at the cell door. Then, a couple of minutes later, the growls faded into an eerie silence.

Moving toward the door, Thomas peered into the darkness. Torchlight moving toward him, so he stepped back and waited for the door to open. A familiar groan filled the room as the door gave way, and Marcus stepped through, handing the torch to Nico. The Roman held his left arm close to his body, blood flowing from a nasty gash just above his wrist.

"How bad is it?" Nico held the torch above the wound.

"Bad enough," Marcus replied.

Rebecca, now standing with the two children, ripped a strip of cloth from her tunic. She motioned for Marcus to hold his arm out. He scowled at her but extended it anyway and watched as she wrapped the wound and tied the end tight. Their eyes met for a moment before he looked toward Thomas.

"We need to get everyone moving," Marcus said as he grabbed a torch from a barrel near the door.

He lit it from the one Nico held, then set off down the tunnel. When they reached the first intersection, he directed them to his right and turned toward Nico.

"Follow this tunnel, and you will reach a cistern. Climb down into it, and you will see an overflow tunnel leading out of the sewers. Follow that until you come to a metal grate near the exit. It is on a hinge so that it can be moved for cleaning."

"And you will be right behind us?"

"I hope."

Nico glanced up the tunnel they had used to enter the dungeon, now blocked by several chairs and a broken table.

"Will that stop the lions from coming back?"

"No." The torchlight danced off his features.

"It seems to be working so far," Nico replied.

The words had barely escaped his lips when a low growl filled the tunnel. A pair of glowing yellow eyes punctured the darkness, making the barricade seem much less imposing.

"Go!" Marcus drew his sword.

Nico led them down the dark tunnel, the snarl of a lion echoing behind them.

A few minutes later, they found the cistern, and one by one, Nico and Thomas helped each person over the edge and down a set of iron rungs. Fifteen feet down, they huddled on a narrow ledge in front of the small passageway that served as the overflow.

Thomas followed Nico down, squeezing past the others as he crouched and moved into the small tunnel. Reaching the end, he knelt before a metal grate. Grabbing it with both hands, he leveraged his legs against the wall and pulled it forward. The metal scraped across the wet stone but only moved an inch or two. Taking another deep breath, Thomas grunted and pulled again. It gave a few inches more, but it would not swing free.

"I wonder how long it has been since this was last moved?" Thomas puffed and sat back on his haunches.

"Let me help." Nico squeezed in beside him.

Taking a deep breath, Thomas counted down. "Three, two, one, pull!"

Together, they strained against the grate, which gave up every inch with stubborn reluctance. Finally, the grate cleared the narrowest part of the tunnel and swung free of the opening.

Drenched in sweat, Thomas wiped his brow and, leaning forward, crawled through the opening. The tunnel was now a pipe extending three feet from the building's wall. They were four or five feet above the sloping banks of a wide ditch that ran the length of the structure. Scattered clouds filled the dark sky, hiding any remnants of the descending moon. Outlines of the nearby buildings crowded in around them and cast dark shadows across the channel. He studied the opposite bank, which rose ten feet above him, but he did not see any guards. Turning back, he found Nico and Isabella waiting near the grating.

"Have them start coming out,' he said.

"All right," Isabella replied as she disappeared into the darkness.

The passage was stifling, despite the cool evening breeze seeping in from beyond the opening. Sweat was pouring down their faces when Isabella finally returned, the others gathering behind her.

"You first," Thomas motioned toward a middle-aged man. "When you get to the far side, help the others climb the bank. Then move into the shadows of the nearest building. Wait for us there."

"Understood," the man replied as he squeezed by and moved to the end of the pipe.

Turning, he swung his legs out the passage, and Thomas held his arms until he was suspended above the muddy bank. When Thomas let him go, the man crumpled into the mud but stood and made his way across the trench. One by one, they helped everyone out until only Nico, Isabella, Thomas, and the two children remained.

"You two go," Thomas said, "and I'll lower them to you."

Nodding, Nico swung out and disappeared into the darkness. Isabella went next, and then Thomas lifted the young girl and swung her out the opening. She started to whimper.

"It'll be fine, little one," Thomas assured her. "We're almost home."

The moonlight reflected off her tiny face. It was full of fear and doubt.

"We are almost home, I promise." He winked, and she nodded in return.

Thomas leaned forward and lowered her to Isabella. Next, Thomas handed the young boy to Nico, and then he swung around and dropped onto the muddy bank. Together, the group moved across the ditch and up the opposite side. Kneeling in the darkness, Nico looked toward the nearby shadows, then back toward the tunnel.

"Nico?" Thomas studied his dirt-encrusted features. He could tell Nico was thinking about going back. "We don't know where to go. You have to show us."

Nico ran a mud-covered hand through his gray hair and nodded. "Let's go. Be sure to keep the children quiet."

They stood and, together, looked back at the dark opening one more time. Their eyes met, then they turned and disappeared into the shadows.

A small group of the adults huddled around the fireplace, murmuring amongst themselves. The two children were sleeping in a second-floor bedroom under Rebecca's watchful eye. The others were in nearby safe houses. Isabella sat at a small table, picking at a piece of leaven bread while Thomas nursed a cup of wine and gazed blankly at the crackling fire. Nico stared at the door.

Dawn was just around the corner, but they would not be moving until the following night. The Emperor would not be happy, and his Praetorian guard would be scouring the city. Staying in Rome would be dangerous, but trying to leave during the day would be suicidal.

Thomas turned toward Nico. "What happened after he resurrected? Your letters were pretty vague. They only said the Emperor took his family, and you were going after them."

"That's true, but we split up in Massilia. He hired a ship and went looking for them." Nico shrugged. "You asked me to stay with him, so I did my best to follow."

"How?"

"I followed the trail of bodies."

Isabella glared at Thomas.

"But he moved faster than standard transport," Nico said. "It took me nearly two years to find him. By then, he had found his wife. She died soon after. He was still looking for his children when I caught up to him in Parthia."

"Why Parthia?" Isabella asked.

"He was out of leads on the kids. So he was chasing down slavers."

"Slavers?" Thomas was cupping his wine but not drinking.

"Yeah. All of them." Nico reached forward and poured himself a cup of wine. "He had already killed the slavers on the ship that took his wife and kids. And the auctioneers. And the buyers. The children changed hands several times, so that trail went cold in Arabia. Somewhere along the way, he decided that the world was a better place without slavers."

"Sounds dangerous," Isabella said.

"It was. He died twice in the first year I was with him. But he always agreed to meet me after he resurrected, so we were able to reconnect in prearranged cities."

"Why would he meet up with you again?" Thomas asked.

"I don't know. We never talked about it. But I think he needed someone, anyone." Nico shrugged. "Everything he had was gone. I think I was his only connection to the world."

Isabella leaned forward. "And why would you want to stay with such a cold-blooded killer?"

Nico turned his head to the side, a confused look on his face. "What else would I do? Perhaps I could help him deal with his pain. Maybe even stop him from killing. Aren't we taught to help those most in need?"

"I supposed. I don't know if I could have stayed with him," Isabella replied.

"It took me years, but I think he's coming around."

"You think?" Isabella raised her eyebrows.

"It's a start."

"And his children?" Thomas asked.

Nico sat in silence, looking down into his cup. His lips quivered as he replied, "We never found them." He met

Isabella's gaze, a single tear running down his cheek. "Not knowing is the worst. It's killing him inside."

They were sitting in silence, the jug of wine long gone, when a loud banging on the door startled them. Isabella looked from Thomas to the group near the fireplace. Several of them jumped when the banging resumed, this time more forcefully.

Thomas stood and moved to the door, Nico by his side. He took a deep breath and unlatched it, then pulled it open and peered through the gap.

A dark form hunched against the doorway, blocking out the night. Thomas recognized him and swung the door open just as the Roman fell into his arms. Dragging him into the room, Thomas motioned for Nico to close the door behind him.

"Marcus?" Thomas pulled back his blood-soaked cloak. "My God..." He stared up at Isabella, eyes wide open as he realized the extent of the Roman's wounds. "We need water and rags."

She disappeared toward the pantry.

Thomas glanced at Nico, then to several of the men standing by the fireplace. "Help me get him to the back room."

The men carried the unconscious Roman to a cot in the bedroom and left him with Thomas and Nico. Kneeling beside the Roman, Nico peeled away the strips of cloth that clung to his shredded midsection. There were five deep gashes with a dozen lesser cuts and scrapes. His left thigh was ripped open, the ivory bone visible in the pale torchlight. A gasp drew his attention to Isabella, who was standing beside him and looking down at the wounds.

Nico took the rags and motioned for her to sit beside him.

"Will he live?" Thomas asked.

"Yes," Nico replied. "But this is bad. It will take several days."

"Then we have to wait," Thomas said.

"What?" Isabella asked. "We can't wait. The Emperor will be looking for us. We have to get out of Rome."

"We won't leave him." Thomas placed his hand on the Roman's forehead and could feel the fever raging beneath. "He did this for us."

"So what?" she said. "If he dies, then he comes back. Why would we risk that?"

Thomas met her gaze. "Because it's the right thing to do."

"He's a pagan and a murderer."

"He's a child of God," Nico said.

"The two of you can say anything you want." Isabella glared at the Roman, "I can't forgive him for what he did."

"That is alright." Nico followed her gaze. "He may never forgive himself."

"Stand still." Rebecca looked up at Marcus's bruised face.

Marcus sat on a stool by the fireplace, watching as she pulled the bandage from one of the wounds. It was already starting to turn pink, so she did not bother replacing it.

"Looks like you will be much better in a day or two."

"Sooner," he replied.

"So it seems."

He pulled his tunic back on. "Thank you."

"No, it is us who should be thankful for getting us out of there," she replied, her soft, brown eyes full of gratitude. There was no hint of anger or hostility.

"You should thank Nico. It was his idea."

"I already have. But it's you who got us out. Why?"

Marcus turned away, his eyes focused on the floor. Then, after a long pause, he looked up and changed the subject. "How were you transformed?"

Rebecca smiled and pulled up a stool. She dropped the bandages to the ground and sat across from him.

"My sister and I were both very sick."

"Your sister?"

"Isabella. She is my older sister."

"Ah."

"We are from a town called Arimathea." She used her hands to smooth the folds of her dress in her lap. "Our mother had already died, as had my younger brother."

"I'm sorry."

"It was a long time ago," she replied. Her voice was lower and laced with sadness. "My father was so worried that we would die as well. Then he heard about a man, a Galilean, who was performing miracles. Several people in our village traveled to him and were healed. So my father took us as well."

"How did you find him?"

"It was not very hard...large crowds gathered wherever he went."

"Those crowds drew the attention of the Roman officials."

"Yes."

"And what happened after you found him?"

"Isabella was too sick to walk. My father stayed with her in the shade of a giant olive tree. I thought she was going to die." Rebecca's expression fell, almost like she had seen a ghost. "I pushed my way to him, but he was already past. I knew that if I could only touch his cloak, I would be healed. Somehow I was able to get my fingertip on his tassel."

"That's it?"

"Yes and no. He turned around and asked me what I had done. At first, I was scared, but his eyes were so gentle, so loving. I told him that I was sick and that my sister was also sick. He smiled at me and said; *because of your faith, your sister is healed as well.* I returned to my father and Isabella, and she was completely recovered. Like she had never been sick."

"Did you go back to Arimathea?"

"No, all three of us stayed. Two weeks later, Jesus was killed."

Marcus looked down as memories flooded over him. The heavy thump of the mallet. The look on Christ's face as he suffered on the cross. The sound of the earth splitting apart and the sweet smell of the desert rain. He looked at both of his hands, expecting to see the blood still on them.

"Marcus?" She leaned forward, placing one hand on his knee. "Marcus?"

Her gentle touch pulled him from the abyss. Closing his eyes, he looked up and opened them again. "Yes, sorry."

"Are you alright?"

"Yes. It can be overwhelming at times."

"I'm sorry, I forgot you were there."

"I wish I could forget as well." He forced a smile.

"Someday, maybe." Her smile was genuine.

"I don't understand."

"Understand what?"

"Isabella hates me for what I did. Why don't you as well?"

She met his gaze, tears filling her eyes. He knew the tears were for him.

"I know that he has already forgiven you, so how could I not?"

He did not reply, but the gratitude in his eyes was enough.

She gathered the dirty bandages and placed them into a sack. When she looked back at Marcus, he was staring at two young children standing in the doorway. They were making faces at him, hoping to get a response from the dark stranger. He raised his lip and snarled, which drew a chorus of giggles. Marcus almost smiled, and for a moment, Rebecca noticed a softer side to his chiseled features.

"Did you have children?"

His expression faltered, then, if possible, grew harder than ever.

"I did."

The two words were said with such finality that it broke her heart.

Despite the warmth from the fire, the room had suddenly become ice-cold. Rebecca stood and, placing one hand on his shoulder, left the room. His eyes shifted to the fireplace, a single tear making the lonesome trek down his cheek.

Is this how it's going to be forever? Thomas thought as they sat quietly in the wagon, a pair of mules pulling them along the narrow road. The rest of their small group was lying down or looking out at boulder-strewn fields on either side of the path. Marcus was scouting ahead.

The Roman Empire might be the largest empire on earth, but there was no place to hide. They had managed to place the children with a family in Italia and smuggle most of the adults to Gaul. The remaining five had made their way to Greece. They stayed with church members when possible, but it was not safe to linger in any one place for more than a day or two. News of their escape from Rome seemed to follow them wherever they went. They'd had another close call in Thracia that required their protector's sword.

"We have to leave the empire," Marcus stated one night as they sat around the campfire.

"Where?" Nico looked up from the fire. "Gaul?"

"No. It would be too hard to double back. We go to Parthia." Marcus poked at the embers with a crooked stick. "They hate Romans."

"I like them already," Isabella muttered.

Marcus ignored the comment. "We'll reach Corinth in two days. After that, we can take a ship to Tarsus. From there, we continue overland to Parthia."

"Tarsus?" Thomas asked.

Marcus looked up at him. "Yes, Tarsus."

"We have a large following in Antioch. It would be safer."

As Marcus glared at him, Thomas felt the hairs on the back of his neck stand up.

"We go to Corinth, or you can go alone."

"Tarsus will be fine," Nico said. Then, he turned to Marcus. "He meant nothing by it."

Marcus stood and threw his stick into the fire. "Be ready at dawn."

As the fire crackled between them, Isabella looked to the darkness where the Roman had been, then back at Nico. "What was that all about?"

"Nothing," Nico replied.

"Don't tell me that...we're sitting right here."

Nico picked at the grass near his feet, then threw the blades into the fire. They lingered for a moment, then curled up as the fire consumed them.

"Antioch was where his children were taken."

Thomas leaned his head forward and rubbed his temple. "I didn't know that."

"Of course you didn't."

"What do you mean his children were taken?" Rebecca asked.

Nico looked at Isabella, who shook her head. "I didn't tell her."

"Tell me what?" Rebecca looked around the fire, trying to get someone to meet her gaze.

Finally, Nico responded, "Marcus lost his children to slavers."

Rebecca gasped. "Why didn't you tell me?"

"I'm sorry," Isabella replied. "I didn't think about it."

"No wonder he's so broken." She stood.

"Rebecca—"

"No, don't *Rebecca* me. He's protected us, the others, the child. He almost died getting us out of there." She glared at

Isabella. "And I don't want to hear about his past and what he did. I know all that. But that was a long time ago, and he has paid the price, a higher price than any of us." She looked around at the faces lit by the firelight. "And if you can't forgive him, then you didn't learn anything from *Jesus*."

Before they could respond, Rebecca disappeared into the darkness, leaving behind the crackling of the fire.

CHAPTER SEVEN

And out of darkness came the hands that reach thro'
nature, moulding men.
—ALFRED LORD TENNYSON

MODERN DAY
PARIS

LAZARUS CUT INTO HIS STEAK as Thomas sat down across from him. The tiny restaurant was empty save for the solitary server standing a dozen feet away. Thomas motioned to him as he scanned the wall behind the nearby bar.

"Double Macallan 18, neat."

"Oui, monsieur." The server scurried away.

Lazarus set down his knife and fork, then took a sip of red wine. "When did you get to Paris?"

"Thirty minutes ago."

The waiter brought his drink and set it down.

"Merci." Thomas took the glass into his hand, swirling the caramel contents. "I was hoping we would have something to toast."

99

"I'm afraid not," Lazarus watched as Thomas took a healthy sip, "at least not tonight."

"What happened?"

"We tracked the phone this morning."

"Why not last night?"

"The fucking French. They wouldn't give us access until we had a court order."

"I'm surprised we got an order that fast."

"We have several judges on retainer. But apparently, none of them work nights. Anyway, we traced them to a block in the Champs-Élysée district. We were doing a sweep of the buildings when he started moving again."

"And?"

"We had him cornered in the Grand Palais. He was unarmed."

Thomas raised his glass to his lips, his smirk disappearing as he took another sip.

"He took nine of my men with him."

"Elusive motherfucker," Thomas noted.

"Yeah."

"Well, at least he'll be out of action for three days. And when he comes back, it will be somewhere east of Paris. Search for him there. And Rome. That's where he's going."

"How do you know?"

"Because that's where I'd go."

"Okay. We made a move on his network, any connection we could find. Assets frozen, contacts eliminated, locations seized. But I couldn't find the priest."

"Keep looking. And put out the word. Marcus is not to receive help from any agency or organization. If anyone violates this, I want to know."

"Will do."

Thomas shook his head and finished his drink, holding it up to the waiter.

The taxi drove through the gate and onto a long, narrow driveway. They passed row after row of grapevines that followed the soft contour of the rolling valley. In the distance, a large grove of trees was the only remnant of what once was a massive forest. Within a few minutes, they crossed a small bridge across a bubbling creek and pulled up to a well-maintained chateau.

The driver put the car into park and hopped out, opening the trunk. Sam slipped out from the back seat and, handing the driver a one-hundred Euro bill, took the bag he had pulled from the trunk and nodded. The driver looked down at the note and then tipped his hat several times in appreciation.

She turned toward the chateau, but before she could reach the top of the steps, the door had already opened. A middle-aged man, dressed in what looked like a newly pressed suit, stepped from the doorway and bowed at his waist.

"Welcome, madam!" His accent was not quite French, not quite German. Quite common for this part of France. He reached forward and took her bag. "It has been quite some time since we have had a guest in the Charlemagne suite. How long will you be staying with us?"

"Just the one night." Sam followed him through the door. "I'm just passing through."

"Yes, of course. Also very common for the guests of this suite." He motioned her to the right side of the foyer. "We will go through here. First time with us, I believe?"

"Yes, it is."

"Wonderful. Then perhaps you do not know the history of our winery?" He led her down a narrow hallway, with several doors on either side, and did not wait for her reply. "We are one of the oldest wineries in the Lorraine region. Legend has it that

101

some of our grape varietals were brought here from Rome by the original owner centuries ago."

Sam appeared skeptical.

"But of course, that is just a rumor." He stopped near the last door. "Here we are!"

He leaned forward, opened the door, and stepped aside so she could enter.

The room was large, with a series of enormous windows that looked out across the grounds, including the creek that meandered through the property. There was a set of double doors that led to the bedroom and bathroom.

"I have opened a bottle of our finest vintage for you to enjoy. Shall you be joining us for dinner?"

"No. I'm exhausted. Perhaps I'll order something later."

"Of course. Enjoy your evening with us, madam. Please call if you need anything."

With that, he left. Sam picked up her bag and brought it to the bedroom, closing and locking the door behind her. She moved across the room and into the nearby closet.

It looked just like the picture Cormac had shown her. She moved to the back of the small room, lifted one of the clothing rods from its base, and inside she found the button as instructed. Sam pushed it and heard an invisible lock click. Next, she pushed on the wall, and it swung back, revealing a stone staircase leading down into the darkness. She used her phone as a flashlight and stepped down the short flight of stairs, which ended with a large metal door. On the wall next to the door was a scanner the size of an iPad. It jumped to life as she placed her hand on it. When it finished scanning, she could hear a subtle clunk as multiple bolts unlocked and the door swung inward.

She stepped through this entrance and found herself in what she could only describe as a bunker. A light had come on as she entered, and she shut the door behind her. It locked shut.

The room was large, at least forty feet across and thirty feet deep. Thick metal support beams held up the chateau above. To the far left was a bed, next to a small kitchen. The opposite corner was walled off, creating a small room. An open door revealed a bathroom within.

On the right was a metal workbench, with several cabinets above, now closed. Next to the bench stood a desk, surrounded by monitors, with a computer station below them. To her right sat a couch, with a remote on a glass coffee table and a large TV occupying the wall opposite.

But the strangest feature by far in the room was the ten-foot by ten-foot patch of dirt in the floor. It was not compact dirt; in fact, it resembled loose potting soil. The hair on the back of Sam's neck stood up as she walked past the area and set her bag down on the couch. She sat and switched on the TV, settling on a local soccer match. Looking at her phone, she noticed the timer had a little less than two hours remaining. She grabbed the remote, scrolled down and opened a saved video file on the TV, but paused it as soon as it played. Setting the remote down, she leaned back and stared at the patch of dirt. Within a few minutes, she had drifted off to sleep. Soon after, the light switched itself off. A single night light cast the entire room in a pale blue glow.

"Who the fuck are you?"

Sam bolted awake to see a dark figure standing above her, the whites of his eyes visible in the pale light.

"Marcus?"

"I said, who the fuck are *you*?" Dirt covered most of his body, and clumps of mud-caked his hair.

103

"I'm Sam! Hold on!" Her hand reached for the remote. "Let me show you something."

"Sam? Sam who? And where are we?" He looked down at himself. "Why did you bury me in that fucking hole?"

"No!" She picked up the remote. "I can expl—."

Before she could finish, he leaned forward and grabbed her by the throat. Stunned, she tried to pull his hand away without dropping the remote. Sam realized she would never break his vice-like grip, so she focused on hitting the play button.

He pulled her closer, rage filling his eyes. "Who are you, and what have you done with Natalia?"

She tried to avoid his rabid eyes and finally got the video started.

"*Hello, Marcus.*"

Marcus turned his head toward the screen to find an image of himself speaking.

"*I know this is difficult, but you need to sit down.*"

Marcus looked from the video back to Sam and let her go. She gasped for air and fell back onto the couch, rubbing her throat. Marcus stood staring at the video as it worked through a series of explanations and descriptions. It talked about events from the past and people Marcus knew. She watched as the confusion faded from his face, and a stark realization set in.

After three or four minutes, he looked away from the TV. "You can turn it off."

She stopped the recording. "Can I get you anything?"

"Water?"

"Sure." She hopped off the couch and moved to the kitchen. Grabbing a glass from the cupboard, she filled it with water from the fridge and walking back, looked down at the opening on the floor. The soil was pushed aside, leaving a significant divot on the surface. She handed the glass to him, and only then realized he was naked.

She walked to the bathroom and grabbed him a towel. He

had finished the water and exchanged the empty glass for the towel.

"How did you..." her voice trailed off.

"I wasn't very deep. Sometimes, I get lucky." He stood, the towel wrapped around his waist. She rubbed her throat again.

"I'm so sorry. Are you okay?"

"No, no. I mean, yeah, I'm fine. It was my fault. I should have stayed awake and started the video earlier. Don't worry about it."

His eyes told her he was worried about it. "I'm gonna take a shower. Can you find us something to eat? Should be a few cans in there."

"Sure."

He buttoned up his shirt as he exited the bathroom, the aroma of canned chili filling the small room. He ran one hand back through his still wet hair and sat at the small table. Sam brought over two bowls and sat down across from him.

"It was in French; I hope it isn't expired." She smelled the chili, then took a small bite from the tip of the spoon.

"Should be fine." Marcus pushed caution aside and shoveled a full spoonful into his mouth.

"What happened?" she asked between bites.

"Shit went south after I headed downtown. Thomas had a big crew, bigger than I expected." He finished his mouthful. "Not having a gun was super inconvenient."

"The explosion?"

"Yeah, that was me."

"Why?"

He stopped chewing for a moment, wiping his mouth with a napkin.

"Do you know how hard it is to kill yourself instantly?" He

didn't wait for a response. "I've tried a dozen times. I was horribly unsuccessful on three occasions. Once, I was skewered on a rock for hours, fucking crabs nibbling on me until the tide came in and I drowned."

A look of horror had settled on her face.

"So, an explosion seemed appropriate." He was about to take another bite when he stopped. "I made sure there were no civilians around."

She nodded, her mouth still open.

He reverted his focus to his chili. When finished, he gulped down the last of his water and then grabbed a nearby cigarette pack and lit one.

"So, what's our status?"

"I went straight to the safe house, then here. No contact with anyone."

"Good." He stood and rinsed his bowl in the sink, cigarette dangling from his mouth. Then moved to his desk.

"Why a winery? And isn't a bed-and-breakfast pretty high profile?"

"Well, I thought a B&B would be less conspicuous. Kind of hiding in plain sight." He sat at the desk and brought the screen to life.

"The manager...does he know you?" Sam brought her bowl to the sink and cleaned it.

"No, it's been a while since I've been through the room upstairs. I visit under more unusual circumstances."

Nodding, she wiped her hands and started across the room. Standing next to him at the computer, Sam rubbed her hands on her hips.

"Can I ask a question?"

"Absolutely." He took the last puff of his cigarette.

"Why here?"

"Yeah." He crushed the butt and pointed at the plot of dirt.

"That's where I was killed for the first time. By a very large and very angry barbarian."

"You probably deserved it."

"Most definitely, though I didn't think so at the time."

"Does anyone else know? Thomas?"

"No. One immortal knew, a man named Nicodemus."

"And where is he now?"

"Dead, killed by the Nazis."

"I'm sorry."

"Me too. I miss him." He glanced at the open patch. "Your uncle was the only other person I trusted enough to bring here."

"And now me?"

"And now you."

"What did you do before? Before anyone was here to help?"

"I dug myself out...or suffocated trying."

"Are you kidding me?"

"No, but that only happened twice."

"And the disorientation?"

"It wasn't so bad. That's only been an issue the last few years."

"Why is that?"

He shrugged. "No fucking idea."

"And who is Natalia?"

Marcus flinched, the smile disappearing.

"You said her name when you were..." her hand moved back to her throat.

He swung back to the computer. "I'd rather not talk about her."

His tone was cold and distant. She had gone a step too far and moved back to the couch and sat down.

There was an unpleasant silence while Marcus typed on the keyboard. After a couple of minutes, he stood and moved over to a cabinet on the workbench. He opened the door and grabbed a bottle of scotch and two glasses. Marcus sat and put the glasses on the coffee table. He poured them both a drink, his quite a bit fuller than hers, then slid the glass toward her.

"I'm sorry." He finished half the glass. "We agreed I would share everything."

She took a sip but did not reply.

"She was my wife. When I die, the same thing happens every time. It starts early in the morning; my wife is asleep next to me. I'm cold because she stole the blanket again." A wry smile crossed his lips as he faded into the memory. "I take a minute or two to realize what's happening. And then it's a mix of excitement and dread, mostly dread."

He swirled the glass in his hand.

"It's real, as real as anything could be. I feel, I smell, I can even taste. But I *know* it's not real because I know exactly what's going to happen. It's like I'm inside a movie, and I can't change anything. It moves from scene to scene. My wedding, my son being born, my daughter's first steps. Arguments with my father. The last time I saw my mother. It goes on for three days. Only they're not memories; I live them."

Marcus finished his drink and poured himself another healthy dose. He took a long swig and said, "And it always ends the same...with the death of my wife."

Sam took a drink, the scotch burning her lips and throat, but not enough to distract her from the sadness in his eyes.

"Why do you think that happens?"

"I don't know. Some kind of emotional connection? Is my life flashing before my eyes? You know, like the old saying? Maybe God is just a fucking bastard and wants to torture me." He drained his glass.

"I'm sorry, you shouldn't have to go through that."

"Well, it's better than the alternative. I have no desire to get caught and stuck in some cell for years on end. If given the option, you can't let that happen."

"I won't."

"Good." He tilted his head toward the computer. "Now, can you figure out why I can't get into any of my accounts?"

"Sure," Sam moved to the desk and started working. After a few minutes, she figured it out.

"Looks like everything is frozen. Your credit card and bank accounts, travel accounts."

"Well, not everything. Just the stuff they know about."

"They? Meaning Thomas?"

"And Ramirez."

She nodded, then she realized. "My uncle?"

"He's safe. I contacted him after I left the coffee shop. I told him to disappear."

"How did you know?"

"Just a hunch."

"Good. Are money or passports going to be a problem?"

"I have everything we need here."

"You know, I've been meaning to ask. But I didn't want to be nosy."

"Now you decided not to be nosy?"

"True. That's not my strong suit." She scrunched her face and asked, "Where did you get all your money?"

He chuckled. "Over the years, I managed to collect a few things. I have a room, a vault, in the wall near the bathroom."

"I didn't see anything."

"That's the point," He said. "It's mostly gold. Doubloons, some bullion, ingots. You could say I had a pretty successful run in the early 1700s."

"You were a pirate."

"I prefer the term *privateer*."

"You were so a pirate." She started laughing. "Tell me you had a monkey."

"I did not have a monkey."

"I bet you did." She nodded. "So gold, that it?"

"Pretty much. I have some artifacts, but I rarely sell them. I had a lot of art, but most of that is gone. And I have some land, but that's a bit trickier to liquidate."

"I figure that's how Thomas made his money?"

"Among other things, yeah. He was big in shipping and trading."

"So, are we gonna have to carry around a sack of gold coins?"

"No," Marcus said. "I have cash."

"Not as cool, but it works." She motioned to the many screens showing various camera angles from outside the winery. "Looks clear."

He looked back at the monitors and shook his head. "I never go out through the room. If you haven't noticed, I'm paranoid."

"So, how do we get out?"

He grinned.

CHAPTER EIGHT

*What is human warfare but just this; an effort to make the laws
of God and nature take sides with one party.*
—HENRY DAVID THOREAU

OCTOBER 732 A.D.
TOURS, FRANCE

IT WAS COLD, the morning air sharp and clean. The heavy
winds from the night before had faded to a soft breeze that
tugged and pulled at the colorful banners. A dense fog
retreated from the field, unwilling to stand between the two
armies.

The defenders formed a human wall across the top of the
sloping valley. Each wing was anchored in the heavy forests
that protected the flanks from encirclement. Some were
mercenaries, drawn by the promise of plunder; many were
farmers, plucked from the harvests. They were a mixture of
Saxons, Franks, and Burgundians. Together, they stood for
Christendom.

At the far end of the valley were the Muslim invaders, a sea

111

of yellow and orange eager to charge across the empty field. Each of the horsemen carried an eight-foot lance with a red ribbon attached below its shiny blade. Most of the army comprised light cavalry or Berbers. They wore chain-mail shirts, pointed helmets, and carried no shields. A select few were cataphracts: armored behemoths who could smash through an enemy formation.

"Will they attack," Thomas looked over at Marcus, "or just nibble for another day?"

Both men were sitting atop giant warhorses, overlooking the field from a shallow knoll. The rest of the court gathered around Charles Martel, Mayor of the Palace and General of the Franks.

"They will attack."

Thomas started to ask why, but a litany of trumpets and drums punctuated the air and signaled the Muslim army's advance. Marcus glanced over at Thomas and winked. Charles prodded his mighty warhorse through a gap in the formation and then turned to face his army.

"Stand firm, Brothers of Christ! God is looking down upon us, and *He* shall not forget your bravery. Let us give these bastards a taste of cold, Frankish steel, and then send the heathen scoundrels back across the mountains from which they came!"

A loud cheer rose from the defenders as each man raised his weapon high above his head. They pounded their weapons against their shields, trying to erase the fear that would fill any man's soul when faced with a thousand tons of horse and steel.

The wall of men looked impressive, but it was not. Charles had too many conscripts, and he knew it. The conscripts wore leather armor, if they had armor at all. Most carried spears and small wooden shields; a few had rusty swords. Alone, they would never withstand a single charge. So, it forced Charles to mix them in with the heavily armed mercenaries, hoping the veterans' discipline would rub off on the peasants. It was a bold move that could easily backfire. Failure spreads like wildfire, and if the peasants abandoned the line, they could take the mercenaries with them. But it was a gamble Charles had to make. Outnumbered, there was no way he could hold the flanks unless he used the conscripts. Fear and faith would have to rule the day.

The Muslims trotted forward, lances rising and falling with the rhythm of their mounts. The pasture disappeared, consumed by the approaching horde. Charles watched the advance from the knoll, his jaw clenched. When they reached the middle of the valley, Charles nodded to one of his generals, and moments later, the first volley of arrows rained down upon the riders. Men and horses fell beneath the downpour, but it did not slow their advance.

Marcus held his breath as the infidels lowered their lances and crashed into the phalanx awaiting them. The impact rippled across the valley as the line buckled but did not break. The screams of horse and man filled the air as the two armies hacked each other to pieces.

The first attack lasted less than fifteen minutes before a horn called the Muslims, so they could regroup for a half hour and charge again. They hoped the speed and weight of their horses would break the line, as it always had. But Charles had planned for such tactics. It was easy to teach a peasant to shove a spear in the ground and stand shoulder to shoulder with his comrade. The tightly packed formations proved impossible to penetrate, and they repelled charge after charge.

This cycle continued throughout the day, each assault resulting in a brief but bitter hand-to-hand struggle before the Muslim trumpeters would signal the retreat. As the battle raged, Charles ordered reserves to reinforce the weakened line. The Saracens rotated units throughout the day, allowing battered elements to regroup before throwing them back into the bloodshed. Marcus and Thomas had asked Charles to join the melee on several occasions, but he calmly denied each request.

They found out why just before sunset. The last charge had almost collapsed the line, and during the brief respite that followed, Charles gathered a group of knights together near the base of the knoll.

"Brothers! The line cannot hold. Our men are exhausted, and we have no reserves. Withdrawal is not an option. And the infidels know this. The sultan will launch one last assault before nightfall, one that I believe he will lead himself." Charles sat up taller in his saddle, the fading sun glinting off his polished armor. "I intend to kill the sultan—or die trying."

He waited as a murmur swept through the tiny force, each man nodding in solemn agreement.

"Thomas, speak with the Saxon leader. During the next attack, his men have to create a gap for us to ride through the Muslim line."

"Yes, sir." Thomas headed off toward the right side of the line.

Marcus guided his horse to a spot behind the thin Christian line and waited for Thomas to rejoin him.

A few minutes later, Thomas reined in his horse. "So, what do you think?"

"I don't like your chances," Marcus said with a shallow smile.

"Thanks."

"Next time, don't ask."

Marcus drew his sword and slid it into a sheath mounted on the left side of his saddle. Next, he retrieved the helmet, hanging near his feet and slipped it on, opening the visor and adjusting it to clear his peripheral vision. He then reached for an angry-looking mace hanging from his pommel and looked over to Thomas, who had completed a similar routine. Within moments, Charles joined their party, brandishing a mighty sword.

"Fellow Christians!" Charles spun his horse toward the men. "We hold the fate of this great struggle and the destiny of Christendom in our hands. I want the sultan's head on a stick by nightfall. I will give a thousand francs to the man who strikes him down. Remember, providence has delivered us to this moment, and before the eyes of God, we shall not fail!"

As if on cue, the distant sound of trumpets floated through the descending twilight. Charles urged his horse to the front of the party, motioning Thomas and Marcus to join him. Together, the trio formed the point of a deadly wedge as they waited for the assault to begin.

The horde rumbled across the valley like an approaching storm. Marcus sat up in his saddle, peered over the line of soldiers and across the bloody pasture. It appeared as if the entire Muslim army was racing up the valley, trampling over the scattered corpses. One last time, the Frankish bowmen unleashed their fury, further darkening the sky. But once again, the Saracens pushed forward, unchecked, and gaining speed. As the shimmering sun slipped below the tree line, the Muslim horde slammed into the Christian wall. Again, the line rippled from the impact, and in several places the Muslim horsemen reached the last row of soldiers. Finally, in desperation, the archers tossed aside their bows and joined the fighting, attacking the Saracens with sword, club, and dagger. As the slaughter raged, the Saxons struggled to breach the Muslim line.

The hearty soldiers crept forward, hacking away at the Muslims. One frenzied Saxon led the push, felling man and horse with his mighty hammer. The Muslims fell back as he cleared a deadly swath through their thinning ranks. With a mighty cry, the resilient Saxons burst through the line, opening a narrow gap. There was no hesitation as Charles spurred his horse forward and led his tiny band into the breach.

The armored knights thundered through the opening, rushing past the Muslim horsemen and careening onto the open ground beyond. Looking over his shoulder, Marcus watched the gap disappear. There would be no going back.

Charles led them toward a mass of cavalry near the center of the valley. It was the sultan, surrounded by a contingent of cataphracts. As the Christians approached, an alarm rose from within their midst.

The Saracens turned to face the danger just as the galloping wedge plunged into their formation. Marcus split two defenders, swinging his weapon in a tight circle. The heavy metal ball caught one adversary in the forehead, shattering his skull and sending him tumbling over the backside of his horse. Leaning forward to avoid a sword thrust, Marcus drove the sharpened tip of his mace into the chin of another attacker, rupturing his larynx and stifling the cry that followed.

As he pulled his weapon free, Marcus saw Charles ahead of him, surrounded by an entire group of Saracens. Marcus urged his horse forward and drove his weapon down upon one of them, splintering his pointed helmet. The impact jarred the mace from his hand. As Marcus watched it fall to the ground, a sharp pain in his side drew his attention to a soldier next to his horse. The Muslim had stabbed him with a broken lance; the tip slipping between the plates of armor and digging into his hip. Marcus spun his horse to the left, knocking the man over as he grabbed the lance from him. Twirling the shaft around, he buried the blade into the man's chest.

As Marcus looked back toward Charles, he was bludgeoned in the head, nearly unseating him. He somehow stayed mounted, but the blow knocked the helmet from his head. Dazed, he twisted to face a new threat, but Thomas had already dispatched the man. Thomas still wore his helmet, his face splattered with sweat and blood. The Muslims had surrounded their tiny party, trying desperately to keep them from the sultan. Just a few feet away, Charles stood up in his stirrups to see over the tangle of riders. His gaze fell upon a bright Muslim banner, less than thirty feet away. As he whirled back toward the others, Marcus could see in his eyes what he planned to do.

"To Charles!" Marcus drew his sword and urged his mount forward.

Thomas and a few other knights joined him, and together they drove through the Muslims, slashing and cutting their way toward the rival leader. The fighting grew desperate, and soon they faced the very last of the Sultan's bodyguards.

"Charles, the sultan!" Marcus drove the tip of his sword into the nearest foe, ducking from the stream of blood that spurted from the resulting wound.

As Thomas and Marcus fell upon the remaining Saracens, Charles galloped toward the sultan. As they tried to follow, a Muslim impaled Thomas's horse. Both rider and horse tumbled to the ground. Marcus dismounted and joined Thomas, turning his back to his old friend.

"Are we the only two left?" Thomas deflected an attack.

"Apparently!" Marcus sidestepped a lance thrust and skewered its owner.

They fought for what seemed an eternity, struggling to stay afoot on the fertile pasture that had now become a gory bog. Both men had lost sight of Charles, and they resigned themselves to the fact they would die upon that nameless field. Marcus dispatched a rather portly man and waited, expecting to find another soldier in his place. But there was none. There was a wide circle of dead bodies around them, and beyond, dozens of Muslims were screaming as they raced for the distant tree line.

"What are they saying?" Thomas stuck his sword into the mud.

"They are terrified of me."

"And me?"

"They seem to be amazed you made it this far." A smile split Marcus's bloodied face.

"Not bad, considering I only started this warrior thing a hundred years ago."

"I can't believe we survived."

"All part of God's plan, I guess. So what are they *really* saying?"

"Something about their camp. I think they said it's under attack."

"Why didn't we think of that?"

"I guess we're not that smart."

As they startled to chuckle, a shadow fell upon them. Fearing a Saracen horseman had stayed to fight, they prepared to face the newcomer. Instead, it was Charles, sitting upon his massive horse. The sultan's severed head hung from the pommel of his blood-soaked saddle.

"What the hell are you two smiling at?" Charles glared at Thomas, then Marcus.

They looked at each other and burst out laughing.

They spent the next day watching the Muslim army. The Saracens had no stomach for prolonged conflict with the sultan dead, and by nightfall, they had slipped off to the south. Charles sent some knights to shadow their retreat, but he was confident the battle was over.

Marcus returned from a reconnaissance mission, guided his horse through the crowded camp, and stopped in front of a large, white pavilion. He dismounted and tossed the reins to a nearby squire.

"Wipe him down and make sure he gets a full bag of oats," Marcus instructed.

"Yes, sir."

Marcus pulled off his gloves and ducked into the pavilion. The aroma of stewed beef intensified the rumblings in his stomach. Grabbing a chalice from a passing servant, Marcus took a long pull of wine and moved toward the back of the tent where Charles was talking with a group of men.

"I don't know where he is," Charles said.

Joining the group, Marcus realized a woman was in their midst. He recognized her, despite the shawl wrapped around her head and shoulder.

"Isabella!" Marcus called.

She rushed toward him. "Marcus! I've been looking for you. No one knew where you were."

"What are you doing? I asked you to stay in Orleans with Rebecca. It's not safe here."

"Can we talk alone?" Her eyes pleaded with him.

"Yes, of course."

They found a quiet spot near the front of the tent.

"Why are you here?" He held both her hands.

"I sent a letter yesterday, but no one answered."

"I didn't get a letter. How did you get here?"

"I rode...I had to find you.".

"Why? What's the matter?"

"Rebecca. Archbishop Rigobert has charged her with heresy. One of her servants went to the Archbishop, telling him she was a witch. She swore that Lady Rebecca had cut her hand on Sunday, and the wound was gone by the following day!"

Marcus clenched his jaw but did not reply.

"He arrested her, and I heard they did awful things to her. And that she confessed. They are going to burn her at the stake."

"When?"

119

"Tonight!"

"I have to find Thomas...and go to Orleans." Marcus looked around the room, finally finding who he was looking for. "Nico!"

The older gentleman was talking to a courtier, but looked up when called. Marcus waved for him to join them. Nicodemus excused himself and made his way over to the pair.

"What's wrong?"

"Have you seen Thomas?"

"I saw him about an hour ago; he asked for you." Nicodemus frowned. "Then he left in a hurry. Is something wrong?"

"I'm not sure, but I need to find out." He looked from Isabella to Nico. "If I'm not back by morning, assume the worst. Stay close to Charles; he'll keep you safe."

"Marcus, be careful." Isabella placed a hand on his forearm.

"Careful doesn't work." He leaned forward and kissed her on the forehead. "I'll be fine."

Marcus walked out of the pavilion. He hurried to the tent he shared with Thomas and stepped inside. A single candle burned on a nearby table. He scanned the room and saw a crumpled piece of parchment on the bare ground. He leaned over, picked it up, and read the contents. The signature at the bottom was Isabella's.

"Damn it!"

Marcus went over to his cot and pulled a heavy cloak from his bag, slipping it over his head and attaching it to his tunic as he ran over to the tent that served as a stable. When he arrived, the attendant was still brushing down his horse.

"I need the fastest horse you have and be quick about it!"

"This one!" The young man dropped his brush and sprung to action. Marcus grabbed his saddle and followed him, throwing it over the back of a jet-black mare.

"She's one of the fastest we got." The teenager slipped the harness on her. "Sir Thomas took the only one who can outpace her."

"It'll have to do." Marcus secured the straps.

Marcus grabbed the reins, pulling the horse toward the exit and leaped onto the saddle, spurring her forward as he slipped his boots into the stirrups. He galloped through the camp, almost running down several men. Once past the tents, he sped unchecked through the picket lines and into the dark forest beyond.

After what seemed like forever, Marcus beheld the welcome glow of Orleans, its dull radiance seeping over the distant ridge. His mount was panting as he reined her in before the city's gate. A single guard stepped out from the portal. The sentry, still a teen, eyed Marcus suspiciously as his eyes fell on his winded horse.

"What business do you have in Orleans?"

"I am a messenger from Charles Martel. I bring news to the Archbishop." Marcus looked through the opening.

"You are the second messenger from Charles." The sentry squinted.

"Where did the other go?"

"He said he was meeting someone at the cathedral. I'll need to talk to my sergeant." His hand moved down to his sword. "I am not to admit anyone without proper authorization."

"And why did you let the other pass?"

"He was already expected."

"By who?"

"The Archbishop."

Marcus's gaze shifted from the young man to the opening beyond. The guard realized his intentions, reached for the horse's reins and yelled back over his shoulder. Marcus spurred his mount forward, leaned over and swung for the chin. The blow caught the point of his jaw, and the guard crumpled to the ground, his helmet skittering across the stone path as Marcus sped forward. Two more soldiers appeared from behind the wall but scrambled away from the approaching mare. Once inside, Marcus guided his mount along the shadow of the city walls.

Marcus knew the cathedral was near the center of town, so he wove his horse through the deserted streets. Twice she almost tumbled, her hooves slipping on the smooth stone. But she was stubborn, and she kept moving forward. On one occasion, she almost threw Marcus from the saddle. He somehow stayed atop her by clinging to the pommel and sitting upright, soon realizing that he was on the edge of an open promenade, on the other side of which stood the towering cathedral.

The hairs on the back of his neck stood up when he saw a smoldering pile of charred wood in the center of the square.

Marcus dug his heels into the mare, raced across the square, pulling the mount up next to another exhausted and trembling horse. He sprung from the saddle and landed at the foot of the stairs, freeing his sword as he dashed up the steps. He pulled open the oak door and stepped over the dead body of a soldier and into the foyer beyond. Two more bodies slumped against the walls, their blood forming a single pool on the cold stone floor. Marcus avoided the growing puddle, and moved into a spacious room beyond, guided by the candles that hung throughout the chamber.

Marcus followed a ghastly trail of butchered corpses to the front of the room, where a shadow enveloped the stone altar. Thomas sat on the steps, holding a charred body in his arms. A sword lay by his side, while three more bodies scattered in unnatural positions all around him.

"Thomas?"

Silence enveloped them as he sheathed his sword and knelt beside his friend. The corpse, burned beyond recognition, was cradled in his lap. Marcus looked down at the left hand, and could see the gold ring that Rebecca had always worn. Marcus covered his mouth with one hand as his body slumped to the ground.

He looked up at Thomas, who was rocking back and forth. His handsome face was stoic, save the tears that cut through the drying blood. Marcus noticed a pool of dark liquid expanding toward the lip of the steps. Standing, he moved toward the platform and the body that lay upon it. The unfamiliar face was gripped with terror. The man's torso was split open from throat to groin, the organs removed and discarded in a pile on the floor. Looking away in disgust, Marcus stepped toward Thomas and placed his hand upon his shoulder.

"Get away!" Thomas screamed. He laid Rebecca's body down and picked up his sword. Standing, he stumbled down the steps, fury consuming his handsome face.

"Thomas—"

"They killed her! Burned her like a witch!" He stepped forward, his face contorted with rage. "They did it in the name of God!"

"These are not men of God. This is not *His* work—" Marcus raised his hands, unable to continue. A long silence hung between them. Marcus pointed toward the altar. "Who was that?"

"Rigobert..." Thomas's response was less than a whisper.

Nodding, Marcus looked around the room at the carnage wrought by this one vengeful man.

"Thomas, we have to get out of here." He glanced toward the exit. "You cannot stay—not after this. Come with me, come with me to Rome."

"No!" Thomas spun back. "For seven hundred years, we preached, fought, and bled for *Him!*" He pointed his bloodstained sword to the enormous crucifix behind the pulpit. "And while I'm away fighting the infidels—defending their land, their church—*He* allows them to do this to *me*? A man of the cloth murders my wife!" He paused, fighting back the tears. "And I'm supposed to walk away? Just turn the other cheek?"

Marcus had no answer. He watched as Thomas paced back and forth.

"The others...I'll find them. I'll kill them all." He moved back toward the front of the room, head lowered as he mumbled to himself.

"Thomas!"

Thomas stopped.

"They will not let you pass." Marcus pointed to a large group of soldiers who had entered the cathedral, weapons drawn. Marcus stepped forward and placed his hand on Thomas's shoulder. This time, Thomas did not pull away. "I know your pain...believe me, I do. But she would not have wanted you to die here tonight. You must leave...these men will not stop until you're dead. I'll hold them off until you are safe, and then we shall grieve together."

After a long silence, Thomas looked him in the eyes. "I can't do this alone."

"You won't have to..."

After a few moments, Thomas nodded.

The emptiness of his farewell almost destroyed Marcus.

Marcus pushed the feeling aside, drew his sword, and turned to meet the advancing guards. Marcus would not see his friend for another seven hundred years.

CHAPTER NINE

History, despite its wrenching pain, cannot be unlived,
but if faced with courage, need not be lived again.
—MAYA ANGELOU

MODERN DAY
PARIS

MARCUS SIPPED HIS COFFEE and watched the heavy raindrops splatter against the nearby window. A winter gale had blown in from the channel, catching them in its chilly downpour. Sam was purchasing tickets for the overnight train to Milan, which would take them about seven hours.

Samantha returned, taking a deep breath as she dropped into the seat.

"You look tired," Marcus said.

"Yeah, I didn't sleep much while you were gone." Sam set the tickets onto the table. "Why aren't we just going to Rome directly?"

"Thomas is expecting us. He'll be monitoring the central station in Rome. It's safer to drive in from Milan."

"Is he watching Milan?"

"Probably. Smile when you look up at the security cameras."

"Now you tell me."

Marcus shifted his attention to the crowd of passengers moving about the cavernous station, some of them looking up at the giant digital timetable hanging on the far wall. Unfortunately, it would be impossible to tell if anyone was following them. When their train was ready for boarding, they paid the bill and headed toward their assigned terminal.

Once on the platform, they found two porters sitting on a pair of wooden crates, engaged in a lively conversation. The younger of the two stood as they approached, his dark blue uniform hanging on his thin frame like a scarecrow on a pole. A wrinkled hat sat atop his black, cropped hair. Ears that would fit a man twice his size jutted out from beneath his cap. He stepped forward to take the bag from Marcus, his smile revealing a mouthful of crooked teeth. The other man reluctantly stood and tossed a mangled toothpick to the ground. His stained coveralls clung to his portly frame, the seams straining against his bulk—the displeasure of having to work written upon his chubby face.

"Tickets, monsieur?" The thinner porter looked from Sam to Marcus.

Samantha pulled out their tickets, which the porter took and scanned.

"Ah, sleeper car six, no? Please follow me, monsieur."

The younger man gestured for his co-worker to take Sam's bag, then led them to a car near the end of the train where they stepped up into the stairwell. The man carrying Sam's bag had somehow fallen behind during the brief journey. Annoyed, Sam motioned for the man to hand her the bag, then waved. Relieved of his burden, the Frenchman shrugged and turned away. Sam shook her head and caught up with Marcus, who was speaking to the porter in the narrow hallway.

"No, we don't want to be notified for dinner. And honestly, I'd like to make sure we're not disturbed at all." Marcus pulled cash from his pocket and removed a crisp one-hundred euro note. "Now, take this as a token of my appreciation. I'll be even more generous at the end of our journey—if things go well."

"Oui, monsieur." Eyes wide-open, the young man accepted the bill and slipped it into his pocket. "I will make certain no one disturbs you for any reason—any reason at all."

Marcus entered the sleeper but paused. "One more thing—"

"Oui?" The porter stopped, eyebrows raised.

"I'd like to know if anyone asks about us. Who we are, which cabin we are in, you know. If that happens, I'd appreciate it very much if you can inform me immediately."

"Oui, monsieur." The little Frenchman frowned and nodded his head up and down. "I will tell you first thing. Enjoy the journey."

The porter smiled as he squeezed past Sam in the hallway.

"You expecting trouble?" Sam closed the door.

"Yeah." Marcus set his bag down near the lavatory door.

"Any reason?"

"Just paranoid."

"Comforting."

Marcus ignored her and pulled down the lower bench to form a makeshift bed. He slipped off his coat and hung it on a hook near the door, rolling the sleeves of his shirt. He pulled off his holster and set it near his bed. Sam prepared the other bunk. When they were both ready, Marcus flipped off the light, and they slipped into their beds.

They were both oblivious to the bustle that accompanied the train's departure from Paris. Their journey carried them east, through the open countryside of eastern France. In the early afternoon, they passed the old Maginot Line and swept through the historically disputed Alsace Lorraine.

Marcus was awake by midnight, but not wanting to disturb

Sam, sat quietly in the darkened room. He opened the shade and watched the shadowy terrain zip past as the steady rhythm of the train lulled him into a trance-like state. A soft knock snapped Marcus back to reality and sent him reaching for his pistol. Marcus stood and glanced at Sam to see if the sound had woken her. Unsurprisingly, she was still asleep. Marcus heard the tap again as he reached the door. Switching on the overhead light, he unlocked the latch and pulled open the door. He peered through the narrow space and recognized the young porter's features, who immediately explained himself.

"Monsieur, I am very sorry to interrupt you—but you wanted to know if anyone asked about you."

Marcus held up one finger. "Wait here."

He closed the door, slipped the gun into the back of his waistband, and moved to where Sam slept. Marcus leaned over and gently shook her shoulders.

"Sam." He shook her again. "Sam!"

"Huh?" She sat up, rubbing the sleep from her eyes, and looked around to gain her bearings. "Are we in Milan?"

"No, not yet. But someone is asking about us."

"Who?"

"I'm not sure, but you need to get up."

"Okay..."

Marcus pulled open the door to find the porter fidgeting in the hallway. When he motioned for the young man to enter the compartment, the porter stepped across the threshold. He nodded to Sam as he moved to one side so Marcus could shut the door. He held his hat in both hands, wringing it back and forth as he shifted his weight from foot to foot. Sam stood up and put their bunks away.

"Let me, madame." The porter stepped forward to help.

"No, thank you. I can manage."

The Frenchman stopped in his tracks, stuffing his hat into

his back pocket. He looked from Sam to Marcus, smiling apprehensively.

"Well?" Marcus glared at the porter, his tone crushing the sheepish grin.

"Oh, yes. I am so sorry. You asked me to tell you—no?—if anyone asked about you. I overheard a man speak to Dotel— the man asked if Dotel had seen any Americans board the train."

"Who is Dotel?"

"Ah, yes, you know Dotel. He is one who carried your bag."

"Oh, that guy," Sam said.

"Well, the stranger he have pictures too. Unfortunately, I no see them—but Dotel see them, and he said the person in pictures *did* board the train in Paris. The man smile and ask which car. Dotel not so sure until man give him two hundred Euros. You see, monsieur, Dotel like to drink wine very much. And women," he sighed, "oh, he really like the women. Most of them are so ugly, but he no care. The women do not like him, but they do like his money, especially when it is in their pockets."

He paused, lost in thought for a moment.

"Go on—" Marcus encouraged the Frenchman.

"Oh, yes. After man give Dotel the money, he then know what car you in, even what cabin." He looked at Marcus. "I did good, yes?"

Marcus stood silently staring at the ground as one hand rubbed the stubble on his chin.

"Monsieur?"

Marcus looked up.

"Of course, you did a magnificent job." He slipped his hand into his pocket and withdrew his roll of money. He handed several bills to the porter, studying the young Frenchman. After a protracted silence he said, "Do you know the name of the man who asked about us?"

"No, monsieur." He eyed the thick roll of money, his tongue sliding over his thin lips. He ran one hand through his greasy black hair, scratching a spot on the back of his head. "If you want, I find out for you?"

"No, no. Say nothing at all to this man—nothing that would warn him about our conversation. Understood?"

"Yes, sir. I no mind—I am very brave person." He tried to stand a bit taller to prove his fearlessness.

"I'm sure you are. What's your name?"

"Navarre."

"It's nice to meet you, Navarre. We appreciate your help." Marcus glanced out the window. "Do you know where we are now?"

The Frenchman dug into his pocket and pulled out a silver watch with no wristband. His features contorted as he stared at the watch and made a series of silent calculations. He looked up and announced, "We are three hundred kilometers from Milan."

"Are we near any big cities?"

"No, monsieur. There is nothing around here but fields and trees—and cows. Lots of cows."

Marcus nodded, then reached over and turned off the light. He moved to the window and peered out into the darkness. The train sped through the night, the full moon bright enough to illuminate the gravel beside the tracks but not the dense forest beyond. Occasionally, a tiny farmhouse occupied a break in the tree line, cold and dark in the winter night.

Marcus cursed under his breath and moved back to the middle of the room.

Sam followed him. "You could make the jump without me."

"Maybe."

"You've got to do it. I'll keep them occupied." Her gaze was unwavering, the shadows from the moonlight glimmering across her face.

"No. We'll find another way."

Sam shook her head and flicked on the light. That was when she remembered the porter, who was waiting near the door. Sam looked to Marcus, her eyes pivoting toward Navarre. Marcus nodded and sat down on the bench as Sam motioned for Navarre to join them. The porter dipped his head and moved to sit next to Sam, across from Marcus. As he settled into the cushion, he stood up quickly, then smiling, reached back to remove his crumpled hat from his pocket.

Can I trust him? Marcus studied the young Frenchman. *Do I have a choice?*

Marcus leaned forward; so did Navarre.

"Can you slow down the train?" The question was just above a whisper.

Navarre recoiled as if Marcus had punched him in the face. His expression wavered between surprise and horror as he looked from Marcus to Sam. "Monsieur...monsieur, I am just a porter, not a conductor. I no can do such things."

"Do you know anyone who can? I pay very well."

"No, no, of course not!" Navarre pursed his lips, squeezing his hat until his knuckles grew white. "Well...maybe I can talk to my cousin—but monsieur, Sefe only a mechanic. I am not sure if he can slow down train."

"All right, please speak with him, then come back and tell me what he says." Marcus studied his watch. "Can you be back in ten minutes?"

"Yes, monsieur. But," Navarre paused for a moment, "My cousin will believe me. He will want to know you very serious."

"I understand." Marcus stood, removing the wad once again. He peeled another ten bills and handed them to the astonished porter. "There will be a lot more if you can help us."

"Yes, sir. I am sure he will help such honest people." Standing, Navarre slipped the Euros into his pocket. He bowed slightly as he backed away from Marcus and

131

Samantha until he bumped into the door. "I be back in ten minutes."

"Remember, not a word to anyone else," Sam said.

"Of course, not a word." With that, he slipped out of the room.

"Can we trust him?" Sam walked over and locked the door.

Marcus shrugged. "Do we have a choice?"

"Did I ever tell you how much confidence you inspire?"

"No, you didn't, but I appreciate you noticing."

Marcus pulled out the pop-up tabletop. He then grabbed his bag and pulled a map from a pocket, spreading it across the table.

"If we're three hundred kilometers from Milan, that would put us approximately here." Marcus pointed to a spot halfway between the French border and Milan. "If we get off in twenty-five minutes, it should leave us here." He moved his finger over a small town. "We lie low and figure out our next move."

"Sounds good."

Marcus folded up the map. "Let's get ready."

"This is gonna be fun. Have you ever jumped off a moving train?"

"No...but someone threw me off one."

"Again, not surprised."

Marcus reached back for the pistol in his waistband and, sliding back the bolt, chambered a round. He stood and picked up the holster, slipping in the handgun before doing the same on his second weapon. Satisfied, he slid on the holster and fastened the straps into place. He moved to the door, lifted his black leather coat from the peg, and slipped it on. Reaching into his bag, he removed another pistol and several magazines, handing them to Sam.

She paused for a moment, then took the weapon and mags, dropping them onto the cushion. Sam put on her coat and placed the gun and magazines into one of the outside pockets. Marcus looked at his watch, then at Sam.

"He's not coming back." Sam slipped her bag over her shoulder and head with the strap across her chest. "You gave him a thousand Euros—there's no way he's coming back."

"Maybe, but I trust in greed...and it rarely lets me down."

"Nope. He's already planning his trip to Monte Carlo. He'll blow it all in five minutes on the roulette tables. We'll never see him again..."

"Wanna bet?" Before she could answer, there was a light knock at the door. "Too late."

Sam smirked as Marcus slipped one pistol free and unlatched the lock, cracking open the door. A familiar face greeted him with a toothy smile. Marcus replaced his gun in its holster and pulled the door open. The porter stepped into the compartment, moving to the center of the room. Marcus closed and secured the latch, then turned toward Navarre.

"So?"

"Yes, I spoke with my cousin, and he will slow down train. But Sefe can only do for very short time—maybe three or four minutes. You will have to jump very fast."

"No problem." Marcus pulled the wad of money from his pocket once again, peeling a stack of bills off and handing them to Navarre. "When?"

The Frenchman shoved the money into his pocket. "He says very soon the conductor take coffee break. He take many coffee breaks; maybe that is why he pee so much. I think I like to be conductor someday; they never have to clean the toilets or take dead animals from the train wheels—"

"Navarre—" Marcus cut him off.

"Yes? I very sorry, monsieur. Sefe will slow the engines down when conductor leave; he said he blow horn, then he wait ten seconds."

"Good." Marcus shot a glance at Sam, then back to Navarre. "That should be perfect."

"One more thing, monsieur."

"Yes?"

"The man who show pictures of you, he was talking with many men." Navarre's hands spread wide apart. "Very big men."

"What were they saying?"

"Well, monsieur, of course it is not so polite to listen to passengers when they talk to each other."

"I understand, but you may have accidentally overheard their conversation?"

"Yes, and since we now are such good friends, I have no reason to keep secrets."

"Good, go on."

"They talking about when they would do *it*—" Navarre raised his eyebrows. "I am not sure what *it* means, but *it* seemed very bad for you."

"I bet," Marcus said. "Did they say when they were going to do *it*?"

"I believe they say they do *it* when we reach the tunnel."

"What tunnel?" Sam asked.

"This tunnel—" Navarre pointed out the window where the trees disappeared into a black wall.

"Are you kidding?" Marcus reached into his coat and pulled out a pistol.

"No, monsieur!" Navarre squealed. "That what they say! Please no shoot me!"

Marcus shook his head and looked toward the door just as the lights went out and the dull emergency lights kicked on.

"Get down!" Marcus knelt beside the wall.

Navarre did not listen. A flurry of bullets filled the room, several of them hitting the young Frenchman. A muffled thump reverberated through the compartment as the door swung inward. Seconds later, they heard a pop, followed by a loud hissing. Soon, the acrid stench of tear gas began filling the tiny cabin. Holding his breath, Marcus scrambled along the floor, stopping as he bumped into the outside wall of the compartment. He reached up around the table and unlatched the window, feeling the cold air rush past his fingers. It helped to dissipate some fumes, but it was not enough to clear the room. As he struggled with the window, a bright beam of light pierced the swirling haze, scanning the room from one side to the other. Lifting his pistol, Marcus fired several shots at the intruder, the rounds hitting his chest and knocking him back into the hallway.

"Sam, cover the door!" Marcus shoved his gun into its holster.

"Got it!"

Marcus braced his legs and ripped the table from its hinges. The echo of gunfire filled the compartment as Sam began firing at any targets that moved across the doorway. Setting the tabletop down on its side, Marcus picked it up and swung it forward, smashing the wooden corner against the Plexiglas window. The pane buckled but did not break. Choking back tears, he tried to regain his grip on the laminate top. Stumbling back, he took several steps forward and heaved the slab against the window. There was a sharp pop, followed by a high-pitched sucking sound as the window disappeared into the darkness. As the crisp air swept away the choking vapors, Marcus dropped the table and wiped away the tears with the sleeve of his shirt.

The train exited the tunnel moments later, filling the room with silver moonlight.

Marcus could see Sam, her sweater pulled around her mouth and nose, shoving home another magazine. He turned back just in time to see a silhouette dash through the narrow opening, his pistol raised. Marcus stepped forward and buried the heel of his boot into the man's chest. He reached into his coat, pulled out his gun, and fired three shots into him as the man fell back toward the door. Before the body had slumped to the floor, Marcus was firing several rounds at each side of the opening through the compartment's thin walls. As the gunfire echoed through the carriage, he barely caught the lonely shrill of the train's horn. Moving toward the door, Marcus dropped the magazine from his weapon and reloaded it in one smooth motion. He freed his second pistol and braced himself against the wall, waiting for the train to slow.

As promised, he felt and heard the engines fade, causing the train to lurch forward and then back. He stepped into the hallway and fired in both directions. The attackers, caught off balance, were easy targets in the tight confines of the hallway. After emptying his magazines, he stepped back into the room and clicked the release on both guns, dropping the empty mags to the floor. Pinning one pistol beneath his arm, he pulled a full magazine from his coat and slammed it home before slipping the weapon into the holster. He repeated the process for the other, but kept it in his hand and looked back toward Sam. She had a thin streak of blood running down her cheek.

"Are you ok?"

"Yeah, it's just a scratch." She looked down at the lifeless Frenchman. "That fucking sucks."

"Yeah, he seemed like a good kid. But we got to go."

Marcus leveled his gun and moved into the hallway. He stepped over the bodies and made his way toward the rear exit. Short stairwells led down both sides, each one ending in a set of sliding metal doors. Marcus leaned down, pressed the emergency exit button, and the door slid open.

They were met once again by the frigid air, which now swept through the hallway and out the broken window. Marcus looked out the door at the passing landscape. True to his word, the mechanic had slowed the train. Satisfied, Marcus motioned for Sam to come down the steps.

"I'll be right behind."

She nodded and stepped down the stairs. She slipped the gun back into her jacket, arranged her backpack, and took a deep breath as she stepped off into the darkness.

Marcus was just putting his gun away when a hand grabbed the collar of his coat and yanked him off his feet. His back smashed into the steps and knocked the wind from his lungs. Gasping, he looked for his assailant but only saw a meaty paw reaching for him as he squirmed away. Marcus tried to wrestle free his pistol, but the stranger wrapped his massive arms around him, pinning one arm to his side and the other across his chest. He was stuck. As the man tightened his grip, Marcus could smell his hot, putrid breath that reeked of sauerkraut and onions. His attacker leaned back, lifting Marcus off the ground and forcing more air from his aching lungs. His vision blurred just as the train picked up steam.

Marcus battled the creeping darkness, arched his back, and then drove his forehead into the man's nose. His assailant grunted and released his hold just enough for Marcus to slide his hand around the pistol grip. Reaching his finger forward, Marcus slipped it onto the trigger and tried to shift the barrel forward. He closed his eyes and squeezed the trigger, gasping as the slug entered his hip just below the waistline. His stunned opponent relaxed his embrace, allowing Marcus to twist the weapon farther. Marcus gritted his teeth and pulled the trigger again. This time the blast was accompanied by a burning sensation along his abdomen, followed by a groan from his captor. The man dropped Marcus to the floor like a sack of discarded laundry. The attacker grasped his stomach with both hands, a look of astonishment on his sweaty, moonlit face.

As the man lunged forward, Marcus sat up and finally pulled the pistol free from its holster, firing round after round. After two empty clicks, Marcus stopped pulling the trigger and watched as the man slid down the steel bulkhead, a glistening trail in his wake.

Marcus shoved the pistol back into its holster and crawled toward the steps. The forest was now streaking by. Faced with no other option, he slid down the grated stairs until he reached the bottom step. He groaned as he swung his legs around and hung them over the edge. Blood soaked his pant leg, and the wound in his hip throbbed. He took a deep breath, looked up into the pitch-black sky, and pushed himself off the train.

The impact of his legs striking the ground sent shards of pain throughout his entire body. Completely out of control, he tumbled forward, his arms and legs battering the loose embankment. He could hear the train continue into the distance as he came to a stop near the bottom of the tracks, pebbles skittering around him. He lay still for a moment, staring at the clear winter night before passing out.

CHAPTER TEN

The path of social advancement is, and must be,
strewn with broken friendships.
—H.G. WELLS

SPRING 1453 A.D.
CHIOS, GREECE

MARCUS LEANED AGAINST THE heavy mast and watched the sailors scurry about the deck as they prepared to harness the fickle winds. For the past two weeks, their tiny flotilla had been storm-bound in the harbor of Chios. It was a pleasant town, with its open-air markets and green rolling hills, but the stay had grown tiresome for the crews. Last night, there had been another drunken brawl, marking the third evening in a row that such an incident had occurred. The captain had expressed his concern over dinner, where he also spoke in hopeful tones about the change he somehow sensed in the stubborn breezes. Marcus was never one to question a seasoned mariner, and the captain's intuition had been on point. They awoke to clear blue skies, providing a welcome reprieve from the gale-force winds

139

that had been their steady diet until this point in the journey. The captain, trusting the weather would hold, put to sea immediately.

Nearly a month ago, while in Rome, Marcus had received news of the danger posed to Constantinople. A letter from Emperor Constantine had described the situation. An army of eighty-thousand Turks was digging in around the city, and unlike previous expeditions, they seemed unwilling to negotiate. In response, Constantine could only muster seven-thousand soldiers, and provisions were scarce, especially gunpowder. The Pope, frustrated by the lack of support from the usual European powers, had asked Marcus to join an expedition bound for the beleaguered city. Their meager force of three ships had set sail at once, but Mother Nature had slowed their progress. In early April, the fleet entered the Aegean, but strong northern winds had driven them into the Greek island of Chios.

As Marcus stood, a commotion that had erupted near the aft of the ship drew his attention. The captain had given the word, and the crew was springing to action. The activity increased to a flurry, as every able-bodied man helped haul up the anchor. He moved to the bow, watching as the local fishermen waved from their tiny vessels, grateful to be free of their bothersome guests. Soon, the convoy was knifing through the placid harbor and sniffing for the open sea. As they cleared the narrow mouth, the bow tore through the foamy crests and crashed against the rolling swells, drenching Marcus with salty spray. The air was cool and crisp as he watched the massive sails billow beneath the stiffening breeze. Strong as they were, he wondered if they would carry them to the city in time.

For three days, they burdened the wind and careened across the sparkling Aegean. As they approached the Dardanelles, a strait leading into the Sea of Marmara, a lookout spied a large galley bearing the Imperial Byzantine standard.

The fleet Marcus was in sailed under the Genoese flag, a longtime trading partner of the Byzantines. The vessels closed to within spitting distance, and the captains parlayed across the short expanse. The galley was a heavy transport stuffed to the forecastle with Sicilian wheat, and despite the odds, her captain had decided to make a run for the capital. The two men agreed to run the gauntlet together, and soon the tiny armada was bearing down upon the narrow strait, ready for anything the Turks could muster.

The Turkish fleet did not reciprocate their enthusiasm, as it had left to join the siege. Disappointed, they navigated the channel, and sailing on through the night, entered the Sea of Marmora. The crew became subdued as they pondered the fate of the ancient city. A few tried to make the appearance of sleeping, but Marcus doubted many were successful in the endeavor. Eventually, sunrise crept over the dark horizon, exposing the beleaguered city. To their relief, the Imperial banners still fluttered in defiance. Marcus moved to the forecastle, where the captain was shaking his head as he lowered his spyglass. Without a word, he handed Marcus the instrument. Marcus put it to his eye and watched as the massive navy slowly came to life. The Turks were scrambling about their ships like ants on a discarded morsel.

"Torquini," the captain called to the first mate, "ready the ship for battle. It looks like the Turks want another lesson in seamanship."

"You didn't think they'd let us sail right in?" Marcus handed him the spyglass.

"One could hope—" He shrugged. "But then again, who wants to live forever?"

Before Marcus could reply, the captain was off bellowing orders to everyone in his path. Marcus moved down the stairs and into his tiny cabin. He retrieved a wooden chest from beneath his bunk, opened the lid, and lifted out a breastplate.

He removed his coat and placed the armor over his tunic, securing the clasps. Next, he pulled a pair of metal gauntlets over his hands and slipped two iron bracers onto his forearms, using his teeth to tighten the straps. Ignoring the helmet, he reached instead for a sword and main-gauche, a small defensive blade. Standing, he slipped on a shoulder harness that held his scabbard and adjusted the hilt at his waist. The other weapon he attached to his belt. Finally, he slipped a dagger into his boot, closed the wooden chest, and made his way back on deck.

The sailors were scampering about, trying to look busy, while most of the soldiers had donned armor and occupied defensive positions throughout the ship. Marcus watched three men scramble up a wobbly rope ladder to the crow's nest, amazed at the agility of these sea-born monkeys. He found a crate, and using it as a seat, waited as the brisk morning breeze propelled the ship into the approaching storm.

Marcus glanced toward Constantinople and saw that many of the citizens had left the city's shelter and settled among the narrow hills at the foot of the great fortifications. He could also make out groups of people perched upon the dilapidated Hippodrome, hoping to catch one last great spectacle. To their right was one of the other Genoese galleys, trailing a half-length behind. The Imperial galley was off to the left, riding keel to keel with the fourth and final galley. Marcus was most concerned about the transport, as it lumbered through the shallow waves, unable to match the nimbleness of the galleys. Nevertheless, he accepted the ship might never make it to the ancient city and turned his attention back to the enemy.

The Turks had arrayed their fleet in a giant crescent, barring the entrance to the Golden Horn. From tiny sloops to hulking barges, hundreds of boats stood ready to halt their advance. Some were sailing vessels, but most utilized one, two, or even three banks of oars. Makeshift barricades of wood and bales of wool adorned the sides of the ships. Beyond the Turks, he could see the giant chain that barred entrance to the imperial harbor.

When the two opposing fleets were less than a hundred yards apart, Marcus and the others saw one man standing near the front of the closest craft. He called for them to lower their sails and allow boarding. It was a request that went unanswered. In response to the silence, a single trumpet blast erupted from a massive ship near the heart of the fleet. Moments later, one of the Turkish ships fired its miniature cannons; the iron balls splashed harmlessly around them. One ball, nearing the end of its zenith, bounced off the Imperial transport's hull and disappeared into the dark blue sea, much to the delight of the Christian sailors.

Marcus stood and moved to a makeshift arsenal where he requisitioned an English longbow, taking a moment to admire the craftsmanship. Nearly six feet long, the shaft was cut from a fine piece of yew wood, caramel-colored with exceptionally long grains. The surface was covered with a mixture of wax, resin, and animal fat. The flax bowstring, reinforced with silk thread, was secured to a pair of ivory pins set into the end of the shaft. He picked up a quiver of arrows, moved back to the front of the ship, and leaned the bundle against the railing. Marcus plucked an arrow from the quiver, slipped the notch onto the string, and drew the bow taut, hearing the heavy wood creak as the feather tickled his ear. He slowly exhaled, focusing his aim on the nearest ship. At the front of the galley stood a fat shirtless man beating a steady rhythm on a large kettledrum, his brown skin glistening; a perfect target. The feather caressed his cheek as the arrow sprung from the bow. Marcus quietly thanked the English as the Turk tumbled forward, the shaft protruding from his shiny back. Those around Marcus erupted in a raucous cheer.

First blood was theirs.

As the two sides closed, the Turks tried to board the galleys, but the vigorous breeze made that a difficult task. Any ship that strayed too close had to deal with a hail of arrows, not to mention the Greek fire spewing from the Imperial galley. But eventually, their persistence was rewarded.

A heavy barge attached itself to their galley, and soon Muslim soldiers were scurrying up the side of the ship. The familiar sound of battle drew Marcus forward, igniting a fire within his soul that only blood could extinguish. He tossed the bow aside and drew his sword, moving into the thickest action. He arrived in time to drive his sword through the belly of one attacker who had just climbed over the railing. As the flailing body fell back over the side, Marcus pulled out his main-gauche and severed the grapple rope, sending three men plummeting back to their ship's deck.

Marcus descended upon a furious mêlée near the forecastle between two sailors and a handful of Muslim soldiers. He moved across the ship, leaving a swathe of dying bodies in his wake. Within moments, the tide turned, and they had pushed the last of the attackers overboard. Two sailors stumbled forward with a steaming metal cauldron. Marcus stepped back as they lifted it over the side and poured the contents onto the barge. Another sailor pulled a flaming arrow from the nearby mast and tossed it over the railing. They scrambled back as the Muslim ship burst into flames, and a chorus of painful screams followed the wave of rolling heat.

As Marcus moved back along the deck, he noticed the Imperial transport had fallen behind the galleys. The Muslims had identified the grain ship as a soft target and concentrated most of their attention on her. Turkish warships now surrounded the galley, and she struggled to repel the hordes of soldiers that clambered up her sides. Greek fire would be suicidal at such close quarters. Marcus looked around and spied the captain atop the forecastle, directing his boatswain.

He sprinted across the deck, avoiding two sailors who were busy dousing a small fire. Taking the wooden stairs two steps at a time, Marcus arrived just as the captain finished his conversation.

"Captain, the Imperial." He pointed to the vessel, nearly lost in the mass of Turkish sloops and triremes.

"I was afraid of that—she isn't fast enough to keep up." He looked around to the other galleys, both of which had broken free of attackers. "Let's see what we can do."

He barked several orders to his first mate as he pointed to the various sails and jibs. He placed a hand on his pilot's shoulder and quietly explained his plan, and waited for the man to nod in response. The captain then motioned to a young boy sitting on a nearby crate. Moving to his skipper's side, he listened to the instructions, nodding occasionally, then bolted off toward the ship's bow. The youngster lifted the horn that hung around his neck and shattered the air with a series of short blasts. After a few minutes, there was a reply from the galley to the right, then one from the third vessel. The captain nodded and waved to the boy, who smiled as he made his way back to the crate.

Marcus could feel their ship slowing as they angled toward the path of the Imperial. She was still struggling but had escaped one of the massive warships. They were twenty yards off the transport and closing quickly when an aggressive sloop slipped between the two. Marcus enlisted a pair of nearby soldiers and pointed down at the Turkish vessel.

"We're going to board her."

Nodding, the men searched the deck for rope. They found several coils, and attached the ends to the railings, then slung the rest over the side. Before the ropes had even reached the ship below, Marcus had vaulted over the side, ignoring the heat building in his gloved palms as he slid down the tether. His feet had just hit the wooden deck when two large sailors set upon him with wooden clubs. Marcus sidestepped one attacker, driving his elbow into his chin. As he crumbled, the second one took his shot, sweeping his weapon in a clumsy arc. Ducking, Marcus stepped forward and caught him with a short uppercut. The man's eyes rolled back into his head as he staggered back over the body of his companion.

By now, the two other soldiers had made their descent. Marcus freed both his blades and focused his attack on the sailors attending the ship while his fellow soldiers moved to engage the Muslims attempting to board the transport. Marcus hacked his way through a small group of sailors, making straight for the captain. The captain saw Marcus's calculated approach, grabbed a nearby sailor, and flung him at the Roman. Marcus bashed the sailor across the cheek with the hilt of his sword, knocking him into a stack of boxes.

Undaunted, Marcus pursued the captain as he scrambled over crates and barrels until he cornered himself against the railing. His eyes moved from Marcus to the churning sea below. He decided to take his chances with the latter, muttering something in Turkish before leaping overboard. Impressed by his judgment, Marcus moved to the railing tied to the imperial transport and severed the lines that joined the two vessels. As the galley slipped free of the sloop, Marcus motioned for the other soldiers to go back to their ship. Then, sheathing his weapons, he grabbed a dangling line and climbed up onto the deck of the transport.

Marcus topped the railing and was amazed at how much damage the ship had sustained. The crew members were putting out various fires around the deck, tending to the wounded or tearing down ragged sails and rigging. He wandered around, trying to find the captain among the sailors. Marcus stumbled into him as he bent over to nurse a wounded boy. The lad, a nasty gash in his stomach, begged for water. The captain helped him drink from a small cup and then watched as the lad died in his arms. The captain laid the boy onto the deck, stood, and wiped his nose with the back of his hand. He glanced at Marcus with glossy eyes before looking back down at the lad.

"Turkish bastards!" He pointed to an overturned bucket. "He was just bringing water to the others."

Marcus nodded. War is an indiscriminate killer, but he didn't bother pointing that out.

The captain was a stocky man of below-average height. His dark olive skin gave way to thin gray hair, matted with sweat and blood. He wore a plain, unassuming tunic, torn and stained in a dozen places. He carried no weapons, though a heavy club lay within reach.

"I'm Captain Phlatanelas, and I thank you for freeing my ship of that Muslim scourge." He extended his hand. "I saw the action from above—you're quite the swordsman."

"Thank you." Marcus returned his iron grip. "Marcus Gracchus. I thought I might catch a ride into the city."

"You're assuming we make the city." The captain peered up into the sagging canvas. "We are at the fancy of the winds."

"We'll just keep sending these infidels back to God. Perhaps he'll get sick of them and send us back the wind."

The captain stared at Marcus for a moment before breaking out into a huge grin. "I think we're going to get along just fine."

As they spoke, the other vessels moved in alongside the transport, two on her port and the other on her stern. They lashed the four ships together, allowing the defenders to concentrate on protecting the two exposed sides of their floating fortress. Soon after, the wind all but ceased, leaving them a good league from the safety of the harbor.

Marcus could see a colorful entourage gathering on the far shore, led by a man atop a white stallion. The mount was nearly chest-deep in the water and reluctant to advance any further, despite the prompting of its master. He waved his sword above his head, motioning to the ships in the Muslim flotilla. Marcus borrowed a spyglass from the captain and studied the rider.

He was dark-skinned with a ceremonial turban that covered most of his jet-black hair. He wore a black silk tunic, knee-high leather boots, and brandished a scimitar, its shiny blade flashing in the sunlight. Even from this distance, Marcus could make out the angry expression that dominated his lean, rugged face. As he directed his horse back onto the shore, his entourage scattered to avoid trampling. He galloped down the beach and reentered the water, trying to gain the attention of his naval commander. From previous descriptions, Marcus knew he was witnessing firsthand the leadership skills of the sultan. The epithets that accompanied his name were often the same: cruel, impatient, and unforgiving. Marcus prayed the city would never feel his wrath.

Marcus scanned the staff that surrounded him and focused on one man who stood watching the majestic rage, a vacant expression on his handsome face. Heart sinking, Marcus closed his eyes and lowered the glass. *Why are you here, Thomas?*

He handed the eyepiece to the captain who ordered his sailors to replace the tattered mainsail, hoping to capture an afternoon breeze. The crew tossed the remains of the dead Muslim soldiers overboard, drawing a school of hungry sharks that transformed the turquoise sea into a bloody froth. Some men wanted to add to the feast by tossing three prisoners into the frenzy, but the captain refused. Instead, he ordered them chained to the mainmast. He gave the somber task of disposing of fallen Christians to a priest and two deckhands, who, one by one, wrapped the bodies in cloth and laid them to rest in the cargo hold.

Marcus found a barrel in the shade of the forecastle and waited. It took the Turks a couple of hours to muster the courage and resolve to rejoin the fight. When the alarm sounded, Marcus stood and moved to the front of the ship. When he reached the railing, the captain handed him the spyglass and pointed to an odd-looking ship lumbering toward them. Marcus leaned forward and focused on the craft.

It looked like a standard river barge, except this one had a giant wooden tower jutting from the craft's center. A long bank of oars propelled the awkward beast. She sat precariously low in the water, almost begging a breeze or rolling wave to send her crashing into the sea. A contingent of elite Janissary guards lined the railings, eagerly awaiting a shot at redemption.

"Now that's interesting." Marcus frowned and handed the eyepiece back.

"If we had any wind at all, my men would sail circles around that monstrosity."

"That's why they didn't use it during the last attack."

When the distance was appropriate, archers from both sides exchanged fiery arrows, the thin black trails crisscrossing the soft blue sky. Marcus ducked as one arrow shot past, burying itself in the mast behind him.

Unlike the previous assault, this attack was well coordinated. The Muslims were taking advantage of their vast numerical superiority to assail the flotilla on all sides, and almost immediately, the Christians were repelling multiple boarding parties. Soon, the barge joined the fray, its pilot attempting, with alarming success, to slip between the Imperial transport and the Genoese galley. His ship's low waterline allowed him to wedge his craft between the bulkheads, where it came to a screeching halt.

Protected in the tower, the Muslim archers backed up the Janissaries as they scaled the sides of the transport and the galley. Not wanting to expose themselves to arrow fire, the defenders were reluctant to engage the attackers.

As Marcus watched the scene unfold, a burning arrow grazed the outside of his bicep. He cursed, looked down at the wound, then out at the bodies that now littered the ship's bow. Knowing the status quo would not suffice, Marcus glanced at the soldiers cowering around him and unbuckled his chest plate, dropping it to the deck. As the captain eyed him suspiciously, Marcus winked and sprinted forward, unsheathing his sword. He dove headfirst, rolled up onto his knees, and stopped near the massive rope that held the anchor. Using both hands, he lifted his sword and brought it down onto the heavy rope. He repeatedly hacked at the giant cord, each strike cutting through several of the stubborn strands. His fifth or sixth stroke severed the rope entirely and buried his sword's blade into the wooden deck.

The frazzled end zipped past the chock as the anchor picked up speed and crashed through the ship below. Marcus ran to the railing and watched a pillar of seawater erupt from the gaping hole, overwhelming the shattered deck. A dozen soldiers leaped from the tower, its wooden beams creaking and groaning as it collapsed. Marcus stepped back from the railing, for a moment fearing that the wreckage might doom the Imperial as well. He exhaled in relief as the structure crumbled in upon itself. An enormous cheer erupted from the defenders as the Muslim craft, groaning in protest, slipped beneath the waves, leaving behind a mass of broken timber and stunned survivors.

Marcus stepped back toward the captain, smiling as he pulled his sword from the deck. The captain shook his head as the Roman approached.

"I wouldn't believe it if the Pope himself had told me—" He slapped Marcus on his wounded shoulder. "Nice work!"

Marcus winced, then glanced toward the rippling canvas and the darkening sky. "Looks like we're finally going to get some breeze."

"Better late than never."

With their behemoth struck down, the demoralized Turks

lost their taste for battle and fell back to their vessels. Some Muslim ships were already retreating when the sails buckled and heaved. Soon, the Genoese vessels and the Imperial transport were breaking free of the enemy fleet.

Marcus looked down at his blood-splattered hands and clothes. "I'm going to wash up."

"Thank you, my friend. Without your sword and quick wits, I fear we'd be enjoying the company of that devilish heathen by now."

"You're welcome." A smirk creased Marcus' lips, "I doubt any enjoyment would've been had."

Marcus reached for his breastplate, slipped it on, and moved to the railing just as two sailors prepared to separate the coupled vessels. Grabbing a rope that hung to the galley below, Marcus slid down the line, releasing it as he reached the bottom. Marcus picked up a bucket of water near the railing and made his way to his chamber, acknowledging the nods and smiles as he went. He set the pail on the night table, unclasped his armor, and set it aside to clean later. Marcus removed his soiled shirt and inspected his sliced bicep. He scrubbed the wound and wrapped a single strip of black cloth around it. Satisfied, Marcus rinsed the blood from his hands and face, repeating a process he had done far too many times.

The sun was just a memory by the time they docked at one of the many wooden piers located beneath the city's watchful eye. Marcus waited for the crew to disembark before he exited down the gangplank. He would come back later for his chest. But as he left the dock, a figure called from the shadows.

"Nice fighting, for a Roman." A familiar female voice called to him.

Marcus stopped and peered at the stranger. They were shorter and wore a dark cloak to blend in with the night.

"Thanks, I get lucky sometimes."

"I doubt you leave much to luck." As Marcus moved closer, the stranger shifted to stay in the shadows. "Why are you here?"

"I'm looking for someone."

"Who?"

"You."

"How did you know?" Isabella stepped from the shadows and lowered her hood. Her face was covered with dirt, and her hair cut short, trying to mask her femininity. It did not work.

"When you moved, you shifted your weight," he grinned, "exactly how I taught you."

She moved forward and hugged him, whispering into his ear, "It's good to see you."

Marcus pulled her body to his, her head resting on his chest. He closed his eyes and smelled the jasmine in her hair. His hands lingered on her back, not wanting to let her go. As they gently swayed in the darkness, the splinter of guilt remained deep in his soul. It was matched by his irritation. He had seen or done unspeakable things and had always buried his feelings of guilt or shame. He knew it wasn't healthy, but it was the only way for him to stay sane. It frustrated him that he could not do the same with Isabella. *Why couldn't he compartmentalize his feelings for her?*

He let go, leaned back, and looked into her eyes. "I missed you."

She winked back at him. "Enough to volunteer for a suicide mission?"

"You're here."

"Where else would I be?"

Marcus grinned. She was as strong and confident as ever. "How bad is it?"

"Let's get something to eat, and I'll fill you in." Without waiting, she headed toward the city walls.

They soon found themselves standing outside a shabby-looking tavern, inconspicuous in its plainness. Languages may differ, but men gather in local pubs to consume prodigious amounts of alcohol in any corner of the world. Some go to enjoy the company of others; some to escape the company at home. Often it was both.

Marcus held open the door as Isabella stepped into the dark interior. As expected, the pub was devoid of its regular patrons, most of whom were manning the city walls. A few older men huddled near the empty fireplace were engaged in a quiet conversation and paid them no heed as they crossed the dim room and sat down at a corner table. A seasoned barmaid in a plain white and tan dress approached them as they settled in.

"Back again?"

"Of course, best meat pie in the city," Isabella replied.

"Doesn't say much. What can I get you?"

"We'll have two pints of ale and two of those pies."

"Very well." She headed back to the bar.

"Meat?" Marcus raised his eyebrows.

"Don't worry, it's not rat meat. The owner is Genoese." She grinned and nodded toward the man behind the bar. "They have a knack for finding things that can't be found. Here, it helps to have a brother in Pera, a city across the bay. There's been a healthy black-market business going on between the two ever since the Muslims pitched their tents outside the city walls."

"Men will always profit from a conflict."

"War and greed go hand in hand."

"What about the siege...how bad is it?"

"The city itself has less than five thousand men capable of manning the walls. Some of them have never seen a weapon,

153

let alone know how to carry one. A couple of thousand foreign mercenaries, mostly Genoese and Venetian. They'd rather sleep with a viper in their pants than fight together, but the emperor has kept them from killing each other."

Marcus leaned back as the server placed two cups of ale between them. "And Mahomet?"

"Damn that heathen!" The waitress hissed, and without waiting for a response, headed back to the kitchen.

"Well, I guess we know how she feels." Marcus took a sip of ale.

"Yep, common response. Mahomet has somewhere between eighty and a hundred thousand men, with more arriving each day. Lots of siege weapons."

"How are you set for supplies? How long can you hold out?"

"I'm sure the supplies you brought will help. Water is of no concern—the wells in the city are deep and plentiful." Isabella shook her head. "No—we shall fall by the sword, or the sultan will give in to the influence of his council and retreat. Either thing could happen tomorrow or a month from now."

"Would he abandon the siege?"

"Other sultans have left when given enough gold, but this one seems different."

Marcus thought back to the scene on the beach. He took a long pull from his cup. "He's here."

Isabella raised her cup to drink but stopped, and set it down, all the while staring right at him. "Thomas?"

"Yes."

"Why?"

"I don't know. I've heard things...they are less than rumors. Rumors of rumors. Whispers."

They sat in silence as the waitress returned and set down two pies.

"I need to talk to him." He pushed the pie aside and leaned forward. "The man in Pera...can we use him to send a message?"

As Isabella stared at her glass, Marcus could hear the crackle of the fireplace. He waited patiently.

"Yes...on one condition."

"You want to go with me."

"Yes."

Not surprised, Marcus nodded. They ate in silence, and when done, Marcus wrote a brief note, signing it *Marcus*. He folded the letter and sealed it with a single glob of wax, which he poured from a nearby candle.

"Let me drop it off with the owner, and I'll get you a room." Isabella stood. "Unless...?"

He forced a smile.

"I know." Without another word, she turned and headed to the bar.

On the morning of the third day in the city, they received a terse reply to the note. It gave instructions for them to return to Pera with the guide at midnight for the meeting. There was no signature.

Isabella made all the arrangements. As the city settled into another uneasy slumber, Marcus donned the clothes of a Genoese merchant and, carrying only his sword and a purse full of coins, walked with Isabella to the dock where they boarded a tiny skiff with their guide. The moon's light reflected off the calm water and guided their craft as they crossed the peaceful bay. The low walls of Pera soon became visible, several torches flickering in the soft breeze.

"Halt!" A deep voice pierced the darkness as they beached the vessel.

Marcus looked at Isabella, then the guide.

"It's just my cousin." the guide said. "I'll need to show him our appreciation for letting us land here tonight."

"Is everyone in this town related?"

Marcus understood the type of appreciation the boatman meant, reached into his pouch, and pulled out several gold coins. He handed them to the young man, who hopped onto the beach and vanished into the tall grass beyond.

He reappeared moments later, waving them forward, before disappearing again. Marcus stepped from the craft, feeling his boots sink into the wet sand. Isabella was close behind. They followed a narrow path that led up the embankment, and found the guide standing beside a Genoese guard, engaged in a quiet conversation that ended upon their arrival. The soldier nodded to his guide and turned back toward Pera.

"Your meeting will take place there." The guide pointed to a copse of trees in the near distance.

They followed a well-used trail, traversing the open field, and stepped into a thick growth of ancient cypress. Marcus could see a lazy stream snaking through the shadowy pasture, spilling softly into the harbor beyond. Their guide disappeared back down the trail, reminding them he would wait at the boat. As they moved further into the woods, they saw a dark figure staring at the distant city, its reflection shimmering on the bay.

"I thought you would be alone." Thomas turned toward them.

"I needed to be here." Isabella took a step towards him. "I deserve an explanation."

"Perhaps." Thomas's eyes dropped to her hand, which rested on a sword. "I trust your intentions are peaceful?"

Nodding, she slid her hand from the hilt.

"Very well then." Thomas stepped forward, arms open. "It's good to see you."

She returned his hug without speaking, her jaw clenched.

Thomas pulled away, then looked to Marcus. "What has it been, 700 years?"

"Longer." Marcus accepted his embrace, then stepped back and studied his old friend.

Thomas had lost weight, and his hair now hung down past his shoulders. A thin goatee clung to his once clean-shaven chin. But the fundamental change was in his eyes; those eyes once shimmered with hope, with a quiet humility that could disarm a stranger with a single glance. Now they were cold and hard. To look into them was like looking into an endless pit. Marcus stood before his old friend and realized this was not the man he knew, but an adversary, one who stood for everything they had ever fought against.

Thomas sensed the uneasiness. "What are you doing here?"

"Helping to defend the church...something we used to do together."

Thomas nodded but did not respond. There was no emotion to his expression, but Marcus could sense a darkness beneath the facade.

Marcus was reluctant to ask but did anyway, "What happened the day you left?"

Thomas flinched but did not respond. Marcus pressed on.

"I tried to follow you the next morning but lost your trail near the coast. I heard nothing of you for at least two hundred years, and even then, only whispers."

"I don't speak about my past—" He shifted his gaze to Isabella. "But as you said, you deserve an explanation." There was a lengthy silence, and when he continued, it was like a different man was speaking. "I remember little, just hearing the news and riding back to the city in search of the archbishop. I found him at the cathedral, and that's where my memory fades. I know there was blood—so much blood." He looked at his hands as if they still carried the stain. "I remember talking to you, then riding to the coast. I boarded a merchant ship to Africa, and it took three days to cross the sea. When I walked off that ship, my mind was clear but broken. I wandered across

157

that continent for years and then to parts of this world you could never imagine. No matter how hard I tried, how far I looked, I couldn't find anything to fill the emptiness. I tried dying, but that only made it worse. It brought back the memories of her. In the end, the pain was all I had." His voice trailed off for a moment. "A few centuries later, I found myself on the steppes of Mongolia. There I met a man whose exploits will become things of legend. I found my purpose, and that's when I made my vow...we were invading Poland when the Khan died unexpectedly. But I found others."

"Mahomet?"

"Yes. I don't have to share his faith, just his objectives. With this army." He pointed to the flickering lights on the distant hilltops. "We will bring Christianity to its knees."

"Why? What will that achieve?" Marcus said. "It won't bring back—"

"Stop!" Thomas's face twisted in rage. "One of us will die tonight if you speak her name."

Marcus studied his wrath.

"No," Isabella stepped forward. "You don't get to erase her that easily. She was my sister, and I loved her just as much as you." She did not let Thomas reply. "You talk about loss? I lost everything...I lost my sister, and I lost you." Her eyes, filled with tears, turned to Marcus. "And you. Of course, *you* left. You probably took out your anger, your guilt, on some poor soul. God, how many people died to ease your pain?"

A single tear slid down her cheek.

"Isabella—" Marcus said.

"No! I'm not done. Do you know what I did? I stayed. I cleaned up the mess. I buried her. Did either of you even think of that?"

She glared at Thomas, who was looking at the ground.

"No, I'm sure you didn't." She looked back toward Marcus. "And then you came back. You always do. But I know it's only a matter of time before you leave again. I don't blame you; that's just who you are."

She paused, waiting for Thomas to look at her. When he finally did, she said, "but I expected more from you. You were the best of us."

"No," Thomas shook his head. "I'm not. I never was. Just look at how I got this *gift*. I know the name they gave me. *Doubting Thomas*. My faith was never strong enough to stand the test."

"So you just quit?" Marcus asked. "Was that the answer?"

"The answer? Is that what you think this is? Is that what you think we're fighting for? There is no answer, only more questions. *HE* started this fifteen hundred years ago, then he just disappeared and never came back. What are we supposed to do? Walk the Earth forever? Live through the hatred, the pain that fills this world? Have you seen the things that men do to other men?"

"Yes," Isabella said.

"So that's the plan?"

"I don't know," Isabella said.

"Shouldn't you be asking yourself what God has in store for you? For us?"

"That's not our place," she countered. "You told me that yourself."

"Maybe I was wrong! Who says we can't question our future?" Thomas took a step forward and pointed to the sky. "God? The Pope? His priests? If God loves us so much, why do such horrible things happen? War, famine, disease...there is so much suffering. Why?"

"I don't know," she answered. "And neither do you. But is that enough reason for you to destroy Christianity?"

"Yes. The Church reflects all the worst qualities of man... greed, corruption, hypocrisy."

"What about humility, charity, and love?" Marcus asked.

"Tell me Marcus, which of those qualities launched the

Crusades? You were there; how much love and charity did you see?" He did not wait for Marcus to reply. "What I saw was brutality, more than any man should see in a lifetime...all in the name of God. But we all know it was about greed and power. And *HE* let it happen...why?" Thomas clenched both his fists in front of him. "Because *He* wants to break us. *He* wants blind faith and devotion...servitude. *He* wants to ensure that no one ever questions the will of God again."

"Again?" Marcus frowned. "What do you mean, 'again'?"

Thomas did not reply.

"You know what? I'm done," Isabella stated flatly. She took a step forward, her eyes fixed on his. "Rebecca would be ashamed."

Thomas stared at her but did not reply.

"I'll be at the boat," she said.

An awkward silence settled around them, a silence that Marcus finally broke.

"You know it's very noble of you to care so much. But I don't think it's about saving the world or freeing man from God's domination. I think it's about you and your inability to deal with what happened. I've heard this all before...a long time ago."

"What?"

"Soon after my wife died." Marcus took a deep breath. "A man came to me. There was something strange about him, something that didn't sit right. He knew everything about my family and me. You sound eerily similar to him. He asked me how a loving God could let such horrible things happen. And he made promises." Marcus shrugged his shoulders. "But I'm not sure he understood who I was, what being a Roman meant. My Gods were vindictive, greedy, hateful...that's all I knew. His story rang hollow, as did his promises."

"You never told me."

"Why would I? I said no."

"And I said yes."

"I'm just more stubborn," Marcus said.

"I'm probably going to regret that someday."

"I think you already do."

Thomas allowed himself a slight grin. "Perhaps."

"We could all leave tonight," Marcus offered. "Go far away from this place."

A long pause provided a measure of hope, but it disappeared with a single word.

"No."

"I had to ask."

"You did." Thomas's face clouded with emotion. "I've been told to kill you...but I cannot. However, I'm warning you—leave the city."

"We can't do that."

"Then you both will die." He took a deep breath. "We've chosen different paths, but it would be foolish to think they'll never cross again."

"Yes, it would be." Marcus met his gaze, emotions welling inside.

"And the next time we meet," the affection faded from his eyes, "there shall be no peace between us."

"I know." He extended his hand. "Goodbye, Thomas."

"Goodbye, Marcus." He returned his grasp and forced a smile.

Marcus walked away, leaving behind his best friend and any dreams they had ever shared.

CHAPTER ELEVEN

There is no fate that cannot be surmounted by scorn.
—ALBERT CAMUS

MODERN DAY
GERMANY

"MARCUS?"

He opened his eyes to see narrow beams of moonlight seeping through the dark wooden ceiling. The musty odor of wet straw filled the stagnant air and had settled around him like a damp cocoon. He tried to sit up.

"Hold on, let me help you."

"I'm thirsty."

She pulled a water bottle from her backpack, twisted off the top, and handed it to him. He gulped it down, nearly emptying the bottle.

He wiped his mouth with his hand. "Where are we?"

"A small farm, next to the rail line. We got lucky. It was right next to where you got thrown from the train."

"I wasn't thrown. I was shot...I mean, technically, I shot myself...twice. Then I crawled off the train."

"Anyway, when I saw you weren't right behind me, I started walking along the tracks. You were a fucking mess. I think this was one of those times where you almost died. Were you trying to kill yourself?"

"No, I wasn't."

"Okay, because it looked like you were. Then why did you shoot yourself?"

"It's a long story."

"Anyway, I half carried, half dragged your ass to this barn. I can't tell if the owners are away or sleeping." Sam flicked her thumb over her shoulder. "There's an old car parked in the driveway."

"That's a start. What time is it?"

She looked at her watch. "Just after 4 AM."

"All right, we need to get moving. That was quite a mess on the train, and either the authorities will look for us, or Thomas will cover it up and his team will hunt us down. We should assume that Thomas will activate his entire network. He's never done that before, but it looks like we've poked the hornet's nest. There's virtually no limit to the resources and access he has at his disposal, so we must stay off the grid as much as possible. Cash only. Landlines or burners."

"Sounds good to me, some real old school shit."

Marcus nodded toward the door. "Can you check the car, see if it's locked?"

As she exited the barn, Marcus pulled out his burner cell phone, and he sent a quick text.

Off the train, forget Milan. Meet in Florence in AM. Send me hotel info. Find a doctor.

10-4. You or Sam?

Me.

Good.

Marcus stuffed the phone into his pocket and lifted himself from the ground, grunting as a sharp pain shot down his hip. As he limped to the door, Sam reentered the barn. She rushed over to help him, placing his arm over her shoulder and her arm around his back.

"It's unlocked. But no keys."

"Damn." He took another tepid step. "Hot wiring is a fucking pain in the ass."

"Just kidding!" She held up a set of keys with her free hand. "They were in the visor. Very trusting farmers."

"Too trusting."

They moved out into the cool, crisp night. Crossing the small courtyard, Sam leaned Marcus against the side of the car. He reached into his pocket and pulled out his wad of money, scowling when he saw the dried blood staining the Euros. He counted out what he deemed a fair market value for the car, adding a few extra bills for good measure, then handed them to her.

"Find a rock or something and put these under it."

She frowned back at him.

"It might keep them from reporting it stolen." He shoved the bills toward her. "And it's good karma."

She shrugged and took the cash. Marcus walked to the passenger side and was just settling in when she returned. She closed the driver's door and turned on the car.

"I hope they are not light sleepers."

"We'll be gone before they get outside."

They were soon pulling out of the drive and onto a narrow country road. When they were a mile or so from the house, Sam flipped on the headlights. Marcus switched on the radio, turned the dial, and settled on a national news station broadcast in Italian. Thirty minutes later, they were merging onto the main expressway.

Just after dawn, they stopped for food and coffee. By noon, they were going through the outskirts of Florence. They parked the car in a long-term storage facility and caught a taxi to a small, independent hotel. Sam grabbed the bags, and they went inside. She walked up to the desk, but Marcus motioned for her to follow him. She did, a confused look on her face.

He got into the elevator and pushed a button for the third floor.

"Did you book something already? I thought we were staying off the grid."

"We are."

They exited the elevator, walked to the end of the hallway, and Marcus knocked on a door. After a few minutes, it opened to reveal a familiar face.

"Uncle Cormac!" Sam sprung forward, hugging him.

"Sam!" He kissed her cheek, then shifted his attention to Marcus. "How bad is it?"

Before Marcus could reply, Sam said, "Shot twice, one bullet still in his leg."

"Hip." Marcus raised his hand.

"Yeah, whatever."

"Okay, come on in. I've made some calls. We can get it fixed after we eat. I'm starvin'."

Thirty minutes later, they were eating room service.

"What's the plan after we get that slug out of you?" Cormac asked.

"The Vatican." Marcus wiped his mouth with his napkin.

"Official visit?" Cormac had stopped eating and had both hands intertwined, his elbows on the table as he studied Marcus.

"No."

"Good, it wouldn't be a very warm welcome."

"Why is that?"

"Over the last 24 hours, everything has gone silent. I've lost access to the Vatican network. And I'm sure you already know the accounts are frozen."

"Yeah."

"Ramirez," Cormac stated.

"That's what I'm gonna find out," Marcus replied.

"Do you know how we'll get in?" Sam looked from Marcus to her uncle.

"There's no *we*. Marcus is doing this alone." Cormac looked over at Marcus. "Right?"

"Yes."

"Why?" Sam asked.

There was a long silence that Cormac finally broke.

"Marcus has a long history with the church. This is none of our business."

Sam was about to protest, but the look on her uncle's face made it clear it would make no difference. She shook her head and left the room.

"That was harsh."

"She doesn't get involved with the church. We talked about that."

"Understood." Marcus took a sip from his water and changed the subject. "Did everything go okay in Milan?"

"Yeah, picked up the car and just about everything else you asked for."

"Just about?"

"I couldn't find Oban, at least not the good stuff. You're stuck with Laphroaig."

"I'll manage." A smile cracked his lips at the thought of half-decent scotch.

"I'm sure you will. Now let's get that bullet out."

Marcus lay back on the cold, stainless-steel table, squinting into the bright lights. Sam and Cormac were sitting on a nearby bench, their eyes averted. Marcus watched as the doctor examined his wound. The doctor was cautious with his questions, careful to avoid being told any information he would regret later. It was good practice, especially when dealing with gunshot wounds and cash.

"How long ago did this happen?" He studied the wound, frowning as he poked and prodded.

"Four days ago," Marcus lied. "My friend has been keeping it clean."

"I can see that. It has healed quickly—I'm amazed you didn't get an infection from the bullet." He tilted his head. "I'll have to reopen it to get to the bullet. I can put you to sleep with gas or an IV."

"Nah, I'll stay awake."

"Then I need to give you a local."

"Fine."

The doctor shrugged and began to work. After numbing the area and cleaning the wound, he sliced along the pink scar tissue that had just formed. Once open, it took less than thirty seconds of probing for the doctor to locate the bullet. Marcus watched him work, gritting his teeth as the slug was extracted and dropped into a metal tray. The physician stitched up the wound, then covered it with a thick gauze pad.

167

"You should avoid walking as much as possible." The doctor put a last piece of tape across the bandage.

"I will."

Marcus eased his legs over the side of the table, wincing as he pulled up his trousers. A few moments later, the doctor reappeared and handed Marcus two pill bottles.

"Pain and sleep."

"Thanks."

Marcus slipped them into his coat pocket and nodded to Sam. She pulled out a stack of fresh Euros and handed them to the doctor. He nodded and stuffed the roll into the pocket of his smock before exiting the room. Marcus limped to the door, followed by Sam and Cormac.

The morning drizzle showed no signs of abating as they moved through a narrow alley to a parked Mercedes. Sam opened the rear passenger door for Marcus, who carefully settled into the soft leather seat. She moved over to the driver's side while Cormac sat in the passenger seat. She turned the ignition and slipped the car into gear.

The drive to Rome took about four hours. Marcus slept, with the aid of the pills, while Sam and Cormac took shifts driving. By late afternoon, they reached the outskirts of Rome, and Sam guided the car through the traffic that packed the crowded freeway. Pointing to an exit, Marcus directed her along the busy streets as they moved deeper into the ancient city. Marcus leaned forward and studied the buildings as they crawled down a narrow avenue, finally motioning for Sam to park in front of a tall hotel nestled between a church and a brick apartment house.

"Wait here." Marcus slipped out of the door and into the hotel.

Ten minutes later, Marcus emerged from the door holding a silver key ring. Sam rolled down the window as Marcus leaned in, resting his arms on the door.

"I got us a suite—it's Room 504. We can unload the bags here, but you'll need to park in the underground garage at the end of the street." He handed Sam a metal disk. "Just show them this token when you go into the garage."

"Will you be using the car later?" Sam dropped the token into the ashtray.

"No, I'll take the bus. It's easier to blend in."

Cormac hopped out of the car as she nodded and popped the trunk.

Marcus grabbed their bags, but Cormac held out his hand.

"I thought you didn't carry these things?"

"That was before you dragged me back into this shit. I always carry my weight."

Marcus smiled and handed him one of the smaller bags.

The room was a standard, two-bedroom suite. After putting the bags away, Cormac made them both a drink from the minibar and settled onto the sofa.

"How's the leg?"

"Good. Stiffness is mostly gone."

"So, how did she do?"

"Good, she's smart." Marcus looked down into his glass. "Still, I almost killed her when I resurrected. It was pretty bad this time."

"Any idea why?"

"No, no clue. I'm more disoriented, and I take longer to remember. We must be getting closer."

"Closer to what?"

"That's just it. I don't know."

"So what next?"

"I'm gonna contact Isabella."

Sam walked in and set her bag on the coffee table before she dropped onto the couch. "Who's Isabella?"

"How did you get in so quietly?" Cormac asked.

"I've been practicing." She looked from Cormac to Marcus. "Who's Isabella?"

Marcus replied, "She's an immortal. Here in Rome."

"Well, why haven't we asked her for help before?"

"She kind of hates the church—" Marcus said.

"And you," Cormac added.

"She doesn't hate me...our relationship is complicated."

"Your relationship with everyone is complicated," Sam noted. "If she isn't working with you or Thomas, what does she do?"

"She helps people in need."

"Bingo, that's us," Cormac said.

Marcus shot him a glare and looked back at Sam. "She has a network here in Rome and connections all around the Med. I just need to see if she's willing to help."

"Well," Sam leaned forward on the couch, "you better talk to her and fix that shit."

"I will. First, I'm going to take a shower."

Marcus got up and wandered into the bedroom. Turning on the shower, he undressed and waited for the water to heat up. He tossed his dirty clothes into a pile in the corner and leaned on the pedestal sink in the tiny bathroom, studying his features in the mirror. Nothing had changed, save for the dark bags under his weary eyes. He peeled off the bandage taped to his hip, examining the wound beneath. The suture was healed entirely now, only his light pink skin revealing the once gaping hole's location. He moved toward the shower, pulled back the curtain, and stepped under the cascading stream of hot water.

Thirty minutes later, he emerged from the bedroom dressed in black pants, a black shirt, and a Roman Catholic priest's small white collar. He buttoned his cuffs as he walked across the room to the large duffel bag Cormac had brought from Milan. He found a double shoulder holster, and after slipping it on, he secured it to his belt. He dug into the bag, pulled out a pair of pistols, checked to see the magazines were full, and then slid them into the holsters. Then he grabbed a few extra mags and locked them into the pouches below the gun. Marcus donned a heavy black overcoat and shook his shoulders so that the coat hung flush. Satisfied, Marcus zipped up the bag and turned back toward Sam and Cormac.

"Be careful. Rome is a big city, but they know we will be here eventually. Don't go out unless you have to—order in. If something goes wrong, remember that you guys are not the target. Do whatever they say and stay alive. I'll get you out."

"That's very comforting—I'll think of that while they're pulling off my fingernails," Cormac responded.

Marcus ignored him. "If I'm not back by midnight, call this number. Isabella will know what to do."

"She's still talking to you?" Cormac asked.

"Just call the number."

Without waiting for confirmation, Marcus left. The clerk was gone when he passed through the lobby. When he stepped out into the street, he could feel the temperature change as the sun gave way to evening. Turning right at the first intersection, he passed an elderly couple walking their miniature dog. They returned his nod as he passed them. Within minutes, he had reached the much busier Via dei Fori Imperiali. To his left was the coliseum, or at least what remained. He crossed the street and stepped right toward the Piazza Venezia. As he made his way past a dozen replica statues, he moved to the edge of the sidewalk and leaned against the railing as he looked down into the excavated area below. The deepening shadows buried the forum, but he could just make out the scattered columns that had once lined the majestic entrance to the square. Over the centuries, the old city's bones were buried, and subsequent generations had built upon its ruins. Much like him, the city had endured, and in doing so, bore the scars of both triumph and disaster.

Marcus pushed back from the railing and started down the sidewalk, eventually recognizing a sign that pointed to the local bus stop. He went around to the back of the stand and studied the map of the city. He traced the bus route he was interested in, checked the timetable, and looked at his watch.

Satisfied, he searched until he found the source of the enticing aroma that floated on the gentle breeze and quickly made his way to the nearby street vendor. He waited in line, reading the menu while the hawker completed a transaction with an American couple. When the two had moved on, Marcus ordered a tramezzino and an espresso, then walked to a nearby bench to eat his sandwich. When he finished the last of his coffee, he headed to the ticket kiosk, where he bought a 24-hour pass.

The bus arrived, packed with tourists and a sprinkling of locals. He climbed into the stairwell, tapped his card, and made his way to the back, where he stood holding onto the metal railing. They rolled down the street, joining the chaotic evening traffic. Stopping at nearly every corner, they made slow progress across the sprawling city. Finally, Marcus spied the familiar silhouette of the Vatican as the bus came to a jolting halt. As they exited the bus, most passengers moved to the right, securing a splendid view of the old towers radiant against the deepening night.

Marcus split from the crowd and stepped toward a street that was little more than an alley. He left the splendor of the square behind and moved through the shadows, a faded memory his only guide. A few blocks down, he found what he was looking for.

Wedged between its neighbors stood an old church, brooding in the darkness. The stone fascia was worn and cracked, as were the two partial gargoyles that clung to a granite ledge. High above, moonlight reflected off the dull surface of an ancient clock. Several of the numerals were missing, and the iron hands stuck at five minutes to midnight.

There was no sign, but those welcomed at this church didn't need one.

Marcus climbed a set of granite steps and pulled open the heavy wooden door. As he stepped from the cool evening into the warm interior, the door creaked closed behind him. A soft radiance leaked from the tall archway that led further into the building. He moved through the opening and down a long, narrow chamber whose ceilings were lost somewhere in the darkness above. Hundreds of small candles cast their light onto the faded plaster walls but failed to pierce the alcoves spaced evenly along the perimeter of the room. An enormous mural that towered above a stone sarcophagus dominated the front wall.

The image portrayed a crimson dragon locked in mortal combat with a winged angel, the latter wielding a sword high above its head as it prepared to strike the fiery serpent. The two stood upon a mound of twisted, writhing bodies. Behind the beast, a host of the other creatures waited to engage the embattled champion. Marcus sympathized with the hero's eternal struggle and sank into the misery of the illustration. The more he studied the painting, the more visceral the experience. He could smell the simmering brimstone that surrounded the pile of bodies and could feel the dragon's fiery breath as it consumed the angel. The ground beneath him quivered as this mountain of flesh churned in anguish. With a monumental effort, Marcus broke free from the trance and found himself standing in front of the sarcophagus, heart pounding.

"Can I help you?"

Startled, Marcus turned toward the nearest alcove and said to the dark figure, "Yes, I'm looking for Brother Bennucio."

A slender figure stepped out from the darkness. He wore a

black habit that hung upon his hunched and bony frame. His shambling steps were deliberate as he moved forward. He stopped only a few feet from Marcus and glanced at the Roman's collar. His soft brown skin was free of wrinkles, but the serenity in his watery eyes spoke of his maturity.

"Very few people know who Brother Bennucio is—and even fewer ask to speak with him."

"I know."

There was a lengthy stillness as the priest studied Marcus in the faltering candlelight.

"Very well, follow me." He moved back toward the alcove, speaking back over his shoulder. "I thought they banned your kind from this place—"

"They did." Marcus followed as the man stepped into the dark nook, then through an opening and into a tiny room beyond. "But these are extenuating circumstances."

"They always seem to be."

Marcus watched as his guide opened a door leading down into the bowels of the building. A faint light from deep in the stairwell guided their progress. They had carved the cavernous walls from rock, the surface rough and glistening with moisture. They reached the bottom of the stairs and stood beneath a single bulb that hung from the stone ceiling, a plain wooden door barring their advance. Marcus waited as his escort knocked several times. He paused for a long moment, and then he knocked again, this time pounding on the heavy panel. A few moments later, they heard the click of the lock, followed by the door swinging back.

"Brother Bennucio," the guide spoke through the doorway, "there is someone here to speak with you."

A low, muffled voice said, "Tell him to go away."

The door started to close, but Marcus stepped forward to hold it open.

"Brother Bennucio." Marcus shifted so he could see the

monk, "I must speak to you. My name is Marcus—we met several years ago."

A shadowy figure leaned into the light as he studied Marcus. As he squinted, the pale skin crinkled around his shallow eye sockets. Thick black hair, cropped short, clashed with his pasty complexion. He was taller than Marcus and much thinner. He wore a dark-brown robe sewn from a coarse material, its hood dangling across his bony shoulders. The thin rope tied around his waist sported a large ring of keys that jingled as he moved. After a few moments, a look of recognition crossed his face, followed by a smile.

"Yes, yes, Marcus!" He extended his hand to Marcus. "It has been a long time."

"Yes, it has." Marcus returned the grip, surprised by the strength in Bennucio's wiry limb.

"Well, now you are in excellent hands." Marcus's escort started back up the stairs. "Please call on me if you require my help. I am Brother Ubertino."

Before Marcus could reply, he had faded into the darkness.

"Come in." Bennucio stepped back, opening the door wide. "Please excuse the mess—I rarely have visitors."

"I understand." Marcus stepped through the door and into the living quarters beyond.

The square room was chiseled from the stone, like the stairwell, but the walls were not as rough. The ceiling was barely a foot above their heads and held a solitary fixture, connected to a hidden power supply by a thin metal conduit that ran to the farthest wall and then disappeared into the rock. The wall opposite the entrance had two identical openings, both dark, empty voids. A bookshelf filled the space between the apertures, extending from floor to ceiling. Most of the shelves were crammed full of leather-bound tomes of varying sizes. The empty spaces on the shelves accounted for the volumes strewn throughout the room, some open and others stacked haphazardly in uneven piles. A simple cot, heavily cluttered, was in the nearest corner, next to a round nightstand upon which sat a glass pitcher and wooden cup. A table filled the rest of the wall with a wooden chair shoved beneath it. One sheet of paper covered the entire length of the table with a book holding down each corner.

"I'm sorry for showing up like this, but I wasn't sure how else to contact you," Marcus said.

"There is no other way." Bennucio shrugged his shoulders. "It's how I like it—it leaves me undisturbed to do my work."

"How's that going?"

"Wonderful!" The monk moved to the nearby table. "I completed all the common chambers and tunnels five years ago." He pointed at the top of the sheet. "I have since been going deeper—I am not sure I will ever find the end."

"And the church? Have they complained?"

"Well," Bennucio twisted his lips into a sly grin, "they cannot complain about what they do not know."

Marcus grinned and leaned over the map, studying the intricate drawing. The monk illustrated each level with astounding detail. He documented every curve, angle, and nook. How the levels were connected was captured on a table occupying the map's left side. As far as he could tell, it had seven levels.

"The Vatican worked with a local university to map—poorly, I might add—the top three levels." Bennucio leaned over, running his skinny finger along the third floor. "I give them too much credit when I say they mapped the third level. They have identified seven or eight tunnels and three or four burial chambers."

"Why haven't they gone any further?"

"They don't know any more rooms exist." The monk pointed to a dotted line near one intersection. "This is a massive stone door—it looks just like the wall. Without knowing how to open it, you would never know how to get to the other part of this level."

"How did you find out about that?"

Bennucio looked at Marcus, a shy smile creeping onto his face. "I'm not sure I want to answer that."

"Why not?"

"Marcus, we have only met once. If I remember correctly, you seem to be a powerful member of the church."

"I was, but things have changed."

"Of course. But you know, the Vatican has tried several times to destroy my religious order. They call us heretics and send their inquisitors around the world to stamp us out. Why should I trust you?"

"Because I don't play Vatican politics. I have supported—even protected—you and your brethren for many years. But most importantly, if I wanted you gone, it would've already happened."

Bennucio studied Marcus, then shrugged. "My predecessor told me I could trust you, so I will. However, there is one thing that still bothers me..."

"What is that?"

"It's been twenty years, but you look exactly the same. I don't believe you have aged one day."

"Everyone ages."

An uncomfortable moment passed before Bennucio realized Marcus was not going to elaborate.

"Well, it seems we both have our secrets."

"Yes, we do." Marcus nodded, "And I've come to take advantage of yours—if you are so inclined."

"You want to sneak into the Vatican." It was more a statement than a question.

Marcus did not respond, but the expression upon his face told Bennucio all he needed to know.

The Italian beamed from ear to ear, a twinkle glimmering in his eyes. "That can be arranged."

Twenty minutes later, they were twisting through a narrow tunnel, following the bouncing beam of a flashlight. Bennucio led him past two gates, down several flights of steps, and then stopped just before a solid wall. He pushed a single stone and waited as the slab moved aside. He stepped through the opening and motioned for Marcus to follow. He aimed his flashlight down the pitch-black tunnel and handed Marcus a smaller flashlight.

"Welcome to the Holy City."

CHAPTER TWELVE

*Life is to be lived, not controlled,
and humanity is won by continuing to play in the face of certain
defeat.*
—RALPH ELLISON

SPRING 1453 A.D.
CONSTANTINOPLE, OTTOMAN EMPIRE

MARCUS AND ISABELLA DIDN'T speak during the journey back across the harbor. The boat pulled alongside an empty dock, and the two helped secure it to the posts. Marcus jumped out of the craft, waited for Isabella to join him, and then headed back toward the gate leading into the city. He was the first to speak.

"The city will fall."

"Perhaps."

He glanced over at her. "It *will* fall."

She only shrugged.

"So, you'll stay?"

"Yes."

"Me too."

They had left the docks behind and were moving toward the city walls.

"Marcus, I'm sorry about what I said, about you leaving..."

"No, you were right." His expression was somewhere between a grimace and a grin. "I do it because I think I'm protecting those around me. But actually, I'm just protecting myself. I'm no different from Thomas."

She stopped and took his arm. "You're not like Thomas."

"Maybe not, but I have my flaws."

"We all do. You're here today, and that's enough for me."

He nodded and together they walked through the city gate.

Two days after they visited Thomas, a swift brigantine disguised as a Turkish vessel sped off to locate any relief force that might be approaching the city. It returned several days later, sealing the city's doom. The western nations had mounted no expedition, and so no hope remained for the beleaguered capital. Despair settled upon the citizenry as they stubbornly prepared for the closing act of the siege. The sultan could sense the hopelessness that gripped the city, and for two days, the Muslims worked around the clock to prepare for their final assault. At night, the campfires stretched around the city like a gaping maw closing in upon its dying prey.

The following Sunday afternoon, Marcus joined Isabella in what many thought would be the last Christian service in the Church of Holy Wisdom. Soldiers, priests, and citizens—Greek, Genoese, and Venetian— packed the cathedral, all resigned to their inevitable fate.

After mass, the pair rode west to a hillock that overlooked the Golden Horn and watched as the blood-red sun settled into the distant mountains, its rays shimmering across the polished surface of the bay. Isabella broke the stillness of the fading twilight.

"These people don't deserve this."

"They never do. They're pawns in a massive power struggle, one that will never end."

"Maybe Thomas is right." She turned toward him, doubt gripping her elegant features. "Maybe there's another way."

"No, I don't think so. There's a flaw in his plan. What if he could destroy Christendom? Something else would take its place. Islam? A tyrant? Some other religion? No, his hatred is misplaced. Which means, someday, it will find another outlet."

"Let's hope I'm around to see it."

"You will be."

"I'm glad you're here." She leaned over and kissed him.

At first, Marcus was reluctant to return the kiss. Something deep inside begged him to pull away. But he ignored the impulse; he gave himself over to the kiss. Her lips felt warm, tender, and welcoming. He looked into her eyes, his hand pushing the hair back from her face. Her beautiful green eyes were filled with doubt and begged him for reassurance.

"We're going to be alright." He leaned forward and kissed her again, and then he sat back down on his horse.

"Not the best timing," she said.

"No," Marcus' gaze shifted to the city walls, "and we should get going."

"Before the night is over, you may regret coming here." Isabella spun her horse toward the trail.

"Not if I live another thousand years," Marcus replied and followed her.

The night was cool and misty as they made their way along the ramparts. Beyond the wall, thousands of campfires scattered across the horizon. As Marcus turned back to follow her, the distant toll of church bells echoed throughout the city and marked the end of another day. As the forlorn peals gave way to a peaceful calm, the Muslim camp vanished into the night. It was as if God himself had snuffed out the twinkling fires.

They moved on to the Adrianople Gate, a section critical to the city's defenses. As they reached the top of the steps above the gate, a group of men gathered around a towering figure, dressed in a scarlet tunic and dark purple cape. His expression was unassuming, but his dignified bearing betrayed his nobility. Marcus assumed he was about to meet the Byzantine Emperor. His muscular build broke with the history of his predecessors, whose corpulence was matched only by their greed. A dozen members of the royal court surrounded Constantine, all of whom stepped aside when Isabella joined the group.

The Emperor was smiling as she arrived. "Good evening!"

"Your excellency." She bowed her head.

"Is this the famous envoy from the Pope?" He looked at Marcus, forcing a smile. "I asked for an army, and he sent one man."

"Your excellency." Marcus nodded. "My name is Marcus Gracchus."

"Well, I watched the sea battle from the walls. If the Pope had sent a hundred men like you, this city would never fall."

"There are not a hundred men like him," Isabella said.

"You're both too gracious."

"Well, no matter." Constantine looked to the surrounding men. "I have 4,000 brave souls. And though I need three times that many to defend my city, we'll give those Turks more than they can handle."

"That we will," Marcus agreed.

"You must join me for dinner tomorrow," a grin creased his lips, "if we make it through the night."

Without a response, he disappeared down the stairs leading to another section of the wall. Marcus looked to Isabella.

"Now that's a man I can fight for."

An eerie silence settled upon the defenders as the hours crept by.

Marcus was standing with one of the Genoese mercenaries when the darkness erupted with a cacophony of trumpets and drums. He rushed to the wall and watched as the Muslim camp suddenly reappeared, campfires blazing anew. In the flickering glow, they could see the entire Turkish army before them, the mass of soldiers waiting beneath the slight drizzle that ushered in the predawn hour.

Marcus had faced the Turks twice before, and as expected, Mahomet had arranged his army with the weaker Bashi-Bazouks in front, followed by the stronger Anatolians. The final line consisted of the Janissaries, who many thought were the finest foot soldiers in the world.

Then it began. The Bashi-Bazouks charged down into the moat and up the opposite side in a frenzied rush, throwing their ladders against the walls. Motivated by the promise of endless plunder, the Bazouks were nothing more than a motley assortment of beggars and thieves. As he expected, the defenders met them with a steady downpour of arrows, boiling oil, and Greek fire. As the attack wavered, he could see Turkish masters, known as *Chaoushes,* beating the Bazouks with chains and clubs to keep them moving. But few made it to the top of the ladders and even fewer onto the wall. They suffered horrific losses, their bodies heaping along the base of the outer wall. The screams of the wounded filled the air, joining the acrid stench of burning flesh.

Marcus believed that battles along fortifications were the

most violent. In open battles, one army would usually break and flee. That is not the case in most sieges, where flight for the defender usually meant death in defeat. Since the point of attack was fixed, the dying combatants collected in heaps at the base of the wall or on the ramparts. He had been both attacker and defender, and neither role was enviable.

As he expected, the Bazouks could not endure the carnage and fell back, overrunning the Chaoushes. As Marcus watched them flee, Mahomet immediately ordered the Anatolians into the melee. These provincial troops were more disciplined than the Bazouks, but just as poorly armed. They crossed the tangled moat, now slippery with blood and crammed with the bodies of their fallen comrades. The defenders were fatigued from the initial assault and hard-pressed by the subsequent wave. The fighting grew fierce along the entire wall, with the Turks breaching the defenses in a dozen places.

Marcus and Isabella were at the top of one of the improvised barricades when a group of Muslims gained a foothold. Most of the defenders had been pushed off the fortifications or killed outright, leaving only Isabella, two guardsmen, and Marcus to face a dozen of the enemy. Realizing that any delay would allow more Turks to reinforce the breach, Marcus charged directly into the Anatolians, who were prematurely celebrating their short-lived success. Isabella was right by his side.

Marcus brought his sword down and caught one man just below his neck, splitting open his light chain-mail and driving him to his knees. He ignored the blood that erupted from his dying body and used his momentum to swing his elbow forward, catching the next Turk directly in the chin. The blow sent him tumbling into the courtyard, where he was pounced upon by a group of older men and women. Marcus spun back toward the wall and watched Isabella sidestep a clumsy attack from a tall, thin Turk, after which she rammed her short sword into his throat. Using her hand to push his body away, she freed her blade and leaned back to avoid a spear thrust from another soldier. Marcus stepped in, sweeping his sword around in a compact arc. The blade sliced through the man's torso and pinned him against the timber of the bulwark. Ducking, Marcus barely dodged a battle-ax as it brushed past him and buried itself into the chest of the Turk he had just dispatched.

Isabella stepped toward the ax-wielding soldier who was busy trying to free his weapon, and grabbing him around the waist, threw him over the parapet. With her hands busy above her head, another Turk tried to skewer Isabella with a broken spear. The tip of the lance caught her heavy breastplate but slid across the smooth surface, slicing into the fleshy part of her shoulder. Angered, Isabella swung at the man with her sword hand, catching him on the chin with the pommel. As the man fell, the spear dropped to the ground, twisting out of her shoulder. Isabella growled in pain, then spun her weapon around and drove the blade deep into the chest of the fallen man.

Marcus shifted his attention away from Isabella and watched as the remaining Turks were killed by a squad of Venetians sent to seal the breach. He turned back to her and nodded toward her shoulder.

"You alright?"

"Yeah, I'll be fine."

"I like the pommel to the chin, very effective. Did I teach you that?"

"No," she wiped her blade on a dead man's tunic. "I figured that out on my own. It works well because I'm shorter. They never see it coming." Isabella nodded her head beyond the wall. "I think they've had their fill."

Marcus could see the second wave was fizzling out, having spent its energy gaining tiny footholds on the walls. They were retreating in mass confusion, stumbling across the crowded moat and abandoning their wounded. Marcus and Isabella took advantage of the brief lull, making their way back to the Adrianople Gate, and desperately tried to reorganize the weakened defenses.

Marcus was redirecting several defenders when the Janissaries joined the engagement. He watched their ferocious approach, and a chill ran down his spine. They methodically crossed the moat and sprung upon the outer wall like lions leaping upon a wounded animal.

By this time, Marcus noticed other citizens had snuck through the gates and joined the garrisons. Women, young and old, stood upon the wall and flailed at the Muslims as they scrambled up the ladders. Young boys, barely tall enough to see over the battlements, poked at the attackers with spears and swords. As before, Marcus and Isabella sprinted to the thickest part of the battle, fighting desperately to deny the Turks a foothold.

Isabella, covered in blood, dispatched a portly Janissary and nodded toward the moat below. Marcus looked down to see that this attack was faltering. From somewhere in the distance, they heard the Byzantine Emperor's voice cry out in the night.

"Christians, you bear yourselves bravely for God's sake! I see the enemy retires in disorder! God has willed it—victory shall be ours!"

A loud cry erupted from the battlements as the defenders waved swords, picks, and battleaxes high into the air. The men tossed the dead and wounded enemy from the ramparts, adding to the carnage below.

During the momentary lull that followed, Marcus and Isabella found a water barrel and took a few mouthfuls. Marcus ripped a piece of cloth from his shirt, wet it, and cleaned the gash on Isabella's shoulder.

"I hope you're not getting used to this," he said.

"Is that even possible?"

"I'm never surprised at what I get used to."

She was about to reply when the drums started beating again. They returned to the walls in time to see Mahomet relaunch the Janissaries against the city. The defenders responded, as best they could. They were out of oil, so they dropped boiling water on the Turks as they scaled the ladders.

A swarthy Turk led the attack on the section of the wall near the gate. Marcus and Isabella reached the barricade just as the giant clambered over the parapet and produced a massive battle-ax from a sling around his shoulder. He stood there shielding the other Janissaries joining him on the bulwark.

Marcus glanced at his companions and sensed their reluctance to engage the Turk. Smirking, Marcus charged forward, diving as the giant swung his ax. Marcus rolled on his shoulder, coming up on one knee as he angled his weapon downward. The blade carved through muscle and bone, severing the Turk's leg just below the knee. The man dropped his ax, howling in pain as he clutched at his bleeding stump. A pair of Greeks, having just arrived, charged at the wounded giant and buried their long spears into his thick torso, then pushed his flailing body back over the side of the bulwark.

Though discouraged by the loss of their champion, the Turks had gained a foothold on the wall. The Greek soldiers rushed past Marcus to engage the attackers as Isabella pulled Marcus up by his breastplate, the latter wiping his bloody hand across his forehead. Marcus turned back toward the city, where a disturbing sight caught his eye. High above one of the main gates flew the crescent pennant of the Turkish Empire.

"Look!" He pointed at the tower.

The blood drained from her soiled face as she saw the fluttering standard. Without a word, they sprinted down the nearby steps and mounted a pair of horses. They galloped across the courtyard toward the tower that flew the foreign banner. A hundred yards from the gate, they met one of the Venetian officers assigned to guard that wall segment.

"What's going on?" Isabella asked.

"They came through a small, unlocked door. The *Kerkoporta*...maybe twenty men." His breath was labored. "I don't know who unlocked it, but they killed the tiny garrison and placed their flag on the tower."

"Are they still there?" Marcus was trying to settle his unruly mount.

"No, they've moved on to loot the palace. I sent men to recapture the tower."

"We have to pull down that flag!" Isabella said. "If the men see it, they'll think the city has fallen!"

Just as she finished, a loud cry erupted from the section they had just left. In the early morning light, Marcus could make out another crescent pennant fluttering from the Adrianople Gate. It looked like the Janissaries had taken the wall.

Marcus and Isabella remounted their horses and sped off to investigate. As they approached the gate, they could see men were fleeing in all directions, screaming that the city had fallen. Waves of Janissaries were pouring over the unprotected battlements and into the courtyard. Marcus and Isabella dismounted and tried in vain to stop the tide of fleeing men. Marcus recognized one other man trying to rally the defenders. Constantine turned toward him, his features stained with blood and soot. Marcus and Isabella joined him, along with several members of his guard.

"Sire, you must leave—" Isabella pleaded with the Emperor. "You can still escape by ship!"

"What? And miss dinner?" He winked, his smile fading to a look of grim determination. "No, God forbid I should live as an emperor without an empire!"

The emperor tore the purple cloak from his shoulders,

threw it to the ground, and drew his sword, ready to face the charging Turks.

Isabella fell in beside Marcus. "Well, this seems to be going as planned."

With no appropriate response, Marcus drew his sword and prepared to meet the horde. They tore into the Janissaries with untamed fury. For a moment, they stemmed the advance, but a renewed assault reversed their initial success. Out of the corner of his eye, Marcus saw several men strike down the Emperor. Only Isabella and Marcus remained as the tide of Muslims broke upon their swords, an island of hope in a sea of despair.

A sharp cry marked her fall. Marcus beheaded her assailant with a lightning strike of his angry blade. He stood above her bleeding body and turned his rage upon those before him. However, sheer numbers overcame his anger and sealed his ruin. A lance pierced his back, its tip puncturing his lung and forcing him to his knees. Marcus swung his sword one last time before someone pulled it from his grasp. As the sun rose upon the captured city, Marcus fell across her body and gave in to the darkness.

CHAPTER THIRTEEN

The Vatican is a dagger in the heart of Italy.
—THOMAS PAINE

MODERN DAY
ROME

THE AIR WAS THICK with the scent of dying books. From a dark recess, Marcus watched an old monk move from case to case, his bony hands slipping the ancient volumes into openings on the various shelves. His name was Brother McLaughlin, but most people called him Brother Mac. Satisfied they were alone, Marcus stepped out from the shadow, clearing his throat in the process so he would not startle the old fellow.

"I was wondering when you'd join me." The heavy wrinkles on the man's face deepened as he frowned. "You've been standing there like a statue. I almost dropped our only copy of Augustine's memoirs—I'm not as young as I look!"

"I had to be sure you were alone."

"Heck, I'm always alone." The monk flicked a thumb over

his shoulder. "Ramirez sent all my apprentices away, and now I'm stuck doing everything."

"Why would he do that?"

"Who knows?" Brother Mac shrugged. "I gave up trying to figure that man out."

"Probably a good idea."

"So, what kind of trouble are you in?"

"What makes you think I'm in trouble?"

Brother Mac rolled his eyes as he took another book from the cart, handed it to Marcus, and then pointed to a slot on the top shelf.

Marcus slid the book home. "Okay, so maybe I got myself into a little trouble."

The old priest glared at him.

Marcus grimaced. "Well, more than a little."

"So, what do you need from me for?"

"I need to talk to you about the last couple of months."

"Is this something *I* could get in trouble for?" Brother Mac eyed him suspiciously.

"Probably—"

"Good! I haven't been in trouble since the fireworks incident in ninety-eight."

"I don't believe that!"

"Maybe that was the last time they caught me." Mac grinned. "Let's sit. My old bones are getting stiff."

Marcus followed him to a long table and several chairs in the center of the room. A single lamp stood in the middle of the table, trying to hold the darkness at bay.

"Want some tea?" Mac called over his shoulder as he hobbled toward a counter on the nearest wall. There was a sink and hotplate, plus a teapot and cups.

"Sure, if it's not too much trouble."

Marcus took a seat, tilting his head to read the bindings of the several books stacked on the table. Most were in Latin, though a few were in Greek and one in Italian. He did not recognize any of the titles.

After a few minutes, Brother Mac returned to the table and handed him a cup.

"So, what do you need to know?"

"Has anyone been snooping around?" Marcus studied the priest, cup poised in front of his lips. "You know, looking for something unusual, or something people rarely look for?"

"Marcus, I've spent the last sixty years of my life working in this library, serving the church and its clergy. One secret to my longevity has been my discretion."

"I understand." Marcus set down his cup. "You know me...I wouldn't be here if this weren't important."

"I know, I know..." He looked down as he slowly stirred his tea with a worn silver spoon. "Two men visited about six months ago, right after the Cardinal became Secretariat. They asked about several subjects but only read through one volume I brought them. It came from the *Domini Restricti*."

"The *Forbidden volumes*?"

"Yes."

"What were they asking about?"

"Ritual Banishment."

"What? Why would they want to know about that?"

"I can't imagine."

"And you don't want to." Marcus fixed his eyes on the worn surface of the wooden table.

"That's not the worst of it—"

"What do you mean?"

"They took the volume with them."

"That's impossible! They never remove the volumes, *especially* the forbidden ones."

"I know—but the Holy Father signed the paperwork." Tears were forming in his eyes.

"Are there any other books that contain references to ritual banishment?"

"A few, but that's the only one that listed the actual steps..."

"Can I see them?"

Brother Mac stood. "Give me a minute."

The crackling flames from the fireplace cast a series of wispy shadows across a massive chamber. A sofa and two wing chairs surrounded a mahogany coffee table sat atop an ancient Persian rug. The cherry-paneled walls boasted several original paintings and twice as many flawless copies. Towering windows lined one side of the room, the heavy curtains drawn to shield the occupants from the Vatican square's bright lights. The opposite end of the room was more functional, with an antique wooden desk resting beneath a drab painting of a long-dead Pope. Two more wing chairs sat before the desk, with a leather office chair nestled behind. A banker's lamp and phone were the only items on the desk. A door near the back corner of the room blended into the woodwork.

The double doors in the front of the room swung open, and a heavyset man in a white and gold-trimmed robe stepped into the chamber, a crimson skullcap clinging to his pale scalp. A second man, dressed in black pants and shirt, followed close behind, his attention focused on a leather portfolio.

"A package arrived by courier." The younger man looked up from his planner. "I placed it in the side drawer."

The Cardinal walked to the desk. "When did the package arrive?"

"Two hours ago."

"And why wasn't I told?" He sat in his chair and pulled off his cap, tossing it across the desk. It skidded along the smooth surface and fell onto the hardwood floor.

"Well, sir," the young man picked up the cap and placed it on the desk, "you were in a meeting with the Holy Father, and you told me you were not to be disturbed."

"Yes, but I wanted to know the moment that package arrived!"

The young priest bowed slightly. "Of course, your Holiness. Please forgive my mistake."

"I always do."

"Can I get you anything else?"

"No. I'll be going to bed soon. Please wake me at five AM."

"Yes, sir. Good night, Cardinal." He closed his portfolio and nodded.

Without replying, the Cardinal watched him leave, then switched on the lamp and opened a drawer. He pulled out the package and reached for a letter opener.

"You won't be needing that."

Marcus stepped out from behind the curtain. The Cardinal looked down at the envelope, a shocked expression on his face, and realized it was already open.

He dropped it onto the desk. "I guess I won't."

Marcus scanned the room as he moved forward and pulled out the chair closest to the window, shifting it so that he could keep both doorways in his line of vision. He unbuttoned his jacket, settled into the soft leather, and crossed one leg over the other.

"I've been expecting you." The Cardinal leaned his elbows on the desk.

"Why?"

"I knew you couldn't walk away."

"And this is where you tell me how perceptive you are...and how well you know me?"

"Perhaps..."

"Save the bullshit."

"Then what do you want to hear?"

"When? And where?"

The Cardinal flinched but recovered quickly. "What?"

"I'm not in the mood, and you're not good enough for this. I've read the report."

Ramirez settled back into his chair. "Then you know it all."

"No...I need to know when and where."

"I don't know."

Marcus glared at him.

"Do you think Thomas would trust me with that information? Would you?"

Marcus let him stew.

"What are you going to do, torture me?"

Marcus reached into his jacket. Ramirez, sweat glistening on his forehead, watched him pull out a pack of cigarettes. Marcus patted one out, put it to his lips, and flicked on his lighter. After taking a long pull, he exhaled. "Forget it. If Thomas were stupid enough to tell you, he'd just change it."

"Yes, yes, that's true."

"So, I guess I should just kill you right now." Marcus reached into his jacket, the cigarette hanging from his lips.

"No, no, wait!" Ramirez stood up. "I can help you."

"I don't need your help," Marcus mumbled past the cigarette.

"Yes, you do...I can tell you where Thomas is."

"I don't care...and even if I did, I wouldn't trust you." He pulled out his pistol.

"I'm sorry!"

"Sorry for what? Sorry you gave up on God?" Marcus pulled the cigarette from his mouth, blowing a cloud of smoke at Ramirez. "Or sorry you got caught?"

"I'm sorry for everything!"

"Too bad I'm not a priest; I could absolve you." Marcus took another pull from the cigarette, then stood up and flicked it across the room.

"I don't want to die!"

"Yeah? Well, you haven't lived long enough." Marcus waved his pistol toward the bedroom door. "Go...I'm not going to kill you, though Lord knows I should."

No longer fearing for his life did wonders for this man's courage. Ramirez glared at Marcus. "You can't stop him."

Marcus motioned him toward the nearby door with his pistol.

Ramirez sneered back at Marcus as he reached for the doorknob. "But you already knew that."

"Unlock your cell phone."

"What?"

"Your cell phone. I heard it vibrate. Unlock it and give it to me."

The Cardinal reached into his robe and pulled out a phone, unlocking it before handing it over to Marcus. The Roman motioned him to step back into his room. Marcus closed the door, holstered his pistol, and took out his phone. He scanned through the cardinal's text messages, finding the one he needed. Pulling up the info, he used his phone to take a picture of the number. Turning, Marcus tossed the cardinal's phone and sprinted to a panel in the wall halfway towards the other exit. He searched where Bennucio had instructed and found a slight indentation on the underside of the panel. As he pressed the dimple, a section swung back into the darkness. Marcus slipped into the opening and pushed the door closed. Less than five minutes later, he was descending deep into the catacombs, his mind still trying to grasp the contents of the envelope.

My God, Thomas, what have you done?

CHAPTER FOURTEEN

I prayed to God to make me strong and able to fight.
—HARRIET TUBMAN

MAY 1849 A.D.
WEST AFRICA

MARCUS STOOD ON THE BOW of the rowboat and scanned the reed-covered riverbank. Isabella was supposed to meet him somewhere along this shoreline. Marcus peered beyond the bank and could barely make out the walls of the stone fortress. He was still surprised that Thomas could have become somehow mixed up with slavers, but then again, nothing should surprise him anymore.

He scanned a break in the reeds, and that was when he saw a figure waving at him. He held up his hand to the rowers, pointed to the split in the vegetation, and waited as the soldiers guided their craft onto the sandy beach. Marcus hopped off the boat as the bow crunched to a halt.

"Isabella!" He hugged her, then leaned back, searching her dark eyes. "Are you okay? I've been worried."

197

"We both know I've been through much worse."

"Don't remind me. Is Blanco still here?"

"No, he left several months ago. The men he left behind are just as bad."

"Any news about Thomas?"

"About that." She paused, seeing his expression change.

"What?"

"Thomas was never involved."

"Then why did you tell me he might be?"

"Because I needed your help, I needed your connections with the British Navy. Without them, I'd never free these people. But you're so focused on finding Thomas..." She grabbed his arm. "Marcus, thousands of slaves pass through here every month. We have to shut this down."

He took a deep breath, shaking his head. His eyes drifted from her to the wall beyond the bank. "Can you tell us how we get inside?"

"No, but I can show you."

"Lead the way."

She motioned for the group of men on the boat to follow her. She disappeared into a gap in the reeds that led to a narrow path along the water, and Marcus kept close behind. Isabella slowed and picked her way up a pile of rocks that formed something of a staircase up the bank. Near the top, she knelt and waved for Marcus to come forward. As he sat beside her, she leaned forward and pointed to the wall above, whispering in his ear.

"There is one guard. We can make it to the door when he is walking the other way." She pointed at a dark recess in the wall's base, ten yards across the open ground.

"Is the door locked?"

"Yes, but I have someone waiting inside. It'll be easy to pass through. The guard is a lazy Spaniard with poor eyesight."

"My favorite guards. Say when."

She watched for the guard, barely visible above the wall. When she was sure he was moving in the other direction, Isabella motioned for one man to cross the expanse. She got three across in the first pass. It took three rounds to get all eight of them across, the group crammed into a small alcove.

"Do you have a pistol?"

Marcus shook his head, pulled one from his belt, and handed it to her.

She used the butt of the gun to knock on the door. There was a long silence, then the sound of the drawn latch. Isabella motioned for them to make room for her to pull the door open. On the other side was a tiny black woman in a dirty blouse and ragged trousers. She grinned, several of her teeth missing.

Isabella motioned the men through, then pulled the door closed behind her. They found themselves in the shadows of the rampart above, the courtyard beyond bathed in pale starlight. Isabella bent over and spoke with the older lady in some strange language that Marcus had never heard before. Nodding, Isabella motioned for her to return to her quarters.

"She'll warn the other servants." Isabella rejoined the group. "What time do we need to open the gate?"

"5 AM, just before sunrise." Marcus pulled out his pocket watch and squinted in the darkness. Unable to read the clock face, he moved to the edge of shadow and held the watch out. "We have twenty minutes."

Isabella motioned for the group to huddle around her near the wall.

"There will be two men in the guardhouse, but they are probably asleep." She pointed to the long building on the opposite side of the courtyard. "That's the barracks. Marcus and I will go to the gate. The rest of you stay here and cover the barracks. Once the gate is open, we will head to the officers' quarters."

The men took up positions behind whatever cover they

could find. Isabella tilted her head toward the gate, and Marcus followed her deeper into the shadows. They crept along the wall, ducking under windows and skirting around the staircase leading up to the rampart. She held up one hand and motioned for them to settle in. They both sat on the ground, leaning against the wall between the gate and the small guardhouse. The building across the square from them was a large one, with three arched openings, each closed off with a tall iron portcullis.

Marcus nodded toward the stone structure. "How many?"

"At least 500, maybe twice that. I didn't see how many they brought in just before sunset."

Marcus looked at the two posts in the middle of the courtyard, standing ten feet apart from one another.

"And those?"

"Whipping posts." She met his gaze. "They pick men at random from each group as examples."

The irony was not lost on either of them that the same empire proved so instrumental in establishing the slave trade was now raiding the most famous outpost of that same trade. The Brits were eager to rewrite history, and in doing so, place themselves in a much more favorable light.

Isabella looked at Marcus and caught him staring at her.

"What?" She asked.

"Nothing," he said. But then he changed his mind. "I'm glad you asked me to help. Even if that meant lying to me."

"You're not mad?"

"No. Of course not. And I know my search for Thomas has distracted me. I see his shadow everywhere I go. Anything evil, I assume he has something to do with it."

"Where do you think he is? America?"

"No, too small. Hard to get lost there. I'd say he's part of the old power structures in Europe. Or maybe Russia."

"Yeah, that would make sense." Marcus picked up a pebble and rolled it in his hand. "I miss him."

"Me too," she replied. "But he chose his path. Maybe someday he'll come back."

"I don't think so."

"Me neither."

He looked down at his watch and then back up again. "It's time."

She nodded and motioned toward the guardhouse.

He pulled his pistol from his belt and followed her toward the door. They took up positions on both sides of the opening, kneeling in the darkness. Marcus pointed at himself, then to her, then to the door, and shrugged. She pointed to herself and leaned up to twist the door handle when it turned all on its own. The door swung inward, letting the light from a lantern spill out into the courtyard. A guard stepped out, his bearded face stretched in a yawn.

Isabella stood up before Marcus could react and swung the pistol by the barrel, catching the man under the chin with the brass plate molded to the grip. There was a sickening crunch as his jaw, and possibly his skull, shattered into pieces. He thudded to the ground, a moan slipping from the bloody mess that used to be his mouth. She flipped the pistol in the air, catching the blood-soaked grip in her hand and stepping through the doorway. Marcus, right behind her, felt a pistol ball slice through his left ear and smash into the door frame behind him as the gunshot echoed through the tiny room. Isabella used the muzzle's flash to locate the second guardsman in a darkened corner of the room and emptied her pistol into his chest. He dropped his weapon and, grasping at the wound, fell backward. She spied several swords hanging on the wall by the lantern. She stepped forward and grabbed one, tossing it to Marcus. He caught it by the hilt and strode over to the lever mechanism that controlled the gate. As Isabella gained a cutlass for herself, the loud report of musket fire filled the courtyard.

Marcus freed the lever, and spun the wheel that opened the gate. They both moved to the door, where Isabella knelt and peered out. The first guard was now crawling away from the door. Isabella reached over and pulled the pistol from his belt before driving her sword into his chest.

Turning to Marcus, she smirked. "The more we kill, the less the Brits can let go later."

A lively firefight had erupted between the Brits and several Spanish guards escaping the barracks. Isabella ignored the action and sprinted to a nearby set of steps, Marcus hot on her heels. She took the stairs two at a time, reaching the top just as a door opened and a half-dressed man stepped out, sword in hand. Isabella leveled her pistol, shot him in the face, and then advanced further along the balcony to the next door. Marcus, confident she could take care of herself, headed the other direction.

Marcus stopped in front of a door and kicked it in. A man inside cursed in Spanish as he raised his pistol and fired, the shot nearly taking off his other ear. Marcus cursed back at him in Spanish and stepped forward, driving his cutlass into the man's chest. He pulled it out and turned to see a young African woman huddled in the corner, a blanket wrapped around her tiny frame. Marcus held one finger to his lips, not knowing if the gesture meant anything to her.

A moment later, Isabella walked through the door, her face covered in blood. She looked at the man bleeding to death on the bed.

"This is the commander. Will he live?"

"Not much longer." Marcus tilted his head to the corner.

Isabella rushed over and crouched beside the girl. She comforted her in her native tongue and helped her to her feet. Marcus led them from the room and to the balcony beyond.

202

The rising sun revealed that the firefight had now ceased with the arrival of more British redcoats. The men who had come with Marcus were emerging from the shadows, one helping a wounded comrade. Two-dozen surviving slavers were standing in front of the barracks, their weapons scattered across the dusty ground. The battle, short and sweet, was over.

They spent most of the day ferrying nearly 800 freed slaves to nearby transports.

"Where will they go?" Marcus leaned on a railing and watched the last of the ex-slaves climb up the rope ladder of a nearby ship.

"Sierra Leone."

"Why can't they go home?"

"It's difficult to find a home for most of them. Many were sold into slavery by another tribe. To go home would be an embarrassment to the local chieftain."

"What will you do now?" He asked her.

"This is the major fortress, but there are many slaver posts."

"You can't stop them all."

"I can try." She met his gaze.

"Or you could come to London with me."

After a long pause, she asked, "How long has it been?"

Marcus looked down at the azure water. "Twenty-three years."

"I've never seen you go that long without dying. But next week, you'll get yourself killed." She reached up to the missing part of his ear. "It's only a matter of time. And when you come back, you're never the same person. I know why—I can't compete with her. At least, not now."

"I understand. Maybe someday I will get over it."

She suppressed a wry smile. She shook her head, placed

203

both hands on his jaw, and leaned forward to kiss his lips, lingering for a long moment before she pulled away, a single tear running down her cheek.

"Goodbye, Marcus."

A moment later, the explosives they had set in the fortifications went off, sending a massive cloud of rock and smoke skyward. Marcus turned back and watched the fortress crumble.

CHAPTER FIFTEEN

Everyone has a plan 'til they get punched in the mouth.
—MIKE TYSON

MODERN DAY
ROME

MARCUS WALKED ACROSS THE SQUARE, scanning the streets as he tore into a breakfast pastry, and washed it down with an espresso. He was late, but then again, it was Rome. He was nervous at the thought of seeing Isabella again, as their last parting had not been on the best of terms. The sexual abuse scandals that had rocked the Catholic Church were the final straw for her. She refused to have anything to do with the Church, its leadership, and especially the Vatican. Marcus, loyal to a fault, had not been ready to walk away, and he knew that had frustrated her. He regretted the things he said.

But she had agreed to meet, so things must be okay. Or perhaps she realized how much trouble he was in. Probably the latter. He stopped near a fountain, tossing his empty coffee cup into a nearby trash can. That is when he saw her standing by a black BMW, waving at him. She was stunning, as ever.

He smiled and met her halfway to the car, where they exchanged an uncomfortable embrace.

He stepped back and kept two hands on her arms. "I'm glad to see you."

She studied the haggard lines on his face. "What's wrong?"

"Not here." He glanced around, then nodded to the car. "Are Sam and Cormac safe?"

"Yeah." She nodded her head toward the car. "I'll take you to them."

When they had settled into the car, he handed her the envelope he had taken from the Cardinal. Without saying a word, she opened it and began to read.

"Can I smoke?"

"Yeah." She nodded, engrossed in the material.

"You want one?"

"No, I quit three years ago."

About halfway through, she reached over and took his cigarette, taking a long pull as she flipped the page. He lit another one, picking his teeth with his thumb as he stared out the window. She looked up at him when she finished.

"You've got to be kidding me."

"Nope. Matches everything we have: DNA, drug formulas."

"Where would he get this kind of technology?"

"I assume he's been investing in this for decades."

"Do we know where?"

"No."

"Jesus Christ." She shook her head. "We have to find out where."

"Does that mean you'll help me?"

"Of course."

"Good. First, we get Sam and Cormac somewhere safe."

"Okay." She reached down and started the car. "I can't believe he's going to do this."

Marcus just sat staring out the window.

They turned down a narrow alley, and Isabella pushed the button on a garage remote. They waited in front of a nondescript warehouse as the door lifted, then they pulled inside. As they came to a stop, Marcus could see a dozen men brandishing automatic weapons and two large black SUVs. Near the back of the garage was a staircase leading up to a loft area.

Marcus left the car and made his way up the stairs while Isabella stopped to speak with her crew. The men responded by unlocking the cabinets and loading various gear into the SUVs.

As Marcus reached the top of the stairs, he could see Sam scanned his dirty clothes.

"Before you say anything, I want to make it clear...I was not shot." Marcus had both arms raised.

"Then why are you so fucking late?" Cormac asked.

"I used the catacombs to sneak into the Vatican, and when I was leaving..."

"You got lost," Sam finished.

"How did you know?" Isabella said, having just joined the conversation.

Sam Smirked. "His problem isn't getting into places; it's getting out."

"Amen!" Cormac crossed his arms. "How did you get out?"

"I wandered around until I found an exit." In truth, Brother Bennucio had found him just before dawn, but he had promised to keep the monk's involvement secret.

"Did you find what you were looking for?" Cormac asked.

"Unfortunately." He pulled the packet from his jacket and tossed it onto the coffee table. The other two stared at the manila envelope. Marcus motioned to Sam. "Go ahead."

Marcus sat down, accepted the cup of coffee one of the men

brought him, and took a sip as he watched Sam read through the documents. Sam handed each to Cormac, who scanned them through his thick reading glasses. He dropped the papers onto the table when done.

Cormac squinted in disbelief. "Can he clone a human?"

"I don't see why not," Marcus said.

"I know we're close, but this all seems pretty far-fetched," Sam countered.

"Maybe, but I can only imagine the money Thomas has poured into this research. I'm guessing his team is at least ten years ahead of the curve...and they are operating outside the legal regulations. For them, human trials are very much an option."

"So," Cormac continued, "the question is who and when."

"*Who* is pretty clear," Marcus said, "*when* is the problem."

"You know who?" Sam asked.

Marcus looked to Isabella, who nodded.

"Thomas is going to clone Jesus Christ," Marcus said.

"For fuck's sake," Cormac mumbled.

"That's ridiculous," Sam exclaimed. "Why do you think that?"

"I know Thomas." Marcus pointed to the folder. "And that's the only thing that makes sense to me."

"How? Where did he get the DNA samples?" Sam pressed him.

"Thomas has several of the spikes used for the crucifixion. He also has the original shroud, which had a lot of blood on it."

"The Shroud of Turin?" Sam guessed.

"No, that is a fake. Thomas has the real one."

"Marcus, he couldn't have gotten much DNA material from that," Sam said.

"Between the three, I bet he did."

"Tell them about the book," Isabella said.

"What book?" Cormac looked from her to Marcus.

Marcus set down his cup. "The Cardinal allowed the removal of a sacred text...one that's nearly fifteen hundred years old. The text has instructions for a ritual banishment."

Sam frowned. "What's *ritual banishment*?"

"It was an early attempt at exorcism. But it was *too* effective —it banishes the soul and the demon. Like throwing the baby out with the bathwater."

Isabella joined in. "You clone Christ, then perform ritual banishment. What that leaves is a divine host with no soul. An empty vessel, ready to be possessed."

"Sweet Mary and Joseph," Cormac said.

"What?" Sam looked at him.

"He's gonna bring Satan to earth," said Cormac, his face ashen.

"I don't get it. It would just be a baby," Sam said. "What good would that do? I mean, that leaves us like ten years to figure out how to solve this problem."

"It won't be a baby," Marcus said. "Remember the growth enhancer formula? The DNA stabilizer? It all makes sense."

"Not really," Sam said. "Why doesn't Lucifer just possess someone already here?"

"He does, periodically, but it's not that simple to find someone vulnerable, and Lucifer can never fully control a host if he has to share it with the original soul."

"Then why not just banish the soul?" Sam asked.

"Because that leaves a mortal host which would someday die," Isabella countered.

"Exactly. Thomas needs a divine host, one that cannot die," Marcus said. "That way, he can stay on earth forever."

Sam sat back in her chair. "Holy shit."

209

Thirty minutes later, Marcus stepped out from the bathroom and was greeted by an enticing aroma that teased his empty stomach. The others were sitting around a table while one of Isabella's men busied himself in the small kitchen. As Marcus took a seat, the Turk brought over a pan of sausage and vegetables, along with a healthy serving of flatbread. There was no small talk as the group reflected on the gravity of the situation.

Marcus was debating a second helping when Hazid pulled off his headphones and came over to the table. He leaned over and whispered into Isabella's ear. Nodding, she gave him some instructions that sent him sprinting toward the stairs.

"We have trouble." She stood. "Ten minutes, maybe less."

"Shit." Marcus tossed down his napkin. "You got a plan?"

Sam followed them up the stairs. "Does she look like someone who doesn't have a plan?"

By the time they reached the ground floor, the other men had already climbed into the two vehicles. Gustaf met them near one cabinet, handing Marcus and Isabella each a small earpiece with a microphone. As Marcus slipped his in, Isabella gave instructions to the Turk.

"I want one in front, the other behind. It's an early Sunday morning, so traffic should be light." She moved to the cabinet, pulling out several weapons. "If we're followed, wait for my signal—then we all head in different directions. Try to draw off as many as possible. These people must get out of Rome alive."

Gustaf nodded and turned back to the SUV.

"Who's driving?" Isabella looked from Marcus to Sam.

Marcus angled his head toward Sam.

"All right," Isabella said. "I'll ride up front."

Marcus moved back toward their BMW, pausing as he stepped past one of the open cabinets. He admired how well-prepared Isabella was and pulled out a Galil battle rifle. Scanning one of the shelves, he slid out a container full of magazines. Marcus handed the ammunition to Cormac, who was already settled in the rear passenger's seat, and made his way around the car. Sam raised her eyebrows when she saw Marcus moving around the vehicle with the large rifle.

"It may come in handy." Marcus slipped into the backseat.

The garage door slipped open, revealing a narrow, cobblestoned alley. The first Suburban turned right, the BMW and second Suburban close behind. After driving for a quarter-mile, they turned right again and found themselves face-to-face with an oncoming black Mercedes. Instead of stopping, the SUV picked up speed and barreled toward the sedan. Sam let the larger vehicle pull farther ahead and hastily clicked her seat belt.

The Mercedes came to a stop, and a man started to get out but quickly closed the door as the Suburban plowed into the car, driving it backward and to the left. The BMW barely slipped by the wreckage and continued down the alley. Marcus watched as the second SUV in their tiny caravan squeezed through the gap, one of its mirrors busting off as it scraped against a brick building. Just behind, he could see the damaged SUV pulling back from the crumpled Mercedes.

"Take the next right." Isabella looked back over her shoulder. "Gustaf, activate the rest of our Rome operatives: code-word Byzantium." After a momentary pause, she said, "Yes, everyone—turn left."

Sam swung the BMW around the corner and down a wider avenue. Isabella shifted her attention down the road as Marcus leaned forward and said, "This isn't good."

Several cars were blocking the way, with a van parked just behind them. They could see men crouching behind the vehicles, their weapons pointed in their direction. Isabella tapped Sam on the shoulder and pointed to a spot just near a massive garage door.

"Pull up there." She motioned toward the barricade as she

spoke into her mike. "Gustaf, pull past us and shield the group. Naref, bust through the garage door." Isabella looked back, a thin smile on her full lips. "This is going to get interesting."

"You and I have a very different definition of interesting," Sam said.

"Are those police officers?" Marcus pulled back the bolt on his rifle.

"Nope." Isabella glanced back at Marcus.

The first Suburban sped past, swinging forward and blocking the others. As it skidded to a halt, the men behind the barricade opened fire, rounds peppering the side of the vehicle. The other SUV had angled toward the building and was backing up to get a good run-up to the garage door. Sam flinched each time a round plowed into the Suburban next to them.

"It's okay, the side panels are reinforced steel," Isabella said. There was a loud crash as the second truck barreled through the warehouse door. "Which also makes them good battering rams."

As the truck disappeared into the building, Sam slid the BMW into reverse.

"It's an auto showroom," the voice filled their headphones. "You should be safe when you first come into the room. We pushed the first two cars out of the way."

"All right," Isabella said.

Sam shifted back into drive and maneuvered the car through the opening. Two Fiat convertibles pushed up over to the side: one partially buried in a sales office, the other had scraped along the wall, taking out a water cooler and several desks. The larger SUV was farther on in the room, parked between two sedans that, along with other vehicles, now formed a semi-circle around a four-door Mercedes. Beyond, the front of the building consisted of enormous glass panels that framed the double doors of the showroom's entrance. Behind them, they could still hear the crack of small arms fire, though the pace had fallen off.

"We need to get moving." Gustaf's voice crackled across the radio.

"Just a minute." Isabella looked at Sam. "Back up so they can get a good run-up."

"Got it."

"Naref?" she asked.

"Yes?"

"Get us out of here."

"Understood."

The taillights of the SUV glowed as it backed up and then stopped. The tires squealed against the slick tiles as the truck shoved the luxury car through the front of the building. There was an ear-splitting crash as the plate-glass shattered in all directions. The Suburban continued to push the vehicle out into the street, disrupting traffic in both directions. A moped, unable to avoid the wreckage, careened onto the sidewalk and into the showroom, where it collided with one of the parked cars, propelling its rider over the hood and onto the roof of the vehicle. He seemed dazed, but otherwise all right.

The SUV was not as lucky. A bakery truck smashed straight into the passenger side, driving the vehicle thirty feet down the street and out of their view. Sam shifted the car back into drive and started forward, the tires crunching on the splintered glass. They pulled out into the street, picking their way through the traffic that had now ground to a halt.

"Naref?" Isabella glared into the Suburban as Sam pulled up next to the hissing vehicle. "Naref!"

"Naref is dead. So is Hamed," an unfamiliar voice filled their earpieces, "and Jarod is wounded very badly."

"Gustaf, pick up Jarod and Yasif when you come through."

"Yes. Uluf has been shot as well—I don't think he will make it."

"Okay, get out of there." She motioned Sam to pull forward. "When you exit the building, follow us to the left."

Once past the wreckage, Sam laid the hammer down. Marcus watched out the back window as the second SUV pulled out of the building, stopping briefly to load in the two injured men. It was soon following them down the street.

"We're close to the expressway." Isabella glanced back at Marcus. "If we can make it there, we have a chance."

"Where are the police?" Marcus scanned the side streets.

"Thomas had them stand down. That's how I knew something was up," Isabella said.

Sam slowed the car as they reached an intersection that forced them to chose right or left. Directly in front of them was a vast open plaza with trees hovering over granite benches. An assortment of fountains and statues dotted the cobblestone landscape, providing natural gathering points for tourists and leisure seekers.

"Turn right." Isabella motioned.

"No! Go straight!" Marcus yelled, "and hit the gas!"

Sam straightened the wheel and stomped on the accelerator.

They burst through the intersection, barely missing a tiny white coupe. A gray van was hurtling toward them, its driver making no attempt to swerve or slow his vehicle. The van clipped the rear bumper of their car, knocking them up and over the curb. Sam fought the wheel as the BMW spun through the open square. They came to a screeching halt thirty feet from the curb, the smell of burnt rubber drifting through the air. As the van came to a stop, the pursuing Suburban rammed it and propelled the vehicle forward until it reached the sidewalk, where it rolled onto its side.

Isabella was unhurt, as was Sam, whose white knuckles were still gripping the leather steering wheel. Cormac had hit his forehead on the window and sported a growing lump.

Marcus, the only one without a seat belt, had fared the worst. He had a gash on his forehead, the result of him hitting the support beam near the door.

Marcus leaned back, a painful grimace on his face. His hand was trying to stem the blood flowing from the wound, but he could only direct it away from his eye and down his face. As Isabella glanced over her shoulder, the anxious expression on her face turned to one of concern. Marcus followed her eyes and saw several men piling out of the overturned van, each sporting an assault rifle and an angry expression. Those onlookers who had started forward to help the accident victims scattered.

"Go, go!" Marcus pulled out his pistol, shattering the rear window with his first shot, and sending the men to their knees.

They returned fire, the rounds plowing into the side of the vehicle. His next two shots dropped one assailant, but they were moving across the square before he could pick off another. Isabella had unbuckled her belt and was now standing, her upper body sticking out of the sunroof. She leaned forward and fired, the shells skittering across the roof. After emptying a magazine, she took a moment to check on Gustaf and the other vehicle. It was then that she realized the mike had fallen from her ear and was now hanging at her side. She could see the tail section of the SUV poking out behind the van, but there did not appear to be any movement. She sat back down in her seat, shoved the tiny receiver back into her ear, and reloaded her weapon.

"Gustaf?" She pointed to the right, directing Sam around an elaborate fountain. "Gustaf? Anyone?"

"Yeah?"

"Status?"

"We're getting moving. Pretty banged up here."

"Okay, join us when you can."

"Isabella." Marcus pointed back through the open window

to where a sedan had swung around the wreckage and followed them across the plaza. A man leaned out the window, spraying rounds in their direction.

"These guys never get enough," she said.

Marcus smirked, lifted the battle rifle, and slipped the barrel out the back window, resting the stock on the top of the seat. Pulling the butt of the weapon snug against his shoulder, he centered in on the pursuing vehicle and fired off several rounds, the heavy report echoing through the car. The first 7.62 mm slug hit the front of the vehicle, with the second shattering the windshield and forcing the driver to swerve.

"Hold on!" Sam tried to steer the car between two concrete pylons that marked the plaza entrance.

The car slipped between the posts, but the right side clipped one of the columns, scraping down the length of the vehicle. Just clear of the opening, the car careened across a narrow sidewalk and into the street beyond, somehow missing a parked sedan. Sam gripped the wheel like a lost lover, slammed on the brakes, and guided the vehicle to a smoking halt.

Their pursuers were not so lucky and piled directly into a pylon. The collision sheared off the post and destroyed the front end of their car. The car skidded out of control with pinned tire and crashed straight into the coupe that Sam had somehow avoided.

Marcus shifted around in his seat, pulled the empty magazine from the rifle, and dropping it to the floor, extended his hand.

"Cormac," after a moment, he repeated, "Cormac, I need—"

He stopped when he saw the older man slumped forward, with only the seat belt holding up his body. A small entry wound just below his left shoulder, a red stain slowly spreading across his back. Marcus reached forward and gently leaned him back into his seat just as Sam turned around.

"No!" Sam screamed and unhooked her seatbelt, flinging open her door.

She moved around the car to the rear passenger door when Marcus reached over and closed the blue eyes of his old friend. Marcus took the magazine from Cormac's dead hand, slammed it home, and opened his door.

"No!" Sam pulled open the door and knelt beside his limp body.

"Marcus!" Isabella started after him. Marcus ignored her, exited the vehicle, and walked toward the crippled sedan, pulling back the bolt of his rifle as he went. Stopping five feet in front of the car, he aimed at the blood-soaked passenger, who had realized his predicament and tried to raise his weapon. Marcus fired three shots into his chest, then methodically fired round after round into the shattered vehicle as the spent casings scattered across the ancient cobblestone. After pulling the trigger three times with no response, he hurled the rifle at the car and pulled out his pistol. He stepped to the side of the vehicle and emptied the weapon into the bodies crumpled in the back of the wreckage. Marcus looked down at the smoking handgun, lowered his head, and moved back toward the BMW.

By now, the SUV had joined them. Only Gustaf and one other man remained, and both helped Isabella move Cormac's body to the SUV. Isabella convinced Sam to join them and was giving them directions as Marcus arrived.

"We'll split up and join you later." Isabella looked at Marcus, tears in her eyes. "I'm sorry."

The distant look was the only response she got.

"We need to go." She took his arm and nudged him toward the passenger door.

He threw himself down into the seat and looked down at the pistol still in his hand. Marcus dropped the magazine, and replaced it with a full one. Isabella drove the car back down the avenue.

217

She swung the vehicle around a tight corner and down a narrow alley. For the moment, it appeared as if they had no pursuers. Following the curves, she eventually exited onto a busier street. Within a few minutes, she turned the car into a parking garage, where she stopped to take a ticket from the dispenser. The gate lifted, and she pulled forward, disappearing into the shadows. They went to the lowest garage level and parked in the most remote location they could find. Isabella popped the trunk, and Marcus rummaged through his bag, pulling out several more magazines for his Beretta. Isabella took a minute to clean the gash in his head with a towel and a bottle of water; the wound had already stopped bleeding. She pulled a baseball hat from the bag and gently placed it on his head. It covered most of the injury.

"There, almost normal."

"What's the plan," his voice was detached.

"The car is too conspicuous, and they would spot us in no time. Our best bet is to blend into the crowds. The other side of this mall has a bus terminal."

"Lead the way."

They walked across the top level of the mall, her arm clasped in his.

"Do you see them?" Marcus kept his eyes forward.

"Yeah. Looks like the bus won't be an option." She let go of his arm and walked over to the railing that overlooked the plaza below. "The Americans make such ugly vehicles."

Marcus followed her gaze to a bright yellow full-sized F150 pickup truck parked on the ground level.

"Do you think the keys are in the ignition?" She asked.

"No, but I bet that young sales lady has them."

"Why don't you go see, and I'll keep our friends occupied."

218

"You sure?"

"Of course."

Marcus entered a nearby elevator, waited for the door to open, and then stepped inside, avoiding a troupe of rowdy teens who burst from within. He watched Isabella through the glass sides of the elevator. She was making her way to an escalator further down the walkway. Stepping out of the elevator, Marcus held the door open for a lady pushing a stroller. She thanked him as she passed. He nodded and walked over to the vehicle.

He pretended he was looking at the truck, but he shifted his glance up to Isabella. He could see three or four men who looked out of place, all alone in a mall. That meant there were probably twice as many whom he had not seen yet. Isabella started towards the escalator when one of the men approached her.

Isabella took a step forward and drove her fist into his throat. As he crumbled to his knees, she grabbed the back of his head with one hand and smashed his face with her knee. He dropped his pistol, falling back onto the descending staircase.

Marcus pulled open the driver's door of the truck, slipping inside, was pleased to see the key fob sitting in the center console. He looked back at the escalator through the windshield and saw half a dozen men running toward Isabella, each one reaching into their jackets. She started down the stairs and pulled a handgun from her coat, taking a moment to glance back over her shoulder. A woman standing on the ascending stairway saw her pistol and let out a piercing scream that immediately scattered the other shoppers.

One man stepped onto the escalator, intent on following her down. There was no one between them, so Isabella calmly raised her weapon and fired off two shots, catching the man in the abdomen and chest. His body tumbled forward, landing several steps above her. As she turned, several men sprinted toward her on the ground floor, weapons drawn. She dropped to her knees as the bullets plunked into the side of the escalator. She spun and fired two shots at a man who had started up the steps, one round catching him in the kneecap, the bone immediately exploding. Marcus could see the sparks as rounds bounced off the metal panels all around her. He laid on the horn, hoping to distract her assailants.

Isabella swiveled her weapon forward, then saw another man trying to sprint down the steps, firing as he went. Leveling her pistol, she fired three rounds, the slugs smashing into his torso. He toppled forward, his momentum carrying his body down on top of her. She squeezed up against the railing and pushed the body down beside her. By now, the escalator was nearing the bottom, so she got ready to exit. Unfortunately, two men were standing less than five feet away, guns leveled. The closer of the two smirked, his white teeth peeking through his thin lips.

By now, Marcus had the truck in gear and barreling towards them. Only one of them realized what was about to happen, but not in time to do anything about it. He flew a good fifteen feet and smashed into the window of a nearby electronics shop, the plate-glass shattering as his body tumbled through a display of large televisions. The second man had jumped just before being hit, so the grill only caught his legs, and it pitched him over the top of the truck. The man tumbled across the roof and fell into the bed of the truck with a thud.

The truck's oversized tires screeched to a halt, and Marcus poked his head out the window.

"Hurry, there's a dozen more."

Isabella stepped off the escalator, grimacing as she sprinted around the back of the truck. Bullets peppered the vehicle as Marcus leaned over and opened the door. She leaped inside while he stomped on the gas. He spun the wheel frantically, rolled through the shattered glass, and barreled down the now empty mall.

"Well, this is much less conspicuous," Marcus said, slamming on the brakes and spinning the wheel, fishtailing the truck around a corner. Unable to straighten up, he slammed into an ATM in the middle of the walkway.

Isabella reached for the grab handle above the window, just as the window shattered, bullets slamming into the dash. In the rear-view mirror, Marcus could see the man he had hit with the truck clinging to the bed with one hand and aiming a pistol with the other. Marcus slammed on the brakes, the truck screeching to a halt. The man slammed into the back of the cab. Isabella leveled her pistol and fired several shots through the back window, knocking him back and over the tailgate.

Marcus sped up again, navigated another bend, and tried to dodge the various stands and booths occupying the center of the mall. He did a horrible job, and within seconds the truck had smashed into several stalls, showering the front of the truck with a range of trinkets. An assortment of earrings, key chains, and cell phone parts stuck to the wiper blades as they hurtled toward the exit. Just before crashing through what appeared to be a large glass wall, a pair of automatic doors slid open. The truck's front caught the door frame, ripping it from the wall and splintering the massive panels. With the metal frame clinging to the outside of the vehicle, Marcus swerved to avoid a hideous piece of art near the sidewalk. His evasive maneuver took them across a short patch of grass and up over a shallow mound.

"Oh, shit," Marcus muttered.

He glanced over at Isabella, who was once again clinging to the grab handle. The massive vehicle cleared the knoll, rocketed through the air, and crashed into a vacant bus stand near the foot of the embankment. The tenacious mall door frame clattered to the ground, along with the shattered elements of the ill-fated booths. Marcus turned the wheel and slammed on the brakes as the vehicle slid into a car parked in a nearby handicap space.

Marcus glanced over at Isabella and hit the gas, the truck scraping its way free of the other car. As they left the parking lot, Marcus waved at the stunned pedestrians who had watched this display of automotive prowess.

"Left here."

An audible hiss filled the compartment as she directed him through a local neighborhood. The truck was sputtering and near death by the time she directed him into the open garage of a nondescript building. As the vehicle lurched to a stop, several men ran behind them and quickly pulled the paneled door shut, leaving them alone only with the fading protests of the dying truck.

Isabella shook her head and opened the door. "Next time, I drive."

CHAPTER SIXTEEN

If there ever was a religious war of terror, it was the crusades.
—MOUSTAPHA AKKAD

1105 A.D.
SAUDI ARABIA

THE HORSE WAS DEAD; it just didn't know it. Thomas clung to the beast as it stumbled up a shallow dune. He would have left it behind and continued on foot, but he was in no better shape than the horse. It had been at least two days since his last drink of water, and he did not know how long it had been since he had eaten. But hunger was the last of his concerns.

A soft breeze drifted across the barren desert. It was too dark to see that it was barren, but he knew it was. He had seen a hundred miles of this desert, and that was barren too. He could walk for another hundred miles, and that would be barren. He was sure the entire earth was barren.

As he dozed off, the earth gave way beneath him. He reached out to keep himself from falling when he realized it was just the horse collapsing. The two of them slid to the bottom of a sandy bowl.

As the sand stopped shifting around him, Thomas lifted his head and looked around. The horse was lying across his leg, its chest slowly rising and falling. Thomas did not have the energy to dig himself out, so he laid his head back and gazed into the sparkling sky. The moon was directly overhead, staring down at him like a curious child. It was clear and bright and beautiful. Everything Thomas wasn't. The damn thing reminded him of things he didn't want to remember. He tried closing his eyes, but they were too dry, and he had to keep them open.

Thomas kept thinking that he should be dead. He should have died a long time ago and should never have seen the things he had seen, should never have done the things he had done. He should never have found Rebecca, and God knows he should never have lost her. And if God existed, he should never see the morning sun.

Maybe that death might finally happen. He could feel his body giving in to the mortality that had stalked him for so many years. He thought maybe his nightmare was finally over, that he could stop running from his fate. But deep down, he knew he would come back again. It had been three hundred years since Rebecca died, and it never ended. The pain would never end.

The moon disappeared, replaced by a pair of shifting ghosts. Thomas was confused. He did not think angels wore robes. Then again, he was not expecting angels. The two murmured something to each other and then leaned over and pulled him from beneath the dead horse. He tried to stand, but with no success. He would have crumpled if not for their sure hands.

"Do not worry, my brother," one of them said, "we will be your legs this night."

"Have you come to take my soul?" Thomas's voice crackled as he looked into the dark cowl.

"No, we are just herding our sheep."

Thomas lay on a bed of pillows behind a wicker partition, staring up at the pale blue and white stripes of a canvas roof. He was still struggling to sit up when a woman appeared from behind the screen. She wore a black robe, with a thin black veil covering her face. She carried a pitcher which she used to fill a cup from a nearby table. She handed it to him and disappeared.

It was the best-tasting water he had ever had. He leaned over and poured himself a second cup.

"Not too much, my friend." The French accent was thick.

Thomas looked up to find a tall man standing beside the bed. His lean face was tan, except where a pale scar ran across one cheek. He too, wore a black robe, and a black scarf over his head, held in place by a triple ringlet. A thin black mustache sat beneath his crooked nose.

"Tastes good." Thomas took another sip.

"Yes...the longer you go without something, the better it is when you finally get it."

"Where am I?"

"The desert. I would have thought you'd figure that out."

"Where in the desert?"

"The ocean is ten days' ride in that direction." He pointed to his right, then to his left. "Or thirty days' ride in that direction. Jerusalem is fifteen days' ride back from where you came." He pointed straight ahead. "That way."

"Fifteen days?"

"With a horse...and you have no horse."

Thomas nodded and took another drink.

"Where were you going?"

"I don't know." Thomas set down the cup.

"Well then, you may already be there."

"Possibly."

"You are fortunate. We have a tradition in our tribe. Any man found wandering in the desert may stay with us and earn his freedom."

"How long does that take?"

"One year."

"And that makes me lucky?"

"Most other tribes would kill you on the spot."

"I still don't understand the lucky part."

"Good, I'm glad to see your sense of humor was not shriveled up like a raisin." He motioned toward the end of the bed. "This robe is now yours. It will be much cooler than the rags you were wearing."

"Thank you."

"You are welcome. You have one day to recover, but tomorrow you must join the others."

"Others?"

"Yes, the other men who work in this community...the single men. What is your name?"

"Thomas."

"Thomas. I have never met a Thomas. My name is Alabar al-wabib. I am the Khalid of this tribe."

Thomas shook his extended hand. He started to leave but stopped.

"One last thing, Thomas. Do not speak to the women. They may not interact with the non-believers."

"Yes, of course."

226

Thomas spent the next two weeks learning his new life. Most of the other men were suspicious of him but fair. As expected, they gave him the menial jobs. Thomas slept in a tent with the other single men and was never allowed to go anywhere by himself.

The camp was built inside a large wadi, surrounded by a labyrinth of river reeds and desert plants. A half-dozen palm trees towered over the tents. A large pool of spring-fed water was the lifeblood of their existence. The resulting foliage provided an abundance of dates and fruits, as well as building materials. Thomas learned quickly how desirable the location was.

He had been with the tribe for a little over a month when the first raiders struck. Sohail, one of the sheepherders, and Thomas had just finished their late-night watch and were lying in their tent. The two sentinels, having just gone on duty, were awake and alert. One of them sounded the alarm by blowing his horn. Thomas scrambled from the tent, along with a dozen other half-dressed men. The others wielded scimitars while Thomas stood there empty-handed. He had no time to ponder his misfortune, because one raider galloped around the tent and into their midst.

The other men scattered, trying to avoid the slashing blade of the marauder. Thomas ducked below his arm, grabbing his wrist as he swept by. Thomas yanked him from the horse and heard his arm snap as he crashed face-first into the ground, the sand muffling his scream. Stepping on his writhing body, Thomas picked up his discarded sword and ran toward the other men.

They were forming a semi-circle near the edge of the spring, with the women and children huddled behind them. Dozens of mounted men were riding through the camp, cutting down those who were trying to make it to the safety of the ring.

Thomas could see a mother guiding two children toward the group. Out of the corner of his eye, he saw the flash of a gray horse as it bore down upon them. Increasing to a full sprint, Thomas angled toward the woman and arrived just before the horseman. He stepped up onto a boulder, leaping into the air and smashing into the raider's chest. Tumbling to the ground, Thomas eventually came to rest on top of him, both of them having lost their weapons. Before he could react, Thomas grabbed his head with both his hands and snapped his neck.

Standing, Thomas looked for his lost sword. As he picked it up, he saw the woman and her children disappear into the circle of men. The horsemen, left with no stragglers to attack, were now milling about the camp. Thomas counted between forty and fifty attackers, nearly twice as many men as lived in the camp.

Thomas made his way to the others, watching the raiders. Sohail was the first to greet him.

"Thomas! I am so glad you made it!"

"Yeah, thanks for giving me a sword," Thomas said sarcastically.

"Oh, you are not supposed to have a sword."

They both looked down at his scimitar.

"Tonight, we make an exception." Alabar appeared by his side. "That was my sister you saved. I would say we are now even."

"We might want to get through the night, first."

"We'll be fine now. They'll not attack, now that we are ready."

"What'll they do?"

"They'll rummage through our belongings and leave by morning."

"And you're going to let them do that?" Thomas studied his face in the moonlight.

"That is what we usually do."

"Maybe that's why they keep attacking."

Sohail was quietly watching the exchange. Thomas could tell that Alabar was debating what he should do. Thomas helped him decide.

"Give me two minutes, then form up your men and go straight for that tent." Thomas pointed toward the tallest tent in the middle of the camp.

"What are you going to do?"

"Even the odds."

Thomas turned and jogged toward the gray horse standing over his dead rider. He grabbed his reins and hopped up into the strange saddle, spinning the horse toward the raiding party. As he had expected, most of them had dismounted and disappeared into the various tents. Thomas assumed the leader would be in the largest tent, hoping to gain the finest bounty.

Thomas spurred the horse forward, guiding him toward the front of the tent where three horses were milling around. He ducked as the horse burst through the opening, trampling one man as he tried to exit with an armful of gem-studded goblets. Slipping from the mount, Thomas dodged the scimitar thrust in his direction. He punched the attacker in the face, probably breaking his nose. Not satisfied, Thomas ran him through with his blade. That's when the third man set upon him.

Unfortunately, Thomas was not used to fighting with scimitars and did not realize they were better suited for slashing. He could not remove his sword from the dead man in time to meet the next attack, so he let go of the hilt and dropped to his knees. Crouched on the ground, Thomas could see a dagger inside the other man's boot. As he swept past, Thomas grabbed the blade and spun around behind him.

Before the man could turn around, Thomas stabbed him three times in the lower back. As he fell backward, Thomas grabbed his forehead and pulled his head back. Knowing brutality was the only language these men understood, Thomas slit his throat from ear to ear. He lay his body on the ground and used the scimitar to finish the job. Grabbing a handful of hair, Thomas carried his bloody head to the exit.

The raiders had gathered around the tent, drawn to the cries of their leader. Thomas stepped through the opening and lifted the head toward the crowd of men. He showed it to each one, then tossed it to the ground. Thomas looked around the circle, but none of the raiders would meet his gaze.

Thomas took a step toward the nearest man, who dropped the loot he carried and scrambled onto his horse. Within seconds, he galloped from the camp. As if on cue, Alabar suddenly appeared, leading a couple of dozen men. The raiders would have none of it and quickly joined their retreating comrade. Within seconds, only a cloud of dust remained. Alabar walked up to Thomas, his gaze dropping to the scimitar. Thomas handed him the weapon, then looked down at his bloody hands.

"You have done this before," Alabar said as he took the sword.

"A few times."

"We are a peaceful people. We defend ourselves, but we do not raid others."

"I understand that."

He studied Thomas for a long while. "You should get cleaned up. We'll talk of this tomorrow."

Thomas nodded and walked toward the spring, Sohail bowing as he passed.

Thomas slept well that night, much too well.

230

They were all staring at Thomas. He had awoken just after dawn and stepped from his tent to find a flurry of activity around the camp. They had disposed of all the dead bodies. The women were busy repairing the tents damaged in the attack, while the men were busy rebuilding the horses' pens.

Thomas stood at his tent exit, trying to find Alabar. He finally spotted him near the storage tent, next to a table covered with various fruits. Thomas made his way to him, ignoring the hushed whispers that accompanied his passing. He was finishing a handful of figs as Thomas arrived.

"Good morning," Thomas said.

"Yes, it is, thanks to you." He wiped his mouth with the back of his hand and tossed him a fig. "Are you hungry?"

"A little." Thomas caught the fruit and popped it into his mouth.

"Walk with me."

He was quiet, and Thomas looked over at him as they walked. Alabar rubbed his hands together as if cleaning them in water. He glanced at Thomas once, but quickly looked away. As they reached the boundaries of the oasis, he finally spoke.

"I used to be a soldier."

"Really?"

"Yes, when I was much younger. I was the fourth of eight sons. My father assumed I would never take over leadership of the tribe, so he sent me away to my uncle, who was a general in the Sultan's army."

Thomas nodded silently. They had passed onto the edges of the desert and into the gaze of the rising sun.

"I have been in two battles and many skirmishes."

"It's not a pretty thing."

"No, it's not." He turned toward Thomas. "I have known many excellent warriors, men who had no equal...that is, until last night. You are so fast! And skilled! You must be the greatest warrior alive!"

Thomas watched the sun shimmer as it crept into the light blue sky. "No, there's one better."

"I don't believe it!" He dismissed Thomas's reply with a wave of his hand. "One thing is for sure...you are no sheepherder."

"You saved my life, and I'm willing to do whatever you ask to repay that debt. I only ask to be treated like any other man."

"But you are like no other man!" He turned and pointed into the distance. "Those cutthroats have been raiding my tribe for three generations...and we could never stand up to them. But you single-handedly drove them away!"

"What do you want from me?"

"Teach my men. Teach them how to fight, how to defend our tribe. That's all I ask."

Thomas did not reply right away. It is one thing to kill a man and quite another to teach others to do it. It was like committing multiple sins at once. But then again, avoiding sin had not worked out for him. Thomas lifted his gaze and met Alabar's dark, anxious eyes.

"Alright, I will train your men."

"Outstanding!" He slapped his hands together. "The others will be delighted to hear!"

Thomas could get used to the heat, but not the sand. It found its way into the mouth, ears, and eyes. It turned sweat into sandpaper and made riding a horse a truly miserable experience. And the wind was picking up, which meant more sand.

Thomas looked to see how his companions were doing, securing his sash across the bottom part of his face. They rode in single file, following in the footsteps of his mount as they clung to their horses. Each of them led a camel laden with goods.

Twice a year, a party went to the nearest town to purchase supplies for the tribe. They would trade dried fruit, wool, and sheep for rice, sugar, and spices. On the last trip, Thomas had gone along as a guard, but this time he was in charge. Many things had changed over the previous year. Thomas was not only trusted; he was their leader.

Given a group of young men, Thomas had transformed them into a lean fighting force capable of protecting the tribe from its enemies. They had nearly annihilated two raiding parties, and the word had spread. There had not been an attack in almost four moons. As a result, they could bring more goods to the city and purchase luxuries for the tribe to make life much easier. The women would be pleased with the tiny treasures they had purchased.

The image of the women running to their husbands after the long absence flashed through his mind. Thomas ignored the tightening in his chest and studied the distant horizon. He could have had any of the single women in the tribe, but that would not have been fair to them. No part of him had anything left to give.

Thomas was lost in thought when they finished climbing a long, shallow dune. As the wind faded, the sky shifted to sunset. A smile crossed his face as he looked forward to a cool bath and a long night's sleep.

"Look!"

It was Sohail, the rider following right behind him. As Thomas lifted his gaze to the horizon, a knot formed in the pit of his stomach. There were several spirals of black smoke rising from the distant oasis.

Thomas shifted in his saddle, directing his gaze toward Sohail. "Pick one man to stay with the camels; the rest follow me."

Without waiting for a response, Thomas spurred his horse down the face of the dune. This close to the oasis, the sand gave way to flat, broken wasteland. As he reached the bottom, Thomas hunkered behind the neck of his steed and urged him forward.

Speeding across the open desert, Thomas should have heard the hoofs clattering against the splintered earth or the labored breathing of his beast as he struggled to please his master. Thomas should have heard the howling of the wind as it battered his robe and blew the scarf from his weathered face. But he did not. He only heard the pounding of his heart as it propelled blood through his tortured veins. And screams, screams that haunted his soul.

The first bodies lay near the oasis entrance, where several guards had made a futile stand. Thomas sped past the bodies and into the center of the camp. Most of the tents were dark outlines on the ground, their contents smoldering in the fading light. To his right, just beyond the broken fences of the animal pen, was a twenty-foot pile of bodies, charred and smoking. Thomas could see the horns and hooves of several goats, but otherwise, the mass was indistinguishable.

His stomach already churning, Thomas guided his horse toward another pile near the edge of the spring.

Alabar was tied to a post and surrounded by his family's bodies, along with the men who had fallen during the struggle. They had then lit the pile, burning him alive. His face was contorted with pain and anguish as he looked up toward the sky. Thomas dismounted from his horse as the others skidded to a halt beside him.

Some were calling the names of their loved ones. Thomas knew they would not receive an answer. Tears of rage rolled down his dust-covered cheek as he turned toward Sohail.

"One hour," Thomas said. "The men have one hour to make their peace. Then we ride."

Without waiting for a reply, Thomas walked away.

Thomas sat on a rock near the shallow pool's edge, staring down into the clear water. Several water bugs scooted along, sending tiny ripples across the smooth surface. He heard the soft crunch of Sohail's boots as he reluctantly approached. He stopped, then started to walk away.

"Sohail."

"Yes?"

Thomas was still staring down at the water. "Are they ready?"

"Yes...and no."

Thomas spun, his dark expression driving Sohail back a step.

"They want to know what we are going to do."

Thomas walked past Sohail and to the group of men waiting near the camp center. They had brought the camels in from the desert and unloaded them into a pile near a tall palm tree. Most of them were staring at the ground but looked up as Thomas approached. He studied each of them closely. All had lost someone in the raid.

"These were not normal raiders," Thomas said.

They looked up, puzzled expressions on their faces.

"Normal raiders would have plundered, not destroyed. It makes no sense to destroy if you plan on plundering again."

"Then who were they?" Mushad asked.

"Christians." Thomas tossed a silver cross onto the sand.

"Impossible." Sohail shook his head. "The closest Christian outpost is five hundred miles from here."

"It was...but they pushed south after consolidating their position in Jerusalem. My guess is they're expanding."

"Are you sure?" Sohail cocked his head to the side.

"Come see."

235

As Thomas walked to the entrance of the camp, the others followed close behind. He knelt beside a set of horse hooves and traced one with his finger.

"This is the hoof mark of one of our horses. Notice how small and sharp it is." Thomas pointed to another one next to it. "This is much wider and compressed. A much larger horse, with a heavier load, made this mark. Knights."

"How many?" one of them asked.

Thomas stood and brushed the sand from his hands. "Twenty-five, maybe thirty. They would have the same number of men in support, squires."

"Fifty or sixty men?" Sohail gasped. "There are only fifteen of us!"

"Yes, the odds are about even." The others looked at him anxiously. Thomas studied each one of their faces. "You have all lost much more than I, but that does not lessen my grief. You accepted me into this tribe, and now I ride to avenge them. I will quench my thirsty blade."

One by one, each man nodded in agreement. Satisfied, Thomas looked to Sohail.

"Bury the goods we brought from the city. If I am right, they may have taken some women and children as slaves. We will need these supplies to start over. Release the camels, they may stay here around the oasis, or they may flee. So be it. Pack the extra horses with all our gold and all the water we can carry. Be quick."

Thomas watched the men work. It was good for them; unoccupied sorrow is not healthy. By the time they left, most were too exhausted to grieve. They rode just as the moon topped the distant horizon, wrapping the desert in its soft brilliance. It was easy to see where the Christians had gone, and even a child could have followed the trail.

Thomas glanced back at the dark figures riding in the moonlight. Each one would have plenty of time to brood before they caught up with their quarry. He figured the Christians hit the camp at dawn, so they had a full day's head start. They would move slowly, with the captives on foot. Thomas calculated they would catch them by the following night.

They camped right after midnight and were moving again before dawn. Thomas was not sure how many of the men slept, but it was vital for them to try. Strung out in a thin black line, they crept across the desert. Early in the afternoon, Thomas sent one man to scout ahead.

He came back an hour later, his smile shining through the dirt and sweat.

"I found them!" He turned his horse around and pointed toward the horizon. "They camp just beyond that hill, near a dried-up well."

"Did they see you?"

"No, they are not looking back."

"That shall be their undoing."

The campfire was visible from a mile away. Thomas stood on top of a large dune and studied them in the disappearing moonlight. He could see several men near the outer edges of the firelight, sitting, not standing. Good, sitting men usually become sleeping men.

His first goal was to rescue the women and children. Then they would see to any revenge. Thomas went into the camp and saw how the prisoners were guarded. He waited until the moon had disappeared behind the distant mountains, then he crept up on the nearest guard. The man was slumped over, almost lying down on the sand. He died in his sleep.

Thomas continued to the ruins surrounding the abandoned well. He knelt in the shadows of a broken wall and carefully peered over the top. No one manned the dying campfire. A couple of dozen men were lying around the embers, rolled up in blankets. There were several other buildings in various states of disarray. The one to his right was the only one with a guard lying next to the door.

Thomas crept around the back of the building, sliding his dagger free as he made his way into the darkness between the two structures. He stopped near the corner of the building, less than two feet from the sleeping guard. Thomas looked toward the campfire, making sure the others were still sleeping. Satisfied they were, he leaned forward and, placing his hand over the guard's mouth, slit his throat. He might have been awake when he died.

Thomas dropped his body into the darkness, then crept back and kicked sand over the pool of blood. Next, he stepped into the room, kneeling by the doorway as his eyes grew accustomed to the darkness.

After a few minutes, Thomas was pleased to see dozens of bodies lying on the floor. He moved toward the nearest one, which was Alabar's oldest daughter. She bolted awake as he slipped one hand over her mouth. She struggled until Thomas leaned forward and whispered to her.

"Ashina, it is I, Thomas."

As she looked up at him, her frightened expression turned to one of relief. Thomas released his grip on her mouth and nodded toward the others.

"Wake them, but quietly...very quietly."

He moved to the door and watched the center of camp as she woke the others. When they were awake, she knelt beside him.

238

"How are we going to get out of here?" she asked.

"We're going to walk out." Thomas motioned for the others to come closer. "You'll go out the door and around the corner into the shadows. Go to the back of the building next to this one, then move straight out into the desert. You will find the others. Do you understand?"

They all nodded. Thomas looked at the two women holding infants.

"You must keep them quiet."

Nodding, they looked down at their sleeping babies.

"Alright, let's go."

He turned back to the door and peered out at the camp. All was quiet. He watched the sleeping men and used his left hand to motion them forward. It seemed to take forever for the last one to leave the room.

Twenty minutes later, Thomas stood watching the tearful reunions. Several of the men stood around the edge of the gathering, realizing their loved ones were not among those rescued. A few minutes later, they drifted into the darkness.

Thomas studied the fading firelight and set his jaw.

The following day, there was quite a commotion in the Christian camp. They scrambled around the ruins and fanned out into the desert. Thomas watched them from the top of the nearby dune, in plain sight. He was sure they saw him, but he did not care.

Thomas had left them only one horse, and as the morning breeze rippled his robe, he imagined the debate. They could try to walk to the nearest town, some forty miles to the north. On foot, they could probably make that journey in two days. But to keep up that pace, they would have to abandon their armor. Or they could send out a rider for help, which is what they

239

attempted to do. Thomas watched the horse streak across the desert, knowing his men waited less than two miles away.

Thirty minutes later, the horse returned without its rider. As the men gathered around the animal, they argued. They were trying to decide if they should set out on foot or wait for darkness and try another rider. Either way, Thomas knew it was only a matter of time. And he had plenty of that.

They broke camp around noon and set out across the desert. They had kept their armor and abandoned their booty. One of them rode into the distance as a scout. Not a smart move. The horse came back an hour later, without its rider. They learned their lesson, and from that point forward, the men took shifts riding the horse within the group's relative safety.

Thomas and his men paced the advance, always within sight. When they stopped, he stopped. The great dunes gave way to an arid, broken land littered with jagged boulders and thorny bushes. As the sun crept across the sky, the beleaguered marauders crept across the desert. They survived the first day but had traveled less than seven miles.

They sent one rider out that night, after sundown and before the moon had risen above the nearby mountains. It took nearly an hour to catch him. Now Thomas had three captives. The men wanted to kill the Christians outright, but he had a better idea.

As the morning sun broke, Thomas sent the riderless horse back. The Christians reluctantly broke camp and started across the desert. Again Thomas followed, his band hovering like vultures. By noon, some of the Christians began to discard their armor. Thomas smiled at Sohail and nodded toward the trail of equipment scattered across the sand.

"It is done."

By late afternoon, the once tight formation of men stretched out across the desert like a string of ants. When stragglers fell back far enough to lose sight of their companions, Thomas had his men sweep down and eliminated them.

Before dusk, the long line came to a stop and gathered around three bodies laid out in their path. They were the captives, stripped naked and covered with squished dates. The latter had attracted all sorts of desert insects. They were not dead, but they wished they were.

The Christians made camp, probably assuming it would be their last night on earth. Thomas' men killed the sentries as soon as the sun went down, and another set just after midnight. He waited until dawn to launch the final attack. Most of the enemy surrendered within minutes. He watched as his men disarmed and lined the haggard Christians before him. Thomas dismounted, looking up and down their number.

"Who is your leader?"

A tall man with short black hair and a long gray beard stepped forward.

"I am."

Thomas took a step toward him and undid the scarf covering his face.

"You attacked a camp in an oasis."

His eyes narrowed, and he raised his head in defiance. "Yes."

"Did they surrender?"

"Yes."

"Yet, you killed all the men and most of the women and children. The rest, you took into bondage?"

"Yes."

"Is this something your religion teaches?"

"We are at war with these pagans; our religion teaches us to defend ourselves against barbarians."

"Like me?" Thomas glared at him. "I have been in your magnificent halls, broken bread with your mighty kings. I have broken bread with your savior. I have forgotten more about

241

Christianity than any man could ever know." A wry smile crossed his lips. "And that is why I shall wipe it from the face of the earth."

The leader started to reply, but Thomas turned away. Nodding at Sohail, he instructed.

"Burn them...burn them all."

CHAPTER SEVENTEEN

There are three kinds of men;
those who are preceded by their shadow,
those who are pursued by it
and those who have never seen the sun.
—GERD DE LEY

MODERN DAY
ROME

THOMAS STOOD BEFORE THE massive window and looked out across the darkening city. The recent showers had discouraged even the most persistent tourists, forcing them to seek refuge within the thousands of cafes that dotted the ancient city.

He turned back toward the room, picked up a wineglass from a nearby desk, and stepped down into a recessed portion of the room. Moving around a coffee table, he settled into a dark leather sofa and took a sip. Swishing the wine gently in the glass, Thomas looked up from the swirling contents and peered at the Cardinal.

"I told you he would visit."

243

"Sure, you told me!" Ramirez said. "You should've beefed up my security. He almost killed me!"

"But he didn't." Thomas set the glass down, leaned back, and crossed his legs. "What did he say?"

"He wanted to know *when* and *where*."

"It's a good thing I didn't tell you, then. What else?"

"That's about it."

"I'm sure you offered to tell him where I was."

"No, of course not!"

Thomas looked down at the vibrating cell phone on the nearby table. He picked it up and looked at the number, then up at Rameriz. "He has my number?"

The Cardinal looked away as Thomas answered the phone.

"Hello. Yes...when?" Thomas checked his watch. "Where... yes, of course. I'll call when I reach the stop." He ended the call and looked at the Cardinal. "I guess he wasn't satisfied with you. He wants to meet with me."

"And you're going to do it?"

"Why not?"

"Aren't you going to trace his calls? Can't you do that with the towers?"

"I could, but he's fully aware of that. It would be a waste of time."

"So why are you going?"

"Because I have no good reason not to."

"He is going to try to change your mind."

"Probably."

"Or kill you."

"I don't think so." Thomas stood and took a long sip of wine.

Thomas sat in the back of the metro carriage. It was almost empty, with a dozen or so passengers seated throughout the car. That was to be expected this late on a weekday. He watched as the train slowed and stopped. Circo Massimo. The next stop would be Colosseo, so he pulled out his cell phone. As they started moving, he called Marcus back.

"I just passed Circo Massimo...Alright...Car 614. Got it."

He thought about calling in a strike team, but that could get messy. Marcus had picked a public place and a mobile one at that. There was no way of knowing which stop he would use to get on or off the train. Besides, every one of these Metro stations had three or four exits. Even Thomas did not have the resources for that. The train slowed and stopped at Colosseo, then started up again.

Ramirez was right, as much as Thomas hated to admit it. There was no good reason to meet with Marcus. It's not like Thomas owed him anything. Thomas knew he should just leave, but he also knew he would not. Something compelled him to stay, something he didn't understand. He never would.

Thomas stood as the train slowed and stopped at the Termini station. Following the other passengers from the train, he made his way to the turnstiles. Passing through, he followed the signs to the Orange line. Thomas held his pass to the scanner, moved through the gate, and out onto the platform. A few minutes later, the Orange train pulled in.

A knot formed in the pit of his stomach. How long had it been? 500 years? More? The sound of the braking train pushed the thought from his mind.

As promised, 614 was the last car. Even though it had an 'out of service' notice, he approached the door, and it opened so he could step inside.

Marcus was seated in the opposite corner, a large gash and

angry expression on his face. His shirt was untucked, which meant he was carrying. Thomas was not.

He sat on the bench across from Marcus. "Hello."

"Hi."

Thomas nodded at the scar on his forehead. "This afternoon?"

"Yeah."

"That was a big mess." The train door closed. "How's Isabella?"

"Pissed."

"I can only imagine." The rail car rolled forward.

"I didn't think you'd come," Marcus said.

"Call me curious."

"Curiosity killed the cat."

"We would be so lucky." He squinted. "What do you want, Marcus?"

"You once told me something; *don't make a mistake you might regret forever—because for us, forever is a very long time.*"

"I'm surprised you remember."

"Well, maybe it's you who forgot."

"No, no I haven't."

"Enlighten me. And don't give me that 'God is horrible' bullshit. We both know that's not why you're doing this."

"It's quite simple. I'm tired." Thomas glanced out the window, then back at Marcus. "I want it over. I don't care what comes next. I've been walking this planet for two-thousand years, and I'm sick of it. I'm sick of man, his greed, his cruelty. I'm sick of knowing I'll never die, that my memories won't go away."

Marcus nodded as the train leaned into a shallow curve. After a long silence, he said, "You're going to start the end of times so that you can die. Or go to the next life, or whatever."

"Yes."

"How many people will die because you made that decision?"

"Everyone has to die. At some point, this has to come to an end."

"Does it? What if it just keeps going?"

"My point exactly. I can't do this for another thousand years." He took a deep breath. "I'm not sure I could do it for ten more."

"Honestly, part of me agrees with you. I'm just as tired, but I couldn't do it. Not to so many people."

"I guess that's what makes us different."

"Perhaps." Marcus leaned forward. "Then I have to ask; Why did you let Isabella live...in Constantinople? The only explanation is that you intervened."

"It's what Rebecca would have wanted."

"You can say her name now." Marcus studied him for a long moment, and he realized. "He stopped it, didn't he?"

"Stopped what?"

"The memories... when you die. You don't see her anymore...?"

Thomas did not answer.

"He did that for you." He stopped and glared at Thomas. "What else did he promise?"

"Promise? Nothing. But what better revenge is there? I get to help the fallen angel regain his glory. Even if I lose, at least I tried. And yes, I don't relive the memories anymore. For that alone, it was worth it."

"You should have said no. I've learned to live with this, so could you."

"You're a better man than me."

Marcus dropped his gaze for a moment, then looked back up with glistening eyes.

"No, I'm not."

247

The train slowed, and Marcus got up, heading toward the exit.

"Marcus," Thomas stood and gripped his arm, "walk away... both of you can leave Rome tonight. Go somewhere and live in peace. I won't chase you, and you don't have to run."

"We're never going to live in peace."

Thomas released his arm and met his gaze. "You will not like how this story ends."

"Probably not." He started to walk away, then stopped and said, "I need to be there."

"Why?"

"I was there when it started, and I should be there..."

Thomas studied him as the train stopped. "The Castel Sant'Angelo. Be there before midnight. But you come as my prisoner. You'll be searched and will have a guard at all times."

"Fair."

He stepped off the train and turned back to Marcus. "And tell Isabella to stay out of my way. I've left her little group alone until now, but if she intervenes, I won't be so restrained."

The door closed, and the train left the station.

CHAPTER EIGHTEEN

We have fought this fight as long, and as well as we know how.
We have been defeated.
For us as a Christian people, there is now but one course to pursue.
We must accept the situation.
—ROBERT E. LEE

MODERN DAY
ROME

"I DON'T LIKE IT." Sam paced the living room of their safe house.

Isabella stood, hands on her hips. "I agree; too much could go wrong."

Marcus sat on a couch, sipping a glass of scotch. Both women waited for him to respond.

"You're right."

"So, what is the plan?" Sam stopped, arms crossed. "And I'm serious this time."

"I don't know. Get inside and kill the clone."

"Is that even possible?" Isabella asked.

249

"I don't know."

"You'll never get close enough...and you won't have a weapon," Sam said.

"Yeah, but I have to try. I'm not saying it's a brilliant plan, but what other choice do we have?" He looked from Sam to Isabella. They shrugged.

Marcus looked to Gustaf. "Can you do it?"

"Yeah," the Turk replied. His expression did not instill a great deal of confidence. "I'm just not sure how much weight it will hold, and for how long."

"What if they move you from the Castel Sant'Angelo? Or what if you can't get out to the roof?" Isabella said. "And why would he tell us where it will happen, anyway?"

"Because Thomas knows we can't stop it. They will have a dozen tactical teams on call. And it's a fortress, for Christ's sake. No, he's confident enough that he doesn't care if I'm there. Which means my only concern is getting out."

"I think it's too big of a risk," Isabella said.

"And I think it's our only option." Marcus looked to Gustaf. "Do what you need to do."

Nodding, Gustaf left the room.

Marcus looked back to Isabella. "No matter what happens, we need to get out of Rome. Get that sorted, but don't give me the details."

"Oh, I wasn't going to."

An hour later, they were sitting around a table, and Gustaf handed Marcus a watch.

"It doesn't look like a smartwatch, and it won't start transmitting until you press both these buttons. Even then, it only records for 10 seconds, then sends the signal out in a quick burst. Nearly undetectable by a scanner."

Marcus took the watch and slipped it on.

"This," Gustaf handed him a belt, "is made from Cordura fabric. It should hold up well to friction."

"Should?"

"I had an hour. I haven't had time to field test it."

"Good point." He looked around the table to Sam and Isabella. "Any other ideas?"

"No," Isabella said. "You'll never get a gun past their security."

"Suicide pill?" Sam suggested.

"Too slow," Isabella said. "If we had time, we could work on some plastic explosive."

"I'm glad you guys have so many great ideas on how to kill me. But I'll be fine. I was thinking about getting out *without* dying."

"Then, no." Isabella shrugged. "The only other option is a helicopter. And they would watch for that. Plus, I can't pull that off on this timeline."

"The belt it is." Marcus slipped it through the loops of his pants.

Marcus climbed on the bus and sat near the back. He stood as they approached his stop and slipped out the backdoor. He found himself standing before the Sacred Heart Church of the Intercession. It looked open, and he was early, so he went in.

It was warm inside, and most of the lights were off. Marcus had never really studied architecture, though he was fascinated by the human infatuation with these majestic structures. He was sure there were a dozen interesting points to the church, but he did not care. He moved to the far corner of the room and slipped into the empty stall, closing the door behind him. Sitting down, he peered through the veiled opening.

"Forgive me, Father, for I have sinned."

The confessor glanced at the dark screen.

"And what sin have you committed, my son?"

"I killed Jesus Christ."

"What?" The bench creaked as the old priest leaned forward. "Is this some sort of joke? I have no time for such things."

"I wish it were a joke—believe me, I do." He studied his hands for a moment before continuing, his voice cold and empty. "My name is Marcus Sempronius Gracchus; I am the son of Proculus Sempronius Gracchus and a soldier of Rome. Two-thousand years ago, I drove my spear into the side of Christ..."

The two suffered through a long, uneasy silence that the nervous priest finally broke.

"I'm sorry, but I don't think I can help you," he replied.

"I'm not looking for help; I'm not sure I'm looking for anything."

"Then why are you here?"

"I don't know. Sometimes, I just have to tell someone new." Marcus stood to leave. "I guess this was one of those times."

"Marcus?"

"Yes?" He stopped and looked back toward the screen.

"May God have mercy on your soul."

A shadow hung across his haggard face. "I think it's too late for that."

He left the warmth behind him and headed toward the Castle. Typically, it would be closed, but a single guard stood next to the open door. He assumed a half-dozen more were hidden around the entrance. Probably a strike team was waiting in a building nearby.

As Marcus approached, the guard stepped aside and waved him through the entry. Following behind, the guard closed and locked the door. Three men waited inside, one with a hand-held scanner.

"Jacket off," he said.

Marcus removed his jacket and lifted his arms. They

scanned him with the metal detector, then used a device to look for a transmitter. Another guard did a pat-down.

"Whoa, buddy!" Marcus shifted when the guard checked his groin area. "I don't even know your first name."

"He's clean."

"Phone." The man held out his hand.

"In the jacket."

The guard looked at his wrist, so Marcus turned it for him to see.

"Timex." Marcus pressed the button, and a little light came on.

Grunting, the guard nodded to the others. They moved to a metal door marked for authorized personnel only. As they waited for a guard to unlock the door, Marcus put his hands behind his back and pressed both buttons on his watch. When the door swung open, they walked through and started down a metal staircase, where another set of stairs led up into the building. They stopped two flights down as one of the men unlocked a door and motioned him through. He noticed all the doors had push levers from the inside.

They walked down a long hallway, stopping in front of a door near the end. They knocked, and a few moments later, Lazarus pulled the door open. He looked Marcus up and down, and nodded for the men to leave.

"In here." Lazarus stepped to the side. "Have a seat."

It was a small viewing gallery with two rows of stadium seating that faced a long window, curtains drawn.

"Medical suite for the Pope?"

"Usually." Lazarus sat a few seats down from Marcus and shook his head.

"What?" Marcus asked.

"I've been chasing you for God knows how long, and then you just show up." Lazarus shook his head. "Fucking annoying."

"Yeah, I have that effect on people."

"But it was fun. I always appreciated your creativity."

"I don't feel very creative."

The door opened, and Thomas walked in. He looked at Marcus, then Lazarus.

"You searched him?"

"Yes, sir. But I still don't trust him."

"I do." Thomas walked over and sat next to Marcus. "I trust him to try something stupid."

Marcus raised both hands. "I have no plan."

Even as he said it, Marcus thought that Isabella and Sam would be listening and probably agreed.

Thomas nodded for Lazarus to open the curtains.

Two doctors hovered over a man lying beneath a blanket on a stainless-steel table; one was administering an IV while the other monitored the diagnostic equipment. A green surgical blanket covered the subject on the table, but Marcus could see some of his hair poking out from underneath. Marcus swallowed past the lump in his throat.

"What are they doing?" Marcus asked.

"A sedative," Thomas said. "He's in a comatose state—for now."

"He's fully mature?" Marcus turned his head, but his eyes stayed fixed on the table.

"Yes, quite—a delicate combination of growth hormones and stabilizers." Thomas squinted. "It took us several tries, but we finally perfected the process."

"And the failed attempts?"

Marcus waited, but Thomas did not reply. Instead, he nodded to Lazarus.

Lazarus flicked on the intercom. "Please remove the IV and clear the room."

The doctors left, and a few moments later, Cardinal Ramirez and two other men walked in, one of them carrying an enormous book. Ramirez opened the book to a predetermined page as they approached the table in the center of the room. The two men went to stand on each side of the table. Everyone but Ramirez wore earmuffs. Marcus remembered reading in the ancient text that the initiator was immune to the ritual.

Marcus watched as the Cardinal read from the forbidden Latin text, his voice settling into a rhythmic cadence. The air grew still as the form beneath the blanket trembled, then convulsed as if gripped by a seizure. The men standing around the table looked to Thomas, who motioned for them to hold the body down. As the ritual continued, Marcus felt somehow drawn to the ancient verse, a longing that grew more persistent with each passing moment. He could feel the words tugging at his soul. At first, it was a tender invite, like the whisper of a lover. But with each reading of the passage, it became more insistent, and soon it called to him like the ancient sirens calling to the Greek sailors.

A low, sorrowful groan, barely audible above the Cardinal's chant, slowly increased to a menacing wail. The Cardinal, with relentless determination, shouted above the howl, both hands extended toward the table. The uproar reached a maddening crescendo, but the Cardinal seemed immune to the din. He made one ultimate gesture toward the body as if he were ripping something from the animated figure, which arched violently and then collapsed onto the steel table with a grief-stricken sigh.

"It is done," Thomas said.

The Cardinal, his face pale and sweaty, crumpled to the floor. Thomas nodded, and several men moved to pick up the lifeless figure.

"What's wrong with him?" Marcus asked.

"Oh, he's dead, heart attack."

"What?"

"The ritual. That's why no one does it—or at least one reason."

"Did he know that?"

"Goodness no," Thomas said. "He would never have volunteered."

"I can't say that I am disappointed...but still."

"Gotta break some eggs..." Thomas nodded his head toward the room. "He'll want to meet you."

A chill ran down his spine, and Marcus could only nod in response. He followed Thomas out of the room and into the medical suite, Lazarus close behind.

The blanket had fallen to the ground, revealing a man wearing black pants and a white cotton shirt. As Marcus came to his side, he saw the clone's empty features and his eyes, dark as pitch, staring blankly at the ceiling. But everything else about him was eerily familiar—too familiar. After a few seconds, Marcus turned away.

"Technology is an amazing thing." Thomas stood next to him, staring back at the body.

"Don't do it." Marcus fixed his gaze on his onetime friend. "Don't—"

"It's beyond my control," Thomas cut him off.

"When?"

"Midnight."

Marcus looked at his watch; it was less than a minute away. He shifted his attention to the clone's hands, and the fingers twitched. A few moments later, the figure sat up, then stood.

As Marcus looked up, his eyes settled on the risen savior. No, not that blue-eyed, blonde-haired savior who Europeans had been painting for a thousand years. This was the true savior. In the flesh.

He was devastatingly beautiful. Not sexually, though perhaps some might think so. He was like a late summer desert sunset or a set of ocean waves crashing against a shoreline; perfect. Though Marcus could not quite pinpoint what made him so striking, taken as a whole, the man was exquisite in every way. That said, there was nothing particularly unusual about him. He was tall for his race, maybe 5'8", with broad but slender shoulders and a narrow waist. His dark skin was smooth and without blemish. A long, broad nose sat between a pair of high cheekbones. His jawline was strong yet subtle. His lips were full but precise. And his white teeth were perfect when he smiled. And then there were his eyes...But were they his? These eyes were dark, complex, callous. It was like Marcus was staring into the abyss, an abyss that consumed all light and hope. The sense of impending disaster was overwhelming, and within seconds, Marcus's soul felt cold and drained.

"Hello Marcus, I didn't expect you here." *He* glanced at Thomas, who shrugged in response. "I'm glad we have the gang all together. I'm sure Isabella is close by."

"She left the city," Marcus replied, having recovered from his initial shock.

"Sure she did." *He* grinned. "So, I imagine you came to stop all this?"

"No," Marcus looked from Thomas to *Him*, "it was too late for that."

"Apparently. Then why did you come? Have you decided to join us?"

"Not interested," Marcus said.

"Then why are you here?" *He* asked.

"Call me curious."

"Curiosity can get you killed."

"Wouldn't be the first time."

He held out his hand to Lazarus. "Give me your gun?"

Frowning, Lazarus looked to Thomas.

"Why are you looking at him?" *He* snapped. "Give it to me."

Lazarus pulled the gun from the holster in his jacket and handed it to *Him*. Marcus watched closely, mentally deciding which of the three men he would incapacitate first. It would have to be the clone since he now had the gun, but Thomas would be second.

He took the weapon and pulled back the slide, confirming there was a round in the chamber. *He* released the slide and flipped the gun around, handle facing Marcus.

"Let's get this over with."

Marcus looked at *Him*, then at Thomas. The latter had a puzzled look on his face. Marcus reached forward and took the handgun. It felt heavier in his hand than expected. He raised it and pointed at *Him*, his finger hovering over the trigger.

"Go on, it's not like you haven't done this before," *He* sneered.

The weapon trembled ever so slightly, then Marcus set his jaw and pulled the trigger. The round hit *His* forehead, right between the eyes. There should have been a tiny hole and a massive blood splatter on the nearby wall from the exit wound, but there was not. There was no wound. His head snapped back a few inches, then the bullet dropped to the floor, bouncing a few feet away.

"I wasn't sure how this was going to work." *He* chuckled. "I thought it would hurt; I'd start bleeding all over the place, then I'd recover. I rather prefer this."

With Thomas and Lazarus just as surprised, Marcus realized this was his best chance to escape. He swung his weapon around.

"Sorry."

Marcus pulled the trigger, the gun aimed at Thomas's head. As Thomas fell to the ground, Marcus spun around and fired at Lazarus, one round missing his head, the second catching his shoulder. Before Lazarus hit the ground, Marcus was already bolting to the door.

He called after him, "I'm not done with you Marcus!"

Marcus reached the door, pulling it open as *He* yelled after him, "I want him alive!"

There were a dozen men in the hallway, all of them holding batons or stun rods. Luckily, the room was at the end of the hallway, so none were behind him. He knew Lazarus would be close behind, so he had to move fast. Most concerned by the rods, he concentrated his initial fire on the two closest men holding them. He used two rounds apiece to take them out. He focused the rest of his fire down the hallway. Several of the men were down by the time he ran out of bullets. He dropped the pistol and quickly bent over to pick up one of the stun rods.

It was tight quarters, but his speed and the ability to take punishment proved invaluable allies. He sprinted forward and quickly dodged the first blow from the closest guard. He then came up hard with an uppercut. But the maneuver slowed him down and left him open to attack. The next guy caught him in the rib cage with a baton. He felt a rib crack, but that also meant the man was closer than he should be.

Marcus smashed his elbow into the attacker, then followed with a vicious blow to his head with the baton. He could hear the man's skull crack as he moved on to the next two. They hesitated. Already, half their team was incapacitated, and Marcus had been in the hallway for less than ten seconds.

He took advantage of their trepidation and sprung forward. Marcus blocked one attack with his baton and drove his foot into the man's chest. The man stumbled back, knocking down the other assailant. Marcus could not avoid the thrust of the other attacker, whose stun rod hit his side. Marcus's torso felt like it was on fire as the electricity exploded through him. He fell to his knees but lashed out with his fist, catching the man in the groin. The man dropped his weapon, clutching his crotch.

Marcus climbed to his feet, still fighting the lingering effects of being electrocuted. One man stood blocking the exit. The guard was holding a baton, but he dropped it and pulled a gun from his jacket.

Marcus grinned and thought, *Good, now I'll have a gun.*

The man fired off one round that tore through the soft flesh of Marcus' shoulder. Two seconds later, the man was lying unconscious on the floor, and Marcus pulled open the exit door, gun in hand.

Marcus fully expected another team inside the staircase, but there was none. He could hear yelling from the levels below and was sure that indicated additional strike teams. He had no plans to go down. Sprinting up the steps, he ignored the sharp pains that jabbed through his side each time he took a breath.

"He's going up!" The familiar voice filled the stairwell.

Lazarus was back in the game. Two levels up, he reached the end of the staircase and burst through the door, finding himself on the roof of the building. The city lights filled his view in every direction. The Vatican, lit up like a Christmas tree, dominated the skyline in the near distance. Above him, the bronze statue of Saint Michael stood upon a square pedestal, behind it a metal pole with several wires hung from it. But those were not the wires Marcus was looking for.

"I'm on the roof." The message would go out in about ten seconds.

Marcus examined the pedestal facing the River Tiber, hoping Gustaf had delivered as promised. At first he didn't see it, then he noticed a metal hook caught around the arm of the statue. Unbuckling his belt, he pulled it out and followed the wire toward the fortress walls. It extended over the wall, above the plaza, before cutting across the St. Angelo Bridge and disappearing over the Tiber river. Marcus assumed it was anchored somewhere on the far side. As he approached the edge of the roof, the door he had exited burst open. Marcus fired several shots in that direction and then dropped the gun.

Standing on the wall, the wire hung a few feet above his head. He wrapped the belt twice in his hand and flipped the buckle over the wire. Grabbing just above the clasp, he stepped off the wall and zipped towards the river.

He heard yelling behind him, then gunshots. He was zipping along at some speed now, so he hoped it would be difficult for them to see or hit him. But the sheer number of bullets they fired made up for their precision. One round caught his calf. He heard several more buzz past his head.

Marcus looked up, hoping the belt would not melt from the friction. He had reached the river, but the wire's trajectory had taken him over the St. Angelo bridge. He was fifteen feet above it when the belt snapped.

"Oh shit," he said as he plummeted.

It looked like he might miss the bridge, his feet just skimming past its walls. But his upper body was not so lucky. His left arm and shoulder crashed into the unforgiving stone, immediately shattering his clavicle and scapula. His head grazed the railing, and he was knocked unconscious. Seconds later, his body splashed into the water.

EPILOGUE

Never confuse a single defeat with a final defeat.
—F. Scott Fitzgerald

MODERN DAY
NAPLES, ITALY

AROUND MIDNIGHT, Gustaf drove them to the docks, stopping near a chain-link fence.

"Good luck," Gustaf shifted the car into park.

"Thanks, we'll need it. Stay low, and I'll be in touch," Isabella said.

The three of them slipped into the cool evening air, and the car pulled away.

"Is he going to be okay?" asked Sam.

"Yeah, he's not on Thomas' radar. He can move around easier." There was a sadness in her eyes. "He wants to see if anyone from his team survived."

"Got it." Sam turned back toward the dock. "Whoa."

Marcus chuckled when he spied the old steamer.

"You were expecting a cruise ship?" Isabella inquired pointedly.

"No," he replied with a smile, "but something built after World War II would've been nice."

"Considering all that is going on, I'd think you'd be a bit more appreciative." She glared at Marcus. "Maybe I should have left you in the river. Perhaps, you could have floated out of town."

Marcus winked and moved to open the door, grimacing as he shifted his weight.

Isabella looked at Sam in the rear-view mirror. "And don't say anything to the captain. He is very sensitive."

"Maybe he should try a fresh coat of paint," Sam said.

Perhaps the steamer had been painted, but the flaking white remnants of the endeavor were all but gone. It was hard to say precisely how old the tramp freighter was, and even harder to know what various names this derelict vessel had sailed under. Currently christened the *Alexandroupolis*, she boasted a Greek flag, to nobody's surprise.

The captain, a short, stocky fellow with greasy hair and shiny olive skin, waited for them on the dock. He stood with both hands buried in his dirty blue overalls while chewing the remains of a cheap cigar, the little brown nub rolling back and forth across his chapped lips. A pair of plump cheeks threatened to blot out his fidgety eyes. He paid particular attention to Marcus, who limped as he struggled to stay up with the others.

"Madame." He nodded to Isabella.

"Captain." Her eyebrows creased when she noticed a smaller tanker alongside the freighter. "Are we not ready to leave?"

He followed her gaze but quickly shrugged off her question. "There was an issue refueling, but that's fixed. We're almost ready." The captain recognized the suspicious eye Marcus was casting upon the freighter. "She does not look like much, but she has two brand-new turbines and a well-seasoned crew. I've navigated more water than a horny dolphin, and not once have I lost a ship or cargo." He paused, a twinkle flashing in his dark-brown eyes. "Well, not one that I didn't mean to lose."

"That's very comforting," Marcus said.

Ignoring his sarcasm, the captain jabbed a stubby finger toward their vehicle. "What's the cargo?"

"Us." Isabella met his gaze.

He paused for a moment, looking at the sling Marcus had on his left arm. A silent war waged between caution and greed. As in most cases, greed prevailed, and he flicked a thumb toward the nearby metal gangway.

"At least human cargo loads itself. Though that one," he pointed at Marcus, "looks like he needs a wheelchair."

"I'll be fine," Marcus assured him.

Grunting, the captain walked away.

Taking their cue from Marcus, Sam and Isabella waited patiently for him to proceed. After prying his gaze away from the vessel, Marcus turned to Isabella. "You trust him?"

"Yes."

He waited for her to elaborate, but she was not so inclined.

"All right. I've ridden on worse old crates—although the last one sunk a hundred miles out of port."

"Wonderful." Sam fell in behind him, shaking her head. "I'm sleeping in a life-jacket."

Marcus watched as the city disappeared into the dark horizon, leaving him alone on the ancient sea. The twin propellers of the old freighter tore through the murky water, generating a bright frothy wake that the undulating swells meticulously erased. The moon had deserted its majestic throne in favor of a more secluded haven behind a set of puffy gray clouds.

"You okay?"

"I feel like I fell off a ten-story building," he mused, "and got shot a couple of times on the way down."

"What a surprise."

Marcus looked up to find Isabella standing beside him, the cool breeze whipping at her hair. She wore a black turtleneck sweater that accentuated the fullness of her breasts and her slender waistline. His gaze met hers, and he quickly realized how much he had missed her.

"Well, at least I had a plan," he quipped.

"Part of a plan."

He tried to smile, but it faded before it could set. She studied the troubled lines that had creased his chiseled features.

"Marcus, what happened to Cormac was not your fault. And neither was what happened this morning."

"Really?" He met her gaze. "Whose fault was it?"

"Cormac knew exactly what he was doing. We all do."

"His death was meaningless." He looked back toward the sea.

"You know better than that." She lifted one hand to his chin and turned his eyes to hers. "Don't ruin the sacrifice he made with your self-pity."

"I'm just tired. Tired of it all. I just want it over."

The words hung between them, finally fading with her soft reply.

"Marcus, it's not your place to choose when and where this journey ends."

"So, what do we do now?"

"We fight on until none of us remain."

"That's the problem...I always remain."

He looked over to see her studying him in the moonlight.

"You should get some sleep."

"I will." He turned back toward the horizon.

"There's plenty of room in my cabin."

His heart skipped a beat as her hand slipped over his. He did not respond. Instead, he kept his gaze fixed on the rippling surface of the water.

"I once thought I couldn't compete with her, but I'm willing to try."

"I know." He gazed into her sparkling green eyes. He felt a yearning to lean over and kiss her, to take her into his arms, and never to let her go. He remembered the years of loneliness and solitude and realized that it could all go away with just one kiss. But the emptiness in his soul prevented him from reaching for her. He was scared that he might pull her into that emptiness and that it would consume them both. His mouth went dry.

"I want to..."

She forced a smile, her frustration poorly masked.

"Our timing is always off." She leaned forward and kissed his cheek, her lips hot and tender on his cool skin. Stepping back, she met his gaze. "Goodnight, Marcus. When you're tired of sharing your bed with demons, you know where to find me."

She disappeared into the night, just like the wake of their ship.

Thomas lay in the hospital bed, picking at the bandage around his head when *He* walked in. *He* had changed into a dark suit, and someone had cut his hair.

"How are you feeling?"

"Fine." Thomas tugged at the bandage again. "I don't need this."

"Two more inches to the right and I'd have been waiting three days to have this conversation."

"Yeah. I'm just fast enough not to get killed."

"I'm glad you brought him. It was worth the opportunity to bottle him up and have him out of our hair." *He* sat down in a chair by the window. "And now he knows I'm invulnerable."

"I think he got the message." Thomas shifted in the bed. "You want me to go after him?"

"No, send Lazarus. He won't catch him, but he's just competent enough to keep Marcus on the run. And out of our way."

"So we can do what?"

He pulled out a pack of cigarettes.

"You're going to smoke in a hospital?"

"Yeah, why not?"

"Because it will set off a bunch of alarms, and we don't need that attention."

"Shit," *He* put the pack away and shifted in his chair. "Have you heard of the Seal of Solomon?"

"It's a fairy tale, made up in the 17th century."

"Most fairy tales have some kernel of truth," *He* replied philosophically. "The seal exists, or at least it did. It's broken into pieces and scattered across the globe. We are going to find those pieces."

"Why?"

"The seal can open the gates of hell and take control of what lies within."

"Demons...?"

"Yes."

"How many?"

"Millions, I suppose, I never really counted." A subtle grin graced his lips.

Thomas hesitated, his mouth going dry. "And then what?"

"Then I take this world."

"And the humans?"

"They'll have their place...someone has to do all the work."

Thomas looked down, a chill running up his spine. He tried to picture those demons spilling out of hell, or at least what he imagined them to look like.

"Don't worry, Thomas. You'll have a place in the new world."

Thomas shook his head. "I don't want one. Like we agreed, when this is over, I'm done. I want out."

"If you say so."

"I don't understand. If that's the plan, why haven't I been collecting the pieces of the seal?"

"What fun would that be? And to be honest, I don't trust you, or anyone, with the seal. Who knows, the seal might even control me." He smiled, "How awkward would that be?"

Thomas forced a smile, then asked, "Okay, where do we start?"

"We have the center piece already, in the Vatican vaults. They just don't have any idea what it is. As for the rest, let's say I have my sources."

"Tell me where, and I'll send teams to get them."

"Nope, we do this one at a time, and I go on every mission. Like I said, I don't trust anyone." The grin reappeared. "You know, this all should have been so much easier."

"What's that?" Thomas asked.

"The plan I brought to *God* was simple; all the souls come down in human form. We let them live their lives, by the rules, of course. We don't let them sin, or stray, or rebel. I promised to return every soul to heaven." His eyes smoldered, and his voice turned to gravel. "But that wasn't good enough. *God* wanted man to have *free will*...*God* wanted man to choose redemption, not be forced back to *Him*."

Thomas swallowed but did not speak. There was a long, painful silence that *He* used to regain his composure.

"So, we disagreed. And I left."

Thomas suspected otherwise, but remained silent.

"And here we are." *He* stood to leave. "Get some rest, Thomas. We begin in two days."

Thomas watched him leave, then tugged at his bandage, smirking; *Marcus, you self-righteous son of a bitch, I can't believe you just shot me!* Then, just as swiftly, his expression shifted to somberness as a new, ominous thought crossed his mind: *My God, what have I done?*

DEAR READERS

Thank you for reading my debut novel!

This book has been twenty+ years in the making. It has endured endless edits, cuts, additions, tweaks and rewrites. My hope is that you enjoyed the end product! If so, then please spread the word! And do not worry, *Book Two: Abyss* will release in late summer or fall of 2021! The final installment is targeted for release in Spring of 2022.

Now, I am going to ask for one more thing. If you enjoyed the book, please take a few moments to leave a review on Amazon and Goodreads (links on the following page). It may not seem important, but reviews are the absolute lifeblood of independent authors. You don't even have to write anything, just tossing me a few stars will suffice (the more, the better). Thirty seconds of your time can help me for a lifetime!

I think this is the beginning of a beautiful friendship,
B.K.

HOW TO LEAVE A REVIEW

Amazon

- Go to your order detail page
- In the US - Amazon.com/orders
- In the UK - Amazon.co.uk/orders
- Click **Write a product review** button next to your book order.
- Rate the item and write your review and click **Submit.**

Goodreads

- Go to goodreads.com
- Search for by author or book title
- Click on the **star rating** under the book cover
- Then you can choose to leave a review

ACKNOWLEDGEMENTS

Thanks to all those that have supported my writing endeavors. My family for putting up with my endless hours of hidden away in my office. Friends who suffered through terrible Beta versions of my book. Professional colleagues who guided me through the publishing process.

I have enjoyed incredible support from my wife Sonya and kids, Chris and McKenna. As well as friends and family (you all know who you are). I am forever grateful for their steady praise, honest feedback, harsh criticism, and above all, endless encouragement.

Any success I have as a writer will be erected upon the foundation of their enthusiasm. Lastly, thank you, the readers, for making it all worthwhile.

ABOUT THE AUTHOR

B.K. Greenwood was born in New Hampshire but moved to Chandler, Arizona as a young kid. In 2014, he relocated to Austin, Texas, where he now resides with his wife and wolfpack of 4 rescue dogs. When not writing, he enjoys board games, taking the pups on new hikes, and building things in his workshop.

B.K. loves to travel and has incorporated his experiences into his writing. He reads works of fiction and nonfiction, emphasizing history, adventure, and classics. His passion for history is on display in his series, *The Last Roman.*

LET'S STAY IN TOUCH!

Click the +**Follow** button on my Amazon author page. **author. to/bkgreenwood**

If you want even more details about upcoming releases, then please join my email list.

www.bkgreenwood.com

Not only will you receive updates on my upcoming releases, but you will also receive a free ebook copy of my short story. *Monsoon*: A Last Roman Story, as a thank you.

facebook.com/bkgreenwood
twitter.com/bkgreenwood70
instagram.com/bkgreenwood70

BOOK TWO: ABYSS - PREVIEW

There is no greater unknown than the sea
and no greater mystery than a lost ship.
—CLIVE CUSSLER

NOVEMBER 1910 A.D.
VIENNA, AUSTRIA

The dull, gray sky glared at him like a tyrant. His ragged clothes, soaked by a recent downpour, clung to his shallow frame and produced such violent shivers that he dropped his leather journal. The notebook splashed into a shallow puddle by his feet. Falling to his knees, he watched in horror as the water seeped into the pages, consuming the charcoaled lines of his grandiose designs. A gust of wind scattered the pages, revealing one ruined drawing after another. He reached back, settling onto the cold stone step behind him. As the water consumed the last of his sketches, he realized the previous three months spent on the architectural designs had been a waste of time. No one would ever see him as anything but a wretched street artist. He was a complete failure.

He snatched up the journal, tore out the pages, and squeezed them in his bony hands as he raised them above his head and cursed the angry sky. A couple strolling by gave him a wide berth as they hurried past. He stared down at the crumpled papers and tossed them to the ground. As the wind swept away the tattered sheets, he skulked up the steps to the entrance of the *Schatzkammer*. At least the museum would provide shelter from the winter cold.

The young man ignored the doorman's scowl, and stepped inside, wandering the cavernous halls of the royal treasure house. He paid little attention to the various items on display, preferring to sneer at the brief descriptions posted by each exhibit. In his mind, none of the relics represented the true origins of the Germanic people. The baubles were merely tokens to appease the mass of tourists that poured through the museum each summer. The Habsburgs needed something to legitimize their rule, so the *Reichskleinodien*, a collection of crowns, scepters, and swords, became the symbol of their crumbling dynasty.

He rounded a corner and paused before a large mirror to inspect his filthy clothes and dirt-encrusted hands. There was no need to reach into his pocket to confirm that no money lay within. All his belongings were in the corner of the rat-infested hovel he shared with a dozen other vagrants. He had lived so long in perpetual starvation that he rarely acknowledged the constant hunger pangs. It was during this appraisal of his bitter existence that a small cluster of foreigners invaded his solitude. Annoyed by their intrusion, the young man tried to ignore the female guide lecturing the group. He was successful in doing so until a single phrase punctuated his sanctuary and shook the very foundations of his soul.

"There is a legend associated with this spear. If the possessor can solve its mysteries, he will hold the destiny of the world in his hands, be it for good or evil."

Heart pounding in his chest, the young man watched the guide and waited for her to continue.

"This is the *Holy Lance*, or sometimes called, the *Spear of Longinus* or *Spear of Destiny*; it is said to be the very weapon thrust into the side of Jesus Christ." She nodded towards the item on display. "The talisman's history is traced back to the Emperor Otto the Great and several other German leaders, including Frederick Barbarossa. Frederick was carrying the relic the day he died. He was crossing a stream in Sicily when he dropped the spear, and soon after fell from his horse and drowned."

The young man shifted his eyes from the speaker and studied the object in question. It was two pieces, both of which sat within a faded leather case. One was the head of the spear, broken off below the blade. A long spike lay along its length, held in place by various colored threads. A second piece, the base, was covered with several gold crosses.

The guide continued, "During the last five hundred years, only one man gave credence to the legend of the spear. After defeating the Austrians at the Battle of Austerlitz, Napoleon demanded the talisman. But his designs went unfulfilled. Government operatives smuggled the spear from Nuremberg, its historical resting place, and hid it in Vienna. It has resided here ever since. Any questions before we move on to the Crown of Bohemia?"

As the group drifted away, the young man stepped closer to the exhibit's rope boundary. The iron blade called to him as if it longed for a familiar touch. He gazed down at his open hand and could feel the cool surface of the spearhead on his sweaty palm. The stirring within his soul suggested he had held the ancient talisman long ago. He lifted his eyes once again to the weapon and fell into a hypnotic trance broken only when the guards announced the museum's closing.

Weakened by the experience, he stumbled down the steps

of the Schatzkammer, oblivious to the driving rain. He had climbed the steps a poor, broken wretch. He came back down them, a driven young man. Adolph Hitler had found his destiny.

MAY 7TH, 1945 A.D.
SOUTH ATLANTIC

"Captain, sonar reports a contact." The young sailor glanced up at his superior.

The captain, who looked more like a schoolteacher than a royal naval officer, grabbed the pair of binoculars hanging around his neck and moved to the front of the bridge.

"Heading, Mr. Hopper?"

Hopper spoke into his sound-powered telephone rig, waited for an answer, then replied to the captain, "Bearing 190 true, speed six knots."

The captain was scanning the horizon. "Who's on sonar?"

"Donnelly, sir."

The captain lowered the binoculars and smiled at the executive officer watching the conversation, then back at the sailor. "Is Mr. Donnelly sure we are not chasing another sperm whale?"

Several of the men around the bridge snickered, but none of them dared to laugh out loud. Hopper, smiling, spoke back into his radio. After a long pause, he nodded back at the captain.

"Mr. Donnelly is positive this is not a sperm whale, *sir*."

"Very well." He nodded to the executive officer. "Mr. Hansen, action stations. Have the plot room determine the vector."

The ship's crew, mired in a midsummer's lull, sprang to life. As the men scrambled across the sizzling deck, the executive officer called down to the plot room. Soon, the destroyer was crashing through the tender sea, making full speed as she began pursuing her prey.

Twenty minutes later, the executive officer finished a tense conversation with Mr. Hopper, then walked over to the captain.

"Well, Jack?" The captain asked.

"I'd say we're right on top of her."

"Let's give it a go."

Jack called to the weapons officer, "Nolan?"

"Yes, sir?"

"Launch a full spread, racks one and two."

"Yes, sir!"

The young man spoke into the radio. A few seconds later, they heard the thump as the launchers fired the canisters into the pale blue sky. The captain studied his watch, lips moving slowly as he counted. He glanced up at his executive officer and winced right as the first charge exploded. A steady series of comparable explosions quickly followed it, and massive plumes of water showered the decks.

"Bring us back around," the captain said.

"Yes, sir." The executive officer spun back toward the helm and barked a series of orders.

"Sir, Mr. Donnelly reports a secondary explosion, bearing 187!"

The captain turned his gaze to Jack. "What do you think?"

"Captain, we either got very lucky, or we ran into the worst U-boat captain in the German navy."

"Oil!"

The cry came from a lookout on the port side of the ship. The captain and executive officer stepped from the bridge and onto the gangway. They leaned over the railing and scanned the sparkling green sea. About two hundred feet away, a dark teardrop stain spread across the rolling swells. Within minutes, several pieces of wreckage floated to the surface.

Jack glanced at the captain. "Not a very big slick."

"No, it isn't." The captain picked at his chin, then looked at his watch. "Bring her back around, but nice and slowly. Let's see if we can pick up anything. She either shut down and went deep or blew this decoy and made a run for it."

"Which do you think it is?"

"I think she ran."

"Then we should pick her up on the next sweep," Jack said.

"Yes, we should."

"Captain, we passed seven hundred feet."

"Keep going."

"Sir?"

"Keep going. Make her depth eight hundred feet."

"But captain!"

"Enough! Eight hundred feet!"

"Yes, sir!"

The men watched the exchange and waited as the walls creaked and moaned. Several pipes burst, spraying the tiny compartment with seawater. The crew sprung to action, closing off the broken valves.

"Seven-seventy-five... seven-eighty."

The captain took a drag from his cigarette, eyes locked on the gauge as it crept into the red. He exhaled and picked at his teeth with his thumb. The first officer placed his hand on the driver's shoulder as the boat reached eight hundred feet.

"Level her off, Johan."

"Yes, sir."

"Fredrich shut her down."

"Yes, sir."

The silence consumed them, only to be broken several minutes later by the deadly whine of distant screws. They waited as the wail grew louder. The screeching reached a near-deafening level, and then it faded. The first mate, sweat pouring down his forehead, smiled at the captain. The captain stared back at his old friend and shook his head.

The first explosion was the closest and knocked everyone to the deck. The captain peeled himself from the metal grating and looked at the depth gauge. It was holding steady. The second explosion was not so close, but still tossed the ship like a rag doll. Water was pouring in from a dozen places, and the hull squealed like it would implode at any moment. With the subsequent explosion, the lights went out, and the sub faded into the icy grip of the Atlantic.

SPRING, 1946 A.D.
MANAUS, BRAZIL

The black river slithered through the emerald forest like a greedy snake. The dark surface, smooth as glass, consumed the noonday sun and gave back the energy as a sticky vapor that clung to the muddy banks. The canopy, drooping in the summer heat, watched the river creep along. Somewhere in the trees, a pack of monkeys shattered the sultry air with their panicked shrieks. The warning sent a flock of bright-colored birds fluttering toward the clear blue sky, their exodus triggering a shower of leaves.

As the last leaf drifted down onto the water, the object that had triggered the alarm floated past a narrow bend in the river. Technically, it was a raft. But it could have easily been mistaken for a random collection of shattered branches, if not for the vines that held it together. Then there was the scrawny, almost naked body wedged into the craft. The man was lying face down, with one arm draped into the water. His skin was scorched and blistered, but what truly set him apart was his long, blonde hair.

The bundle continued down the river, somehow avoiding

the eddies that marked the lazy bends. By early afternoon, the current had carried the raft to a mile-wide section of the river, and it was there that its long journey ended. The makeshift vessel floated into the shadows of a muddy bank, eventually coming to rest near a group of dugouts.

The local fisherman had retreated from the river to avoid the sweltering heat, but returned as the sun dipped below the distant canopy. It was a young boy, not much older than twelve, who found the new arrival. The lad stomped into the shallow water and used a stick to poke the lifeless body. There was no response, so he poked it again. He was ready to give the man up as dead when the fellow groaned and tried to roll over. The boy jumped straight up into the air, clearing the water by at least a foot. When he landed, he was facing the other direction.

"Father! Father!" He splashed through the water and up the bank.

The older man, not much taller than his young boy, looked up from the net he was mending. He rolled his eyes and returned to his task.

"Father! It's alive!"

"What's alive?"

"The man!" The boy pointed at the pile of wood in the shadows.

The father scowled at this son and dropped the net into his dugout. He motioned for the boy to step aside and crept along the river and into the shadows beyond. When he saw the body, he stopped and extended his hand.

"Don't touch it!" the boy yelled.

The man stood and glared at his son. "Shut up!"

He shook his head, leaned over again, and laid one hand on the bony shoulder. The skin was soft and warm, but the man did not respond to the touch. The fisherman shook his shoulder, which elicited a soft groan. Standing, the elder looked up at the clear blue sky and exhaled. He climbed back up the riverbank and called to several of his companions who were about to launch their craft.

As the men gathered around him, the fisherman started an impromptu council, fielding the various suggestions on dealing with the sudden and unwelcome visitor. The most common proposal was to push the raft back into the river and let it float downstream. They were all sure this was how the villages upstream had dealt with this issue.

Two of the men, who were brothers, suggested they tie the man to a single log and float him down the river. They pointed out that the other pieces of wood might work well in the fire pits. The others quickly agreed, another even hinting the newcomer did not need the single piece of wood since he was close to death, and it would only delay the inevitable.

The unconscious man never found out how lucky he was. The boy's father had spent a summer in a Christian school and had taken on some of his teachers' qualities. Although he did not believe in the Christian God, he knew they had rules. He did not remember the specific rules, but he was sure they did not involve sending a man down a river on a single log. The blonde hair meant this man was one of them and should be returned to them. He would take the man down to the Christian mission, even if it meant missing an afternoon of fishing.

Having decided, he elicited several men to help. Of course, they disagreed with his decision, but he had found the man, or at least his son had, so the man belonged to him. That was the rule of the river, and they all lived by it.

The two brothers helped load the unconscious man into the bottom of a dugout, then walked back to their nets. As the young boy climbed into the craft, the father pushed them from shore and hopped inside as they entered the current. They floated down the river for nearly an hour, meaning the return journey would take three. The boy steered while the man kneeled at the front of the boat, staring down at the stranger.

He was unnaturally skinny, but that was common for most men who appeared at the various villages along the river. His hair was matted with dirt and twigs, as was his long, scraggly beard. The fisherman leaned forward and studied the tattoo on the stranger's right shoulder. It was an odd symbol, with no meaning to him. He reached forward to touch the design when his son called him.

The man sat up and looked toward the shore. They had rounded a bend and now approached a fairly busy set of wooden docks. Beyond the landing, it appeared the hand of God had reached down and swiped away the jungle, exposing the chocolate brown earth. A jumble of huts and buildings littered the barren landscape, peering out into the river. Two buildings seemed out of place. The first was a huge cinder block structure with a corrugated roof. The jungle had crept toward the building's back walls, and no one seemed interested in keeping that from happening. The second building dominated the town center. Made primarily of wood, the architect had used an assortment of bricks and mud to complete the structure. The most striking feature was a rough-hewed cross perched precariously on the highest peak of the roof.

After directing the dugout to a muddy beach, the boy jumped out and helped his father pull the craft from the water. The man stared at the church and then back at the stranger. He decided it would be easier to bring the holy man here, so he told his boy to watch over the man. He trudged up the slope and made his way through the crowd into the church. The boy, who was always happy to visit the bustling town, sat on the edge of the dugout and took in the sights and sounds of the dock. He was busy staring at an old steamboat preparing to leave when his father appeared, the priest in tow.

The priest, a middle-aged man with a pockmarked face and receding hairline, peered into the boat and shook his head. He moved closer, reached down, and placed two fingers on the stranger's exposed throat. Nodding, he motioned for the two others to help him pick the fellow up.

Disappointed not to see the steamer's departure, the young boy scowled, but helped his father lift the stranger's legs. Soon, they were stumbling toward the church. After depositing him on a cot, the priest thanked the fisherman and dismissed them from their charge, but not before rewarding them with a sack of flour and several strands of colored beads.

The father nodded, instructed his boy to pick up the bag, and both disappeared.

The priest leaned over and touched the man's forehead, which was covered with sweat. He was burning up. The priest went to the refectory and opened the cabinet above the sink. He pulled a small tin and pried the top off. Inside was a dark powder, made from grinding the bark of a cinchona tree. It was often referred to as Jesuit's bark, having been introduced to Europe by Jesuits. The bark contained quinine, and if administered in time, could save a patient suffering from malaria.

He boiled a pot of water, and then mixed the powder in a small cup with the hot liquid. As he let it cool, he found a large bowl that he filled with water and a few rags. He secured the help of one of the nuns to carry the items to the sick man. The priest managed to pour some of the medicine into the man's mouth. He then placed a cool, wet rag over the man's forehead.

For three days, the priest sat by his bed. The man often cried out and rambled about lost comrades and hidden treasures. By the second day, the priest started recording specific details in his journal. He determined the young man's name and concluded he was of German descent. That was as far as he got. Near midnight on the third day, the

291

young man died, taking with him the secret of his sudden appearance.

Abyss: Book two of the The Last Roman series will be available on Amazon soon.

Follow my Amazon author page for notification when it is published.

https://Author.to/bkgreenwood

Made in the USA
Coppell, TX
18 February 2023

13056271R00173